THE
CHIMES

THE
CHIMES

ANNA SMAILL

SCEPTRE

First published in Great Britain in 2015 by Sceptre

An imprint of Hodder & Stoughton
An Hachette UK company

2

A CIP catalogue record for this title is available from the British Library

Hardback ISBN 978 1 444 79452 6
Trade paperback ISBN 978 1 444 79453 3
eBook ISBN 978 1 444 79451 9

Typeset by Hewer Text UK Ltd, Edinburgh

Printed and bound by Clays Ltd, St Ives plc

Hodder & Stoughton policy is to use papers that are natural, renewable
and recyclable products and made from wood grown in sustainable forests.
The logging and manufacturing processes are expected to conform to
the environmental regulations of the country of origin.

Hodder & Stoughton Ltd
338 Euston Road
London NW1 3BH

www.sceptrebooks.co.uk

For my parents

Then music, the mosaic of the air,
Did of all these a solemn noise prepare:
With which she gained the empire of the ear,
Including all between the earth and sphere.

Andrew Marvell

MANUAL SIGNS OF TONE IN KEY.

NOTE.—*The diagrams show the hand as seen from the left of the teacher, not as seen from the front. Teachers should particularly notice this.*

soh

The GRAND or *bright* tone.

te

The PIERCING or *sensitive* tone.

me

The STEADY or *calm* tone.

doh

The STRONG or *firm* tone.

ray

The ROUSING or *hopeful* tone.

lah

The SAD or *weeping* tone.

fah

The DESOLATE or *awe-inspiring* tone.

For **fe**, let the teacher point his first finger horizontally to the left. For **ta**, ditto to the right. To the class these positions will be reversed, and will correspond with the Modulator. For **se**, let the teacher point his forefinger straight towards the class.

The Arrival in London

Burberry

I've been standing here forever. My arms and legs and head and
even my bones are heavy with sleep. Clothes heavy with the rain
that won't stop falling. Shoes heavy with mud. My roughcloth
bag is slung over my shoulder and it jostles against my leg as I
shift from side to side to keep warm. It's heavy too, weighted with
objectmemories. The ones I've decided to take.

Deep in the drilled-in mud of the fields behind me, our bulbs
are wrapped in their brittle skins with their messages of colour
stored inside. Blue iris, yellow crocus, tulips of all colours. I won't
be here to see them open. Longcup, double trompet. Daffs with
the flowers in papery bunches and their smell of pepper like the
air as it is just before Chimes.

Along the horizon, the fields are lines of grey that get darker as
they reach the sky. I stare at them hard to make a picture I can
take, but it's only objectmemories you can trust in the end. And
I'm carrying those in the bag already. You can't force them to
flower either. Like bulbs, they show their secrets in their own time.

A trader rides past. A handful of farmworkers cross the fields to
the neighbouring farm. A swagman sings the there-and-back of
his day's journey, a song whose cadence closes at our village
square. All journeymen, lighting their way through near distance
with a day's tune. Most people won't venture further than a day
– tarry longer from home, and the memories kept there, and risk
losing the melody back.

At last a horse and cart come to a stop. 'Whoa,' says the carter
and the horse blows steam. The cart is covered in a big tarp, and

the carter sits up front and says nothing, just jerks his head to show 'get up'. He waits there while the horse stamps.

When I'm sat in the back with the wool bales, he takes an old burberry from his shoulders and passes it. I'm wet through. I gather the burberry over my shoulders, and to save speech I sign the solfege for 'thank you'. He shrugs to say it's nothing. Then he shrugs two more times, not from choice, I realise, but because his muscles are dancing. I look away from that. The stink of woolfat is strong and I bury my nose in the sleeves of the burberry.

'How far are you headed?' he asks.

'Into the city,' I say. 'Or close as you're bound.'

'You going in to be prentissed?'

I shake my head. 'I'm going in to trade.'

He studies my farmclothes and my single roughcloth bag and is tacet awhile. 'And a ride back?' he says. 'You'll be looking for one, I suppose?'

I meet his look and there's nothing in my eyes. I don't need a ride back. I have a name and a song to find, a thread to follow. But it's not something to share. With my gaze I dare him to ask again, but he turns to the front and hitches the reins. We go forward and the cart's bumping goes through me.

'I'm bound for Leadenhall. I can set you down where you want. But take my advice and get prentissed soon as you can. Instrument makers are always on the lookout for young fingers.' He flexes his own hands, cracks his knuckles. His head jerks rough again on his neck. 'Don't wait too long,' he says.

I keep my eyes fixed on the road ahead.

Around one toll after Sext we set down in Romford, where the carter buys lunch of cheese, bread, dried blood sausages. He spears one, passes it to me. I eat presto, like I don't remember my last meal. Then we are back on the A-road, straight as a viol string stretched under the sky. The further we go, the wider the road and the thicker the knots of people. And with each step closer the city's music grows.

4

At first it's just the shouts and calls of song from traders. Then there are driving bursts of melody from highboy, viol, clarionet. We trot in past blankfaced buildings with hollow windows and buckled mettle and narrow cobbled streets. Music spills from the living quarters above shops, spins up from groups of musicians standing in door frames. Trompets send out brassy martial calls along the roof turrets. Viols speak with voices high and yearning and full of ache like human song. And under it all is the hard horsehoof beat of tambors. It grows and grows in a vast crescendo.

The carter looks at me with my mouth hanging open. I am gobsmacked. My face is up and ears peeled in what? Joy? Amazement? I know I have been to London for trade before. I had forgotten this.

The whole city is talking in music.

We move through the crowded streets. I turn side to side as if I could hear it all, but the melodies move presto and the meanings slip past. At home those four notes strung together mean one thing, but here the tune's words play a kind of trick on the meaning, pull against the notes so it says something else altogether.

After a while my ear begins to hold the tunes in my head long enough to unpick them. The official conversations are loudest – roll calls for choir and orkestra rehearsals, poliss warnings, the announcement of a funeral mass. Below those are striding public conversations – calls for new prentisses, invites to buy food or beer. Then threading through narrow and low are the in-between melodies. The songs people sing piano to their loved ones, calling to their minds the good things of home and reminding them of the streets to take to get there. A woman's voice makes me lift my head. It's a song for a child, a simple lilted lullaby, and the sweetness of it hits me hard and for a while I can't move. I see the carter look at me again as I sit there with my face raised and eyes wet, and I shrug the burberry up, turn away.

And that's when I hear something else. Deep under the sound-fabric of the city, somewhere to the south – a voice of silver announcing itself. Like a hole of silence down there, a rip in the hubbub. I do not understand what it means. And voice is not the right word, either, as voice is sound. What I hear is the absence of sound, its opposite. The carter does not remark it, though, so I do not ask.

It's long past None when the horse pulls to a halt and the carter turns to say he's going into the small streets now to visit his daughter before market tomorrow and do I want to get down? In where he points the houses grow close together. Their roofs are red tile. I nod. But I am tacet.

'Remember. Find a prentisship,' he says. 'Don't wait too long.'

When I go to give him back the burberry, he shakes his head. 'Keep it,' he says. He sketches the formal solfege for 'farewell' in the air as well. 'And keep your memories close.'

I hear the common phrase for what it is: a warning.

Alone with my bag of memories and the burberry, I move through the crowds of traders and prentisses. On the street's north side, I pass an enormous white crosshouse with its crushed mettle dome open like a mouth to the sky. I repeat the two things I have to hold to, the ones my mother gave me. A name and a humdrum, homely melody. A stranger's name – Netty. A melody that has in it the sound of food cooking, water bubbling.

Shops and people, trades and secrets. A tune for all of them. A special price today for blue linen. Best-quality clarionet reeds. Tarp hoods for rain. Pennywhistles. Oranges. And all I've got is the name and the song. No placename, nothing with directions in it. And no idea how I'm meant to find one solo melody in the midst of all this din.

So I do the only thing I can think of. I follow my stomach.

Bar of Chocolate

The first street I pass carries the waft and song of peanuts cooked in caramel and sausages on a grill. I keep down the same wide road and pass bakers singing yeasted bread. Hot coffee. Beer. Nothing close to my mother's tune, though.

Then a short, busy street to my right and at its end a broad, high-arched building where the smells gather, rich and thick and heavy. The sounds of a market place are familiar even if the accent and the tunes are strange.

I walk through broken pillars and down steps and find a corner to watch and count my tokens inside the vast market square. My stomach is turned with loneliness and strangeness. The people move around me and I am invisible to them. But I sniff; I listen.

A plaintive three-note cry from a sweet-potato man who sings as he pedals a bellow wheel. A tune of golden meat pasties sung by a fat woman with a wink. There are tunes for sandwiches and for potatoes fried in goosefat, and there is a seabrimmed song sung by a boy with dark hair and a shucking knife. A song with a gleam of pearl in it for the oysters he sells. The oysters are from Essex, the song says. Like me.

And then the homely note of one tune weaves its way out of the rest. There is something in it that catches and tugs. A solo voice singing, though it's not a tune so much as a quick underbreath patter to match the rhythm of boiling water and hissing butter.

Four beats down is the small vending cart, its blue tarp awning just wide enough to cover a tiny bench with a three-ring sterno plate and two beaten-mettle stools. Behind the stove, there's a woman with greyflecked dark hair caught into a bun. She is wearing an apron and moves presto between two huge pots and a small cast-iron skillet. The pots simmer and she croons to them, '*Bubble and squeak, neeps and tatties.*'

In my mind the voice is joined and doubled by another voice: my mother's. The tune is the one she gave me.

My throat aches with relief, right up under my ears.

'Netty?'

I try to keep the hope out of my voice. I try to keep out the questions I want to ask.

When she looks up, she does so lento, as if she'd known I would be standing there. A flicker in the brindled eyes.

'Netty,' I say again.

She silences me with a *tssk* of breath. 'Sit down,' she says, sharp. And before I can say more, she places a plate of hash in front of me.

The food silences me better than her warning. While it's in front of me, I eat like I can't remember my last meal.

While I eat, the woman called Netty clears up her stall. She tidies a pile of gold-wrapped bars into a neat stack. Wipes down the bench and the stove. Picks up a steelo and starts to scour the skillet. All the while her head is bent and her movements are clipped tight. At last she walks past the bench and looks presto both ways before she pulls the furled tarp down, closing us off from the rest of the market. The late-afternoon light comes through the tarp and makes everything a pale blue colour, old and sad.

She looks at me then. Though her gaze is steady, I see that she is afraid.

'What do you want?'

'My mother gave me your name,' I say. 'She sang me your tradesong. I've come all the way from our farm in Essex.' This time I fail to keep out the note of desperation.

'Keep your voice down, boy,' she says. A presto look to the tarp. Then she returns to scouring. 'There's no one left in Essex,' she says. There is a sour pleasure in her voice and for a second I see the people massed in our village hall for Chimes. Her words make no sense.

'You don't understand,' I say. 'My mother told me to find you. She meant you to help me.'

Netty sighs and lowers her chin, looks me hard in the eye.

'Who is your mother, then, when she's at home?'

'Her name was Sarah Wythern.'

She says nothing, but she is listening.

'What else did she tell you?' she asks.

I try to remember. I search through the last few days of grief and strangeness and I come up empty. My mind is closed tight so there's nothing in it but the rain on the road and the bumping of the cart and the hubbub of the city. A low dread rises up in me.

'Nothing.'

'Then she must have given you something. Something to prove who you are?'

I shake my head.

She hisses under her breath, like the sound of potatoes in fat. 'A song? No other message?'

'No,' I say. 'Only your tradesong.'

Netty is silent awhile. Her face is blank and closed, as if whatever was once warm in her has gone cold long ago.

'Every fool and his prentiss knows my tradesong, boy. I can't help you if you have no proof.'

At first I am unsure of what she is telling me. Then she speaks again. 'I don't know anyone called Sarah Wythern,' she says. 'There's no place for you here.'

I shake my head against what she says and fix my eyes on the bench, stand still as if she might yet change her mind. I have nowhere else to go. In front of me is the pile of gold-wrapped bars, each purple paper band embossed with the same jingle. I hear again the flat, refusing note in her voice like a door shutting. And as if it doesn't belong to me, my hand moves out toward the bars and I take one, weigh it in my hand, hear the tune on the paper that is sweet and rich. There is something else in her voice too, I think: she is lying.

'That wasn't a question,' Netty says with no flinch in her eyes. 'Take your memories and get the hell out of my stall.'

I leave the market by the opera house, shouldering through the crowds to get free. My heart beats like a tambor under my ribs, tight and loud with anger. In one hand I hold the bar of chocolate I snatched from Netty's stall.

The crowds follow their own paths through the streets, pushing and pulling around me, paying no mind. Only the prentisses watch as I pass, step back to leave an exaggerated berth. Scorn on their shut-in faces. From an open window a man half screeches a tune and all at once the noise is too much. Too many stories speaking tutti, too many melodies demanding notice. I stop there in the middle of the street, as if I could stand solo and be the one still point of the noise and dance.

Then someone shoves past me and my feet slip and I'm flat out on the cobbles. My memory bag across the ground and out of my grasp and all subito the other voices seem to stop as if silenced by some high-raised baton. I leap forward. I stretch out full to grab back the bag from under the tramping feet. Down on the ground, people's legs move above as if I am not there. A voice curses and there's a sharp kick to my hipbone, but my hands grip roughcloth and I pull the bag to my chest and kneel there with it cradled like a baby.

After, I stand under the eave of a building, out of the surge of the crowd. My breath comes in short bursts like the carter's horse. I wind the leather straps of the bag round my hand and wait for the horror to lift. How long would it take if I lost them? How long before you're one of the nameless, wandering ones? Clustered for comfort with the rest of them, like a sheep on the public green: memorylost.

Bodymemory would keep you going awhile. After all, muscles and bones have their own trick of remembering what to do each day. The habits go right down, deep in there with your breath and blood. My body remembers the shape of fields, though, the right weather for planting, the feel of the earth. My arms know how to turn a seedbed; my hands the depth a bulb will thrive at. And that's no use here. Only objectmemories can tell me who I am. That's where you keep the pictures of what happened, stored in scraps and oddments salvaged from passing days. When I hold them, the objects, the pictures come up. My whole life is in my bag. Bits of my childhood. Pieces of the last days on the farm. Everything I ever thought important enough to keep. I fight the urge to reach down right now and touch one, let the pictures cluster and pull me down.

She was right, Netty. There is no place for me here. No place, and the thread I followed my way in on hangs loose already. My mother not two days dead and I have failed her. The city slips outward around me in its awful din and its smell of bilge and rosin.

Then I hear it again.

That whisper of silence somewhere in the south. A cool current through the clutch and noise. It comes like the promise of a place I can draw breath.

I use my hands to carve through the crowds and through the melodies. I take corners as they come, moving blind. Past boarded buildings and vendors and more people. Across a broad street with grand buildings. Through duos and trios of musicians, their instruments flashing silver, maple, gold. Down a narrow grey alley, into a park, two spiked fences vaulted, a push through the scrub and at last, over a wide concrete road, there it is.

A river like a clear, flat highway. A river wider than I've ever seen. Greybrown water. The boats like toys on it and the ripples pushing through as it runs east to west. Calm, like it's been there forever and seen everything.

My arms shake as I look, like I've just put down something that was much too heavy. This is where I'm standing when I hear the sky's half-cough half-shiver. The warning so deep in bodymemory that my muscles are the first to answer. I have lost track of the tolls and it is a narrow minute from Vespers – and Chimes.

At Matins the Carillon sounds Onestory piano – quiet, amabile. Onestory is antiphony: question and answer, call and response. Our voices fill in the melody gifted by the Carillon. We give the right answers, always the same and the same for all. If life is music, as it is, Onestory is the bass. Which is to say the burden, the constant truth beneath everything. There to walk on and also to steer with, each and every morning.

At Vespers, though, Chimes is another thing altogether. Solo and forte, strong enough to bring you to your knees, put you in your place. Different every time, and always changing.

Across the road is a stone platform guarded by two strange catlike creatures made of black stone. One has its face broken clean off. The other still wears its whole smile, calm and pretty as a girl. A glance at the catgirl but no time to make a better acquaintance as I slip beside her and through the twisted mettle bars that keep me from the water. I crouch tight at the top of the stairs that walk down into the water's mouth. The best I can do is empty my mind as the air pulls in and out like a tide, like a set of lungs, and the smell of pepper comes.

Chimes is like a fist. It unclutches, opens. Starts like a fist, but then it bursts like a flowering. Who can say if it's very slow or very fast? Chimes is always different, and even after the thousands of times, I couldn't venture to say what it's like.

On the south side, people have come out of buildings and houses to form a ragged line along the bank. They stretch up one by one into the great calm of the music. My arms stretch up too, kin with the joints and muscles of those distant strangers.

It's the melody simple first. We follow in solfege. Hands in concert as the sky is carved by it: *Soh Fah Me Doh Ray Me Soh Fah Me Me Ray Doh Doh Soh Soh.* Then the melody is repeated, but turned upside down. Then it comes again, but up an octave and another voice takes the inverted melody and they weave together. The chords wash over. They clean and centre me. The weight of the tonic goes down my spine and into the ground.

Follow the melody through its variations, through its opening and flowering. It tells of harmony and beauty. It tells of a beauty wider than any of us. My mind opens with it and everything there is in the world is shown in perfect order in the music. There is no space for any other thought.

The sides of the river unfold. The forward and backward of all objects walk out and present themselves – brick, man, boat. The river thickens as if it's going to curdle – as if you could walk out on it, right over the crenelling waves and eddies.

It is not painful, not exactly, but nor is it without pain. I've seen men crying, certainly. But who's to say what it is they're crying for? It is so strong that one by one we crouch. Our foreheads in our knees, our skulls open to the sky.

Riverstone

The melody simple returns at the very end. Like a firm hand nudging me awake.

I open my eyes, blink my way clear of the blur and the ache. Above, the wide grey sky is held in pink bars of sunset. The step I am sitting on is a rough brownish grey, one of a flight that goes down to a river the same colour as the stone. My memory bag is stowed between my knees, and there is a muddy burberry over my shoulders. Fear grips me. Vast chords echo clean and upright through the far and near of my head. I try to push under them, into the stilled watery hush. Nothing. I wait and breathe and lento it comes back, up out of the murk. I am in London. I have arrived.

I look down at my hands. In them is a bar of chocolate wrapped in gold mettle foil and purple paper. The chocolate has melted through the foil and into the creases of my palm. I see a woman holding a skillet and punishing it with a steel pad. Her face is grey and cold. 'Who is your mother, then, when she's at home?' she asks, and turns her back on me.

My mother. I look for her outlines. All I get is the feel of her standing next to me in a light-filled earth-smelling room. She smiles and crooks her hand at me as if to say, 'Over here, Simon, come.' I pick up my bag, feel the weight of the memories inside. I will have to trust them. A task, I think. A thread to follow.

The sounds and songs of the city are beginning to fill the air, and the tide is ebbing, so I walk back along the concrete way. With the river at my side and the city crouching heavy and dense with song above, I feel a measure of calm. I will find a park or a cross-house yard to sleep in down on the embankment, away from the clutch of people. I will find a prentisship tomorrow. I will trace my way back through my objectmemories. I won't forget. Then it comes again. The silence sits up and calls me from deep in the river.

I shake my head to clear it. Nothingness. Flashes of nothing-ness like quiet silvery blinks. The need to find that silvery silence grips me hard. Though I have no idea what it is or what it means, I walk towards it like it's calling my name. And then subito I am running. Without any other thought and with my memories bang-ing at my side. Until, past the embankment's broken stone, the river is low and there is a huge bridge with blue mettle struts that swoop up into the sky and I can see the bed.

My hands in oily greenness. Deep in the shell and rock and debris and mud. I claw so far down into the silt that the water soaks the pushed-up sleeves of the burberry I am wearing and I almost overbalance. Clenched handfuls of mud and shell and fragment pulled up and cupped under the silted surface of the water. I shake my hands from side to side so that the pieces sluice between them. There is a gulp in my throat, a lump there.

The movement is in my bodymemory, so deep in muscle I don't even think it. I push down again and I'm in our fields digging for used-up bulbs. Shells and stones prick and scrape against my fingers and palms. Pieces of mettle press under my nails. I push down into the glut of the river's belly and bring fistfuls back to the surface to sluice. And then again, presto, with a rhythm form-ing as if there is a purpose to it.

And it's like my hands have ears. My fingertips reach out and at last touch something. Something that is smooth and cool. Alive in its silence, or with silence growing from it like roots. My hands close.

When I lift them clear, I'm holding a lump slicked with muck and grit. The thing, whatever it is, pulses with milky light and a weird world-calming silence. I wipe it on the coat, spit on it, wipe again and hold it up in the fading light. A fist-sized nugget of silver mettle. All twisted as if it's been kneaded by some great heat.

I stand there and my heart slows and I feel the silence come into me and with it a kind of peace. Then there is a loud splash and I jump. About a foot from where I'm standing heavy ripples spread out in the oily water. I take a step forward and something flies past my ear and lands next to me in the dirt and grit with a thump. I stoop to look – it's hard as a brick, slick in greybrown mud. Then the world cracks open in stars.

Pain in everything. Pain that is blackness. Blackness broken by stars, veined in red. It licks the side of my head and moves off to leave me still in the water at last. Tacet dark with the watery light and my head in the stillness halfway between strand and sky, halfway between water and air. And there is old code flickering down at me to say, ENTRY TO THE TRAITOR'S GATE, whatever there is of meaning in the letters blinking, and what is it? Bricked high and stretching up into whatever sky's still left. Old letters blinking and old brick stretching, and my upsidedown mind shifts against my will and a snatch of song buried deep dislodged too late. With words that go together with the tune. *In the quiet days of power*, it says against my will too late, *seven ravens in the tower.*

And subito I am with my mother. We are standing in a forcinghouse. She is singing the song to me in notes that I repeat after her.

> *In the quiet days of power,*
> *seven ravens in the tower.*
> *When you clip the raven's wing,*
> *then the bird begins to sing.*
> *When you break the raven's beak,*
> *then the bird begins to speak.*
> *When the Chimes fill up the sky,*

then the ravens start to fly.
Gwillum, Huginn, Cedric, Thor,
Odin, Hardy, nevermore.

I wish to hold on to my mother's voice with its dark vowels, but she is insistent and tells me that I must repeat it, that it is very important. The notes go down, down, down.

Head in the river, I go down with the song into the place of cool darkness where mud will cover my eyes and stop my mouth and—

Wrenching.

A slap.

Something shakes me and I spit out water, gulp in air. Rough hands roll and pull me and I'm out of the water and blinking light again.

In front of me stand a pair of legs in ragged jeans. Then a face pushes into mine. It's broken in a grin of contempt. Brown hair in hacked clumps. Anger rising like a smell. A thickset guy of prentiss age, anywhere between fifteen and eighteen winters on him.

'What the god d'you think you're doing raking our fucking turn?'

Before I can move the prentiss drops his full weight onto my chest, pins my shoulders with his knees.

The silver nugget.

Something in me fights to keep it. I tighten my grip and try to roll, but he is too heavy.

'You fucker. What've you got?'

His mudgritted hands scrabble at mine, pulling up fingers one by one; then he wrenches the nugget from out of my grasp and I am left with nothing but a handful of thamesmuck.

The look on his face as he holds it up to the waning light is strange. The mettle has given him confidence. He shifts his weight on my shoulders.

'You're on our run.' The weight gets harder; his face pushes closer. 'What do you think happens to riverscum we find on our run?'

There is no guildsign on his shirt. He is not a prentiss at all. Which makes no sense. No guild means no work; no work means no bodymemory; no bodymemory and it's a quick step to memoryloss for certain. But his eyes are sharp, and his movements are smooth and sure.

Then from behind him I hear a second voice. It says, 'Leave him, Brennan.'

It is cool and clear, the voice, like at the very end of Chimes when the pain shifts off and it's just the notes hanging in the air.

The one called Brennan shifts his weight from off my shoulders and sits back on his heels lento. I'm into a crouch so that I can run if I need to. His heavy threat behind me.

But I cannot run.

For one thing, Brennan is holding my bag. He has my memories. For another, I want to see the owner of the second voice. The one with the cool silver in it like the last notes of Chimes.

He's standing a few paces back on the strand. He is lean and tall and pale, and he's wearing too-large trousers made from green roughcloth, and no shirt. His trousers are pulled in with a thick leather strap. He has wide, bony shoulders and there is light in his curled hair.

But none of that matters. What I stare at are his eyes. They are so pale he must be close to blind, each with a pinprick blank pupil in the middle of its milky white. With these strange sightless eyes he looks straight at me. He walks forward and when he is close, he stops and proffers his hand. The gesture is like a mockery of introduction, and I don't want to give him the satisfaction of a response. He stands there for a little; then the edge of his mouth twitches up.

'You'll have to excuse Brennan,' he says. 'He's very protective of our territory.'

They take me to a storehouse on a place they call West India Key. In the middle of the room is a drum with a glowing fire in its belly. The wood of the floor is cut out from round it, and the drum has been lowered into that and banked with riverstones to keep in warmth. A big black beaten-up teakettle hangs from a mettle wire strung over the drum's open head.

Another one of them is in the room, standing still as a frighted rabbit in the light of the stove. They call him Abel and the leader cuffs the back of his head friendly enough as he passes. He is a good few planting seasons younger than me, with a thin-lipped scar down the far side of one cheek that ends a narrow step from the vein under his jawbone. Whatever happened was a close-run thing.

The storehouse is warm. On one side, hammocks hang from the roof beams. I am floating with tiredness in the warmth, and I have my coat and my bag close by. I wind the leather straps round my hands, pull them tight to my fingers so the blood gets painful and the pain keeps me awake. I see the one called Brennan notice what I am doing, shift his eyes back to the fire.

The leader's pupils are larger here, as if he can see more in the half-darkness of the storehouse. He sits both inside and outside the small circle of light. And then he interrupts the silence.

'So, what's a lone farmboy doing prospecting in London?'

I don't say anything.

'Did you lose your parents in the market?'

The small one called Abel speaks then, piano. 'Maybe we let him get his bearings awhile, Lucien?' he says. 'He looks half drowned.'

'We took pity on him on the strand. We've given him dinner. We have been altogether very friendly and hospitable. But you know, Abel, we can't afford to keep a houseguest.' Lucien glances at me and the corners of his mouth twitch again, as if we're both in on a grand joke.

'He got lucky today stumbling on the Lady like that. But look at him – just another scumsifter. Likely doesn't even know his rudiments. I'd bet in a dark room he couldn't tell his nose from his arse.'

I'm angry, as I see he means me to be.

'I don't know what the hell you're talking about,' I say, slow and cold. I am treading water.

He fixes me in his gaze and I see again how strange his eyes are – almost white, and with that bright, sharp pupil. There is something wild and clear in the eyes and they make the hairs on the back of my neck prick.

'So you had no idea what you were fighting for down there? You just didn't want anybody else to get their hands on it. Is that right?' He comes closer and there's a smell of woodsmoke off him. In his hand the silver nugget. 'I'm afraid we all have to let it go, sooner or later,' he says.

I look at the nugget lying on his palm, milky silver and its strange grip of silence.

'What is it?'

'You should pay more attention at Matins,' he says. 'This is the mettle in the river. What rose out of dischord's ashes. This is what they pay us for.' He closes the mettle in his palm.

'I don't understand.'

'You don't need to understand, farmboy.'

'What's it for?' I ask. 'Who buys it from you?'

He looks at me as if unused to questions. His expression has changed and he speaks lento now. 'What do you need to make harmony? A conductor. And for the biggest harmonies of all? A superconductor – the Pale Lady.' His mouth quirks like it's another joke I don't understand.

'The Order wants it, of course, and the Order pays. We harvest it from the river and the Order buys. The Lady goes to build the Carillon,' he says. Watching me. Though watching is not correct. Listening, rather. Ears keen to the measure of my blood and breath.

The Lady goes to build the Carillon. It's strange, but at Chimes my mind never moves to the instrument. I don't think of where the sounds are coming from – of what is playing. Only of the music leaping through until every part is commingled and one. Not pipes or bells, but the air's own orkestra. A sky shrouded in curtains and the chords pulling them back and back until all is revealed clean and bare.

There's tacet in the storehouse for a while. Lucien breaks it. 'What's your instrument?' he asks. Brennan raises a brow. He's surprised by the question.

'The recorder.'

Brennan sniggers and Lucien silences him with a raised hand.

'Get it, then, if you please.'

The flames are flickering and the lamps that hang from the beams sway in the wind coming in off the river. They cast long shadows all over the wooden walls. The two called Abel and Brennan go to their hammocks and come back, Brennan with a round, flat tambor about two handspans in width, Abel with a viol.

I reach inside my bag. A moment of panic, but the case is still there, undamaged. I unfasten the small brass clasps. Inside, the leather is lined with blue velvet that fits neat to each part of the recorder. Fits the chestnut wood, the ivory-tipped beak. In there it's cold and separate, but as soon as I pick it up, it feels light and warm and alive. My hands find their places without thinking, each finger in its stop. Happiness pricks in the fleshy part at the base of my thumbs.

I walk into the circle and Lucien turns to me.

'Do your best to keep up,' he says.

Without accompaniment he starts to sing.

He sings and time stands still, as if he is walking on water. His voice is stark and true, and in it there are stretches of empty skies and a bright rime of salt.

The tune starts with a glee and a lilt. The words don't say much, but I can follow the melody's meaning. It is about when innocence is really blindness. How when you want something very much, so bad you can taste it, your mind likes to trick you that it's in your grasp.

That is the gleeful, lilting, funny bit. But then the second theme comes, and that's bitter. It is about when the beauty is false and yet you still somehow desire and still cannot have it.

Lucien sings the first theme through once again with no words now and no solfege, just sounds that curl and change. Then, lightly, Brennan comes in on the drum. He lays down a four-four rhythm. Then he spreads and patterns it until it tells the same story. But his part has a relentless tread: the warning of what will be lost, and the punishment to come. Then Abel brings in another voice on the viol. It starts an argument with Lucien's, a quickwitted patter of running triplets: scolding, blustering, mocking Lucien's plaints.

And I listen. I listen until the flickering walls of the storehouse drop away and the three new figures with their intent faces and movements disappear. Abel and Lucien and Brennan disappear and all I can see is the melody unfold and the music tread.

In the midst, though, there is something missing. Something waiting. I can feel it, and with each moment it grows stronger. It is coming maybe from the three of them, who though they don't look at me, are watching. But more than that, it is coming from the music itself. A whole voice is missing. The song has three parts: a yearning, a warning and an urgent scolding. But nowhere is there the voice of the beautiful thing, the one that is waiting to be found and claimed. The one they are all searching for.

I pick up my recorder and I start to play, even though I don't know how to make the voice that is missing. When I have played all my feeling into the first part of the tune, I still don't know, but by then it is too late and I no longer care, so I just play it. I play it high and reckless and free so that it flies above all the others. I play it with some of the anger I feel and some that I throw in for extra. I play a voice that has never known anything except for luck and beauty. I don't know where it comes from, just that it was missing.

The tune goes on and on and on. Lucien pulls the song one way and then the other. He offers a new key, tells a joke, breaks into a new rhythm. After a while I hear that the viol has dropped out. And then the drum falls away and I hear that it is only Lucien's voice and my recorder. I follow him. It is like running and running in the dark, without looking down. The dark streams out around me, exhilarating. For a while I run and it seems that I am following close behind the pale bright light that Lucien's voice sheds. It is a running that is more like a falling. My stomach drops out.

And subito I get a glimpse of a strange new territory. Not the close, light-flickered wooden walls of the storehouse after all, but a vast illuminated maze like a spiderweb. And at that moment I see Lucien ahead, laughing in his mastery. His voice lights the maze. Or does it make the maze come into being?

I stop, breathless, and the heavy wooden walls come back and I can see Lucien looking at me through the cookstove flames. He draws a circle in the air with his finger, still singing. He slows and his voice drops piano and he sings the first verse through to the end. I stand there.

Across from me, through the fire, I see Brennan and Abel. They hold their instruments quite still, listening.

I blow air through my recorder, hold it in both hands and wait. Tired, as if I have run a long way. I do not like being tested. But the fire of their music is moving through my arms and chest and it warms me. Abel sits back down by the stove. He spits on a piece of cloth, then rubs at the rosin dust under the fretboard of his viol and looks sidelong at me, thoughtful. I watch his careful movements. Where did the tricky dry repartee of his playing spring from? His eyes go to Brennan and I see a look move between them. A look with a tacet agreement in it.

'I see,' says Lucien. 'I see.'

Then he smiles a slow smile. And like an exchange for the mettle they took, he reaches into his pocket and tosses something to me that I catch. I open my hand. On my palm sits a small river-stone, dry and dull.

'Not bad for a farmboy,' he says. 'Which is lucky for you. And lucky for us too, I suppose.'

Lucien makes a gesture and Brennan sits, and then he sits down himself and the fire makes gilded shapes over his face and the eyes that are strange and pale. He stretches his shoulders and folds his long legs and then by some half-shrug he shows that there is space by the fire for me to join them, if I wish.

'Tomorrow we'll teach you how to run in the under,' he says.

Memorylost

thirteen months later

Matins

I wake up and I'm hanging. Up above, the beams of a wooden roof thick with old oil and smoke. The light is thin and grey and blurred, and for the life of me I don't know where I am. Panic starts up in my stomach and chest like some trapped thing flapping. I look around for a clue in the grey that will tell me what I am doing here. Something lost down deep in the sleep I just came up from. Some word or meaning for the sadness in me that I cannot name. I wait and I sway, and at last an answer comes up out of the riverine murk. Not sure if it is the one I was looking for, but it floats up and it brings a sort of relief. It comes in the sounds of morning. *Listen*, it says. *You are home.*

Dry sharp half-echo of coldness. That comes first. Down low to the ground so it makes the distances stretch. Then the storehouse grows up from that – four walls solid and stripped bare like a beat for marching to. Then I listen for the others. I listen for their different sounds, their rhythms. Clare's clipped tread in its forward and back of impatience. Brennan heavier. Abel light and uncertain, like each footstep wants to change its mind. Lucien? Not yet.

Next I try to hear the water out past the storehouse walls. The boatpeople are already travelling downriver to trade from Richmond. They sing the sightlines of the river and the metre of the tide upstream and down. Their melodies follow each curve of the bank so if you listen close, you can almost see it. Voices low and wordless in the half-song of navigation, a sort of *la la leia la* that is almost the sound of the river itself. Above that, different messages curl in and around with the small schooners and flatbottomed boats. There are words to these, some working sly against the music's message. A burst bank at Leaside. A poliss barge moored this morning at Hammersmith to check for smuggled goods. Poppies for sale at Columbia Road. A girl gone missing off a boat down Lambeth way.

At last I pull back the blankets and swing my legs over the side of the hammock. As I do, something clatters to the floor and I fetch it up. A riverstone, dry and gritted – a memory I must have visited last night. Whatever it holds it is silent now and I get it back in the memory bag presto. Bodymemory trumps object-memory, and bodymemory says, *Join the others*. It says, *Eat, downsound, get down to the river*. It says, *Night is for remembering*. And in a sidelong voice, it says, Before *is blasphony*.

My name is Simon, I think. I live in the storehouse on Dog Isle, in the city of London. I am a member of Five Rover pact.

I push the curtains aside and go out into the day.

In the storehouse, the embers of the cookstove are aglow and the rest of the pact are there, which makes my heart rise up. Abel stoking the stove. Clare slicing bread at the workbench. Brennan stretching by his quarters. If you listen right, the whole thing has its rhythm. Abel fetches the caddy and spoons tealeaves into the water. Clare pours milk into a copper pot, adds honey, nutmeg. Brennan skewers bread on the toasting forks. We each take a fork to the fire, in our circle round the stove, and we drink tea with sweet spiced milk. Bodymemory keeps us in our places. No one speaks in the mornings, not until we've gathered ourselves enough to know who we are and what we're about. Not until after Onestory.

If you listen now, you'll hear the steady tread of feet on the streets outside. Jostling, moving fast. People walking to cross-houses, parks, public spaces, gathering to hear and sound Onestory ensemble in public, grouped together for companion-ship and comfort. We, Thames pact of the run from Green Witch to Five Rover, gather to sound it with mugs of sweet tea around the cookstove, our voices an undercurrent muddy with sleep,

Lucien leading. Same every morning. In the pops and cracks of the fire, with the sweet tea and the river moving slowly beside, and with the under calling to us already.

I hear him before I see him. The long-legged walk in from the balcony. Lucien comes in and it's hard to look at him first thing. When you go from darkness into light, it's the same, isn't it? I see his profile first, then the sharp swing of his arms. He passes the kettle to me and I take it, hang it by its hook over the wire that sits inside the cookstove mouth.

Then there's the ripple in the air that signals it's almost Chimes. A kind of hitch or lift, a clearing of the throat before a grand announcement. And a question comes up with it. It rises out of the silt of sleep in my head. Not sure if it's my voice or someone else's. *The arrival in London*, it asks, *what was it like?* I look to my side as if there might be someone there to tell me where it comes from, what it means. But not enough time to puzzle it now, as in the middle of the room Lucien's arms lift up and with them the first notes of the Carillon. It is Onestory.

A leap of joy inside me, fierce and bright. I open my mind and let the music and the words come. The rhythm as familiar as breathing. The chords sure and full of beauty. Lucien makes the solfege, spells it out by hand so that we see it and hear it inside at the same time. That is how it works. *Doh Me Lah.*

What happens in the time of dischord? the music asks.

And we sing the right response:

> 'In the time of dischord, sound is corrupt.
> Each one wants the melody;
> No one knows their part.'

Onestory tells it like it's always still happening. Always here and always telling the tune. Every piece of it just a strand of the bigger melody. But that's taught too: *The part is the whole, and*

29

the whole is the part. The way I think of it, Onestory is a circle that connects up the end to the beginning. No before and no after. Start at one point and sooner or later you'll meet yourself coming up the other side.

> *'In the time of dischord, there is no score.*
> *Music without meaning*
> *Knocking at the door.'*

How does sound become corrupt? the Carillon asks.

> *'In the time of dischord, worship only words.*
> *Greedy is the lingua.*
> *Greedy are the swords.*
>
> *'In the time of dischord, worship only talk.*
> *Devil in the music.*
> *Put the sound to work.'*

What happens in the cities? the Carillon asks.

> *'Sound becomes the weapon, sound becomes the gall,*
> *Sound becomes the screaming,*
> *All the cities fall.'*

The answer is harsh and punishing. At the height of dischord, at Allbreaking, sound became a weapon. In the city, glass shivered out of context, fractured white and peeled away from windows. The buildings rumbled and fell. The mettle was bent and twisted out of tune. The water in the river stood in a single wave that never toppled. What happened to the people? The people were blinded and deafened. The people died. The bridge between Bankside and Paul's shook and stirred, or so they say. The people ran but never fast enough. After Allbreaking, only the pure of heart and hearing were left. They dwelled in the cities. They waited for order; they waited for a new harmony.

The words are simple, because words are not to be trusted.

Music holds the meaning now. No one is unaccounted for. Even us, plundering the last of the Lady from the under.

> 'Mettle in the river, out of breaking's harm.
> Calm and consolation.
> Bright and balm.'

The notes come off my tongue as they always do. Repeat it forte, over and over and over, until it's locked in a place deeper than memory. A great calm enters with it. The ragged worry of the morning's waking, the blur and the striving, they all drop away.

> 'Out of dischord's ashes, harmony will rise.
> Order of the Carillon.
> Music of the skies.'

I don't know if it's just me that does it, but sometimes I try to see Onestory as a line that starts in one place and moves to another. I can't, though. I never can. It's blasphony to try, I think. Instead, it moves round its circle and through its changes, and each moment is always happening – the glass floating, or the bridge stirring, the people running.

Dischord lives with us, even in the harmony of the Order. You can see the fallen buildings of Allbreaking if you look to the other side of the river. The bridge between Bankside and Paul's shakes and stirs. The people run but never fast enough. There is no bridge between Bankside and Paul's now, but in the streets and markets, the kids sing the old forecast, like it is still taking place, like it is always taking place. *London Bridge is falling down, falling down, falling down. London Bridge is falling down, my fair Lady.*

At Prime we get dressed for the under. Wool longjohns first, jeans over that. On our feet, another layer of wool to wick the water and keep warm. I put poly overshoes on over this, then gaiters. Brennan binds stickwrap round his feet, then gaiters. Says it keeps the water out better, though I have my doubts.

We pack matches, canteens of fresh water, a stack of oatcakes in some greased paper, some dried strips of rabbit meat.

It's a lean line of us that emerges from the storehouse. All dressed the same, our faces pale as dawn. Quiet out on the race. The flat tables of cracked concrete stretch right down to the wrecks of the two cranes that guard the way in. The water runs in a narrow inlet right along, dividing our side of the dock from the city almost like an island. The mettle struts of what must have been a bridge once, wrongly tuned and bent out of shape.

The sky is white and still. We walk past the old twisted cranes and from there, speeding now, pushing a bit, we take the Liver Street steps three at a time.

I breathe the old tea smell of the river and see the familiar shapes of the strandpickers, who walk like storks on straight legs with their backs hunched and their divining forks twitching. They're like blind people, led by a rumour of the Lady's whisper and rare generosity – the hint of a fragment left in thamesmud.

Onestory doesn't tell you much about the Pale Lady.

When the weapon of dischord was destroyed – and most say that happened in the scar, out past Batter Sea – what they found in the remnants was palladium, the Pale Lady. The Lady was driven by the blast far and wide, and then she settled down, easy as you like, into the river. It's there that we prospect her. Because palladium goes to make the Carillon. Hundred per cent of her. Superfine. *Out of dischord's ashes, harmony will rise.*

What Onestory doesn't tell you is that, in the time of dischord, they used the Lady for other things too. Where she's less pure, she definitely got around. You can find small dabs of her in secretboards, and in lots of small, silent electricks. Fleet, one of the pacts to our west, have the pick of the old car graveyards, and though they don't have any hope of securing the pure, there's a lot of her hiding in the piping there. That kind of prospecting is messy, of course. You need aqua regia, and patience.

The easiest way to imagine the Carillon is as pipes. The Order each carry their own small pipe, or flute rather, which has the meaning *one part of the whole*. And in the Citadel, the heart is the Carillon, which is all the many pipes put together, and is what is called an organ, which is just another word for heart.

My name is Simon, I think. I live in the storehouse on Dog Isle, in the city of London. I am a member of Five Rover pact. We run in the under, and in the under we search for fragments of the Lady. We sound Onestory. We trade in the markets of London. We go silent for Chimes at Matins and Vespers.

In the Under

The bare edges of the morning are only just beginning to show as we enter through the stormwater drain near Five Rover. The mouth of the tunnel is wide and black. There are small ferns round it and moss like green velvet on the rocks beneath where water spills onto them. Lucien in first, then Clare, then me and Brennan and Abel last.

For the first four beats there's still light with us. Then dark closes in. At first I don't like its hands on me and I fight. Then I forget to fight, and the dark comes closer, gets friendly.

The tunnel widens into a small room. Our ears sharpen. Lento I can hear the amphitheatre and its shape. The air is cool and still and there's a shiver to it – the wind moving through the tunnels and the echo from old mettle. I can hear the four main tunnel-mouths. I can hear where they give onto the tracks of mettle rails, or the worming wet casings of the sewers and stormwater drains. Lucien hums and we move round so that he's in the centre. Then Lucien listens for the Lady.

We all hear her in our own way. For me, the Lady's voice is like a current of silence, far off. Not sure where the picture comes from, but often I think of it like mudflats at the very end of a grey day, when the water lies at the far edge of the sky. The line of silver, that's the Lady. So thin you can't quite make her out, but still you know she's there from the shining.

But Lucien hears where she lies and where we will run to find her. This is what we wait for. I do not understand it. His mind running far, far ahead, tuned to her smallest shifts and scatters. Lucien hums a low note again. It's the tonic, the home key. We

34

sing it back to him as a chord, first major, then minor. Our hearing's keener now and our singing sets up a low thrum in the
amphitheatre that dies lento.

First, as always, he sings the haunted silvery tune that is the
Lady's song. To remind us of why we're down here, what we're
searching for. The silver flashes for me as he sings it, almost as if
it could light up the dark. Then he sings our bearings in his reeded
voice. He starts with the melody of where we are, this dark room
under the city, and from there his voice moves through several
keys until he sings the exact shape of the river, the part that is our
territory. This is for his benefit, not ours. Lucien is the only one of
us who can hold the whole map in his head at once. After he has
his bearings, he sings us the tune of where we will run, and where
we will find the Lady.

Standing still in the darkness, I follow Lucien's melody as far as
I can as he sings. Standing still with my imagination running
onward. To get to the curve of tune that tells of the Limehouse
Caisson, he has moved back round to the fourth chord, setting
that as the tonic, by gesturing across the circle to the wistful pulling tone of the flattened seventh. He sings the banks of the
Thames from Wapping to Mill Wall. My body moves with it so I
feel the weight of each chord in the muscle. How to explain? The
tonic steady, stable like standing upright on solid ground looking
forward, that's your north. The fifth chord is that moment just on
the edge of a new balance, one foot and one arm aloft, almost
ready to swing round and upward to the new scale. North to east.
And with each modulation, so on. I listen hard, feel the shifts in
my body and in our planned direction, feel the melody swing me,
modulate. He sketches our direction onward and outward in the
pattern of notes and cadences we will follow under the river.

After a while my memory falters and I'm back to standing
where I was all along, in the main amphitheatre with the network
of tunnels spreading out their mystery around. Listening blind for
the tune that will be our thread through the dark.

35

At last the melody comes to its end and we stand and smell the tunnel's cool breath, waiting for the sounding to settle in our minds. Then the run begins.

The way is hard at first because the tunnel is narrow and low. I run with Clare. Our hearing fits well. She has a good recall for rhythm, which means she can keep the distances in mind. We're in water halfway up our shins, and there's the shock of the cold as it makes its way through my overshoes. Then it warms and the warmth is trapped in the layer of wool and leather and we settle into a good half-jog.

The tunnel is as Lucien sung it, and the tune keeps us following straight for a good while until the first cadence comes upon us, and we follow the tune he gave us sharp west. There are no steps upward to the mouth of the new tunnel, and I have to pull myself up first and then turn to give Clare an arm up. This tunnel is wide and dry with a bricky, sandy smell. We take the twists and turns that the tune tells us, and before long we are running straight again. And then we're just waiting for the first tunnel that will lead us toward the fourth chord.

We're closer to the surface and every few beats there's a small crack of light above us. Not sunlight, but a softer, grainier darkness. We're running now, and past a knot of openings to the east Clare starts counting out the beats that give us the exact distance: 8, 2, 3, 4 . . . 7, 2, 3, 4 . . . 6, 2, 3, 4 . . . and so on, hearing the tune underneath. And right on time the next cadence appears, as Lucien sang it, and I see the right-hand tunnel that will lead us northeast, right onto the spot that Lucien sounded. Clare is a few paces ahead and gestures to me as I join her, so I drop to a walk and stand close. We both wait for our hearts to stop thudding so we can listen and see if we've dropped down on the right tunnel.

Ragged breath in the still, close air, and the scritching sound of the feet of small creatures, mice or rats, scurrying in the sandy tunnel. I stand and wait. My breath slows. Then a long silver blink, a pale ellipsis of silence. *Husssh*, it whispers, like a pulled-back tide. I feel my thumbs prick and I can hear Clare's slow smile in the darkness. I imagine the sharp white of her teeth. 'It's clean, and close,' she whispers. And I nod. She speaks from a distance, though. Like her mind is clouded with some worry.

We can hear her now, but it's needful to keep the tune still. Follow the Lady and lose the tune, and though you'll have her, she'll not show you the way back. They say there are pactrunners who have died down here, lost forever in the tunnels.

I lead now, and the Lady's call gets stronger. The tunnel narrows again and curves downward. It rejoins the floodwash of another drain. There is a grille to the outside that drops stripes of early morning light onto the small rush of waters.

I hold my breath and go to a crouch and use both hands to sluice through the debris at the grate below. Leaves and old stick-wrap bags, wads of old wet papermoney. Then I lift my hands and hold them out and Clare's breath makes a small, wondering 'Ha!' in the silence. On my palm is a nugget of Pale. About three ounces, and shined with soapy, idle gleam in the thin light, as beautiful as anything I've ever seen. It pulses with silence. With a brisk few steps Clare's next to me and we look at it closer and I give her shoulder a squeeze, in gratitude for her hearing and the glow of her triumph. I slip the Lady into my back jeans pocket and grin.

'Not bad for a morning's work,' I say.

Following our path backward is harder. You need to remember the tune and turn it inside out. But by that time we've been down long enough that my ears have slowed and sharpened and I can hear some way ahead. The cooling shift of air around a tunnel-mouth, the echoes bouncing clipped and clean in concrete. I hear something else too.

Behind me, Clare's breathing has a halted rhythm. Pent up, then every few minutes an irritated burst of breath. I slow, let her set the rhythm and judge what distances she needs. Running with

Clare is all quick conflagration and offence. Keeping away from her temper is like balancing on a wire.

Sure enough, after a while her mood flares. She lights her words with it and flicks them at me.

'What are you and Lucien doing?'

I almost slip on one of the pipes underfoot. I had expected some imagined slight. A courtesy not supplied, some overstep or understatement.

'What do you mean?'

'At night,' she says, presto. 'I hear voices.'

'What do you mean, voices? Saying what?'

'I don't know. Just voices. Someone asking questions, like downsounding. Singing.'

'When? Was it just the once?' I have a sliding feeling. A feeling of blur. Our jog is lento now, half bent under mettle girders. There's water to our shins and the current tugs against us.

'You tell me.'

Grey light through a grating to the street above. A noise that must be the blood in my ears. I force myself to hear the inverted tune, sound it through. I have no idea what she is talking about. We must be nearing the amphitheatre now. Two phrases or so off. Two tunnel changes. Soon we will rejoin the others and be folded back into the quiet hum of the successful run and the rest of the daily rhythm.

'He asked about your memories,' she says. 'Why?'

And that is when I stop. We don't speak of memories. Remembering is done solo. Each of us keeps them. But glimpse a box or bag in someone's quarters with that guarded look and you look askance so as not to see. There is a problem with these questions. And not just with the questions, but with Clare asking them. Clare keeping something that I have forgotten at just a day's distance.

'How did you remember?'

'You mean, how did *I* remember when you didn't?' I hear her

38

shrug. 'I might not keep them close like you, but I've my own ways of remembering. Anyway, sometimes stuff just comes up from nowhere, doesn't it? What's the point spending all that time putting your memory into objects? You can't get something back if it doesn't want to come.'

She is right. It happens to me too, the sudden bubble that pops on the surface and subito there's a clue to what's hidden that you don't know. *It'll come up in its own time or not at all.*

'What's so special about your memories, then?' Clare asks.

'Nothing,' I say. But there is another part of me that stands separate and watching. A part that says maybe there is something special about my memories. And a tugging feeling. Something I am meant to do.

After the run is over, Lucien leaves with a curt salute and quick-step down a side alley, off to his own blind business. Abel back to the storehouse to practise. Clare splashes down to the strand. As she goes, she swings the long mettle bar she uses for mudlarking. Iron for raking the river.

I follow her, walking a few steps to her side. Every few moments she throws a look at me that flicks out sharp, then back. I keep my own counsel and my gaze fixed ahead.

After a while she stops. Pulls her gingerish hair back and knots it behind her head. So tight it makes her cheekbones more than ever like knives. She stands widelegged and gouges a narrow gulley into the mud's surface. I site a spot nearby and dig also. Something has opened inside me like hunger, but not for what's hid in the rivermud.

We dig in silence. When she discards the spot and moves off, I follow.

'What are you looking for?' I ask.

'Nothing. What do you care?'

There's not much to say to that. Lucien in my quarters, I think. Downsounding. Singing. And the voice that was in my head on waking, familiar and strange at once. A blankfaced, emptyhanded question. One with no answer that I can supply. *The arrival in London*, it asks, *what was it like?*

'Tell me what he wanted.' She's facing square to me but I shake my head that I do not know. I think.

'Clare,' I say subito, 'do you remember when you joined the pact?'

She goes tacet; then she takes a few strides and pushes the tyre iron down. She levers it back and forth to clear a space, then pulls it out and looks down at the rush of water that has filled the hole. She doesn't turn round.

'What do you mean, joined?' she says.

A feeling of blankness, like the moment before the run starts. Eyeblind, ears grasping at imagined sounds. A dark room that could stretch forever or end in a wall two steps beyond your face.

'I mean, how did you come to be here? On the river. In Five Rover. How did you find the pact?'

I hear the tension in her. She bends and pushes her hands into the brief opening she's forced; then with her two palms cupped she pulls something out, covered in muck.

'I've always been here,' she says.

I don't know what to say to her dead certainty. 'But you had parents,' I start. The word is unfamiliar in my mouth. Ignoring everything that says not to ask. 'Do you remember them?'

Clare narrows her eyes, curls lip back from teeth. She is holding herself tight in all her muscles from neck to feet. 'What's your major problem, Simon?'

'I don't know.'

'You want to see my memories? Like Lucien wants yours?'

I shake my head before she's even finished the question. 'No.'

She walks toward me until she is standing close and the mud from her hands drips down my jeans. Her face is in mine, blood flushing her thin skin. The look on it is something not far from contempt.

'It sounds to me like you do.'

40

I step back. 'No,' I say. The flinch is deep in bodymemory.

'You've seen them already anyway.'

'No.'

'Yes. You've seen them. You just didn't know what they were.'

I step off, kick the sand. I'm sick to my stomach with the whole conversation, which seems to have spread into places I don't have any knowledge of.

What Clare does next is roll up the long sleeve of her T-shirt. She rolls it high up, with a look on her face of challenge. Mud from her fingers is left in streaks. Her sleeve is tight, but she gets it rolled almost to the shoulder, so I can see her whole forearm and from the elbow up past the biceps.

I look at her arm, tacet.

It is covered in scars. They are too clear, too straight, too regular to be accident or injury. She has done them herself.

I have to walk away for a bit and it is a while before I can come back. She stands there until I do, not moving. Her arms at her side and her hands dripping mud.

'Why did you do that?'

Clare won't look at me.

'Why?'

'Why do you do what you do? I do it because I hate the day coming again and again and never changing and nothing to hold on to. Because I hate waking into it with nothing there. You remember better than me. But this way I can measure something at least. Do you know what it means?'

I don't answer. I'm still livid with her.

She looks at me, testing. 'It's time,' she says, with a sort of satisfaction. She points to a raised cut, hard with pink scar tissue. 'This is about an eightnoch. I know that it's recent because it still hurts.' She points to a pale, spidery healed scar on her forearm. 'This one is older. I don't remember doing it, but at least I know I did it, and I can see them changing. Once that one heals, I'll start another.'

41

The outline of her face is keen against the sky. She stares me down. I'm still angry, but what is my anger worth? And what does it change?

Who am I to question her need for something sharp and sure to keep on her own body? At least she holds them with her. At least they'll never be consigned to thamesmuck and dug up by a stranger. I put my arm across Clare's shoulders and hold her as we stand there on the strand.

'Shit,' I say.

'What?'

'Nothing. I have to check the snares.'

'Did Lucien give you the tune?'

'Of course.'

Clare has a strange look on her face then. As if she is just meeting me for the first time. As if none of the conversation we've just had has happened. I feel a shiver down my own arms, though I'm not cold. *How long does memory last?* says the voice in my head.

'What?' I ask out loud.

'Nothing. Off you go. You'll have to run presto if you want to make it back to the river by Chimes.'

I leave Clare on the strand, follow the tune along the north road that goes all the way from the river with Covent Garden market to my west, up past the hulk of Euston and Pancras, toward Fleet territory. The crowds thin past Pancras and the air is colder there, like it's been left behind from a darker season. Clare cutting a path through time on her own skin, I think. I take two rabbits from the snare in the old Battle Bridge crosshouse and a squirrel from the estate gardens opposite. The buildings are empty, with sightless windows looking down.

I should go back now, but I don't. I sit on a bench that still has a few of its wooden slats. Lucien in my quarters at night. Downsounding memories. The sound in my head of a note struck. A chime or echo. Sometimes things come up from nowhere, I think. A bubble just pops on the surface. Doesn't mean it's true memory. What Clare heard and what Clare thinks she heard are two things far apart. But I don't believe what I tell myself.

I sit on the bench and I try to go inside my head. I think about waking at Matins and that is easy. But when I try to trace my way back from there to yesternoch, my mind shies from the *before* of it. I force it anyway. Yesternoch I woke. I sounded Onestory. We ran in the under. We checked the snares. Then in the night, like every night, I chose an objectmemory from my bag and I remembered. I entered the memory and I lived inside it for a little. Then after that I slept.

I try hard to think what memory it might have been. I breathe in the green smell of the tangled weeds, and my hands move over the wood of the broken bench, and after a while the voice comes in my head again. *The arrival in London*, it asks, w*hat was it like?*

That is all. Just an echo like the thrum in the air after a note has ended. Try as I like, all else is left behind on the banks of waking.

What is it that tells you to make a memory? I can't say. Something that sits raised and raw against the skin of the day. Something that presses at you. And I see that even if Clare remembered false, I have to keep it. I start by looking around for an object that could hold the memory. Something with rough edges of its own to give a grip for the picture. But I can't find anything that feels right.

When the answer comes, I try to ignore it. I push it away off into the shadows of the garden. But because it's the right answer, it skirts round and comes back unbidden. What I am looking for is a thing not subject to the tides of whim and chance. A thing that I'll keep whether I like it or not.

I take my knife from its strap at my ankle. Then I stand up, stamp my feet and roll my sleeve as she did. I press the blade into the fleshy part at the top of my arm.

There is numbness first. Blood pools up lento through the cut skin as I watch. An airy rushing in my head. Then pain at last and its sharpness somehow a relief. I push the knife in further. I think hard as I can until I make a picture. The picture is the two of us. Clare kneeled in thamesmud, her wet hands raised toward me in a question. I put the thought of Lucien in there too. A ghosted pale figure between us. Half there, half not, like forgetting. *What's so special about your memories, then?* asks Clare's voice.

And the memory is made and finished and it's done for my own sake, as, if you're honest, you have to admit all things are done in the end.

Yet isn't it also true that I do it for her? For Clare born to parents who don't exist and who's lived on the river maybe forever or maybe for a twelvenoch, it makes no odds which. It's for Clare who never joined the pact but has been with it always. And who's angry at the world but also at me for some reason I don't know. Some forgotten betrayal. Or maybe some betrayal yet to come.

Parly Hill

I bind a strip of cloth from my shirt round my arm. I walk and I think and the pain comes and goes like mist. I keep to the narrow streets. People step out of my way as they walk home to their families. When I finally come clear, I see from the sky that it's close to Vespers and that I won't be able to make it back for Chimes. There is a hitch in my stomach for the river and the smell of it, an urge to be back there next to the moving water. But not much I can do.

I'm in Fleet territory, near the heath. There's no danger from the rival pact as long as I'm not prospecting or down in any of the car graveyards. The city's up for grabs, really. It's only river we fight for, but I move presto anyway.

Into the heath from the bottom end, past a crumbled brown-brick building with letters of old code like a badge on its brow. Three letters only: one like the tail of a crochet. Then D, which is part of the scale. Then a round one like a breve. Or like a full moon, but empty. I D O, it says. Inside the smashed walls is a huge basin filled with rubble and tile.

I follow the old path up to the flat. It's half hidden by a tangle of bushes, and the thorns and branches catch my clothes as I go. A sharp smell of new buds and unwashed bodies and at last I push through to the flat expanse of trodden grass that rises up in a slow slope to Parly Hill.

It is covered with memorylost, ragged and threadbare, thin as sticks. Eyes either empty or fevered. They wander aimless around the green, or they sit leaned against the fat-girthed trees that line the path. Bivouacs of blue tarp, mantles of grey wool. Rubbish of lives scattered.

I skirt the sloped field and pass the flat red track that circles endlessly under its busted lights. As I walk, I sign solfege for the directions I'll need to follow to get back to Dog Isle. I think about memory and what it is. *Keep your memories close*, people say. Say it to children as often as they can. Keep them schooled up in body-memory from early on. Give them an instrument for their own. Get them prentissed. And make them mind their memories.

I think about what it means to keep them close. The trades-people who live and work in the city and trade in the market, they keep them on their bodies at all times, in pouches or pockets. The moneyed guilds, instrument makers and such, have elaborate bandoliers, belts with many pockets. The strandpickers port theirs in stickwrap, rather than linen or leather. Even Harry who reads the weather, whose house changes with the tide and whose head is loose as muttering, still keeps his wrapped in whatever he can find, and pushes them in his old shopping trolley along the strand or the embankment.

But for all that everyone keeps them and coddles them, I tend to think most adults wouldn't know their own memories from anybody else's. Something in their eyes and how they greet you in the market. At a certain point in your life, it's like you have to choose what to keep.

'Hey!' A low whisper, and I jump. Behind me, in the eave of a half-standing brownbrick wall, a shadow leans out. Then it peels itself away from the wall and walks out.

It's a young boy. His brown eyes fixed on me like those of a keen dog. He's slight and wiry, his red hair dark with dust. And it's clear by his bright eyes as well as by his age that his thoughts are still his own.

'What do you want?' I ask, too loud. My heart is beating presto.

'You did hand signals,' he says.

Back in the darkness is another shape. Someone lying down, asleep.

46

The boy walks closer.

'I never learnt it. Does it help?'

'What do you mean?'

'Does it let you keep things longer?'

'Things?'

'The pictures in your head. Of what happens to you.'

I wonder how long he has been here. I don't remember a time I didn't know solfege. It's taught to everyone. Soon as you get your instrument, so it's deep as breathing.

'It helps you remember music,' I say. He looks confused. 'Look, it's easy.' I sketch a scale in the air. 'Each step has its own sign.'

He wrinkles his brow and stares at me. He doesn't have a clue what I'm talking about.

I shake my head and talk lento. 'First is *Doh*. You know that one.' I clench my hand in front of me like a rock. To my surprise, the words of instruction are just under the surface. 'That's the firm note, the tonic. Next is *Ray*, the rising note, so your hand points up. Like a sunray.' I show him. 'Then *Me* is steady, so pretend you're calming something.' I reach out to pat an imagined dog. '*Fah* is the desolate tone.' I point downward. 'Then *Soh* is bright. Open. Like, um . . . like a handshake.' I reach out to shake his hand and he draws back. I keep going, hardly knowing what for. '*Lah* weeps – hear it?' I show him my wrist slumped as if in despair. 'Then *Te*.' A pointed index to the sky. 'Piercing. Like Chimes. Then you're up the octave and back at *Doh*.' I look at him, feeling somewhat foolish. It would take a long time to teach solfege so you could hear it and talk in it. More time than I have spare.

'You use it to help you keep the way, to stop getting lost. Not to think of things that happened before.' I hear the blasphony, but he doesn't seem to notice.

He looks disappointed. 'I don't care much about keeping music. I just don't want to end up like them.' He looks at the dazed men and women wandering the grass.

'What are you doing in this place?' I ask.

47

'We've got nowhere else to go. We came in from the south yesternoch so my father could get work, but he isn't well. I'm looking after him.'

His eyes have a sort of hunger. Something unfamiliar moves in me. What to tell him? The usual.

'You should get work yourself, quick as possible. You've got to get work to keep memory.'

He holds his hands out, flexes his fingers. 'I know,' he says.

'Get a prentisship with a guild. What's your father's trade?'

The dusty boy turns and looks back into the shadow of the buttress. 'He was a weaver, but his hands shake now,' he says. 'I guess I could try for piecework. But I can't become a prentiss as I can't leave him. He wanders off.'

I look again at the figure lying in the shelter along the wall. I hear a sound. It is the sound of legs and arms pulled in tight, again and again. It goes on and on until a heavy sigh tells that it is over. It is familiar. Something rises up that I cannot name. The boy moves to his knees and places a hand on the man.

'It's OK,' he says to him. 'It's me. It's Steppan.' His voice drops to a cajoling whisper. 'We're in London . . . Yes, I've got them. It's OK. Back to sleep now . . . Yes. Yes, I've got them.'

He reaches to his father's side and picks up their bag of shared memories. Keeping them close though he doesn't have a word for them.

I want to tell this boy to leave presto, as soon as he's able, not to risk losing any knowledge he has in his hands for weaving. I want to tell him that bodymemory is more than just skill. It ties you to your self. And then a dark thought comes. I want to tell him to leave his father while he can. He'll forget the pain of that soon enough, and at least he'll still have something to hold to.

The deep, low throbbing sounds of the early summons. Like someone clearing their throat before they talk. There are a few minutes before it starts. Most of the memorylost look around

48

blankly and seem not to guess what is coming. But streams of people emerge from the hillpaths and from the houses that give onto the heath. Up the threadbeaten grass of Parly Hill they climb. The hill is rounded under the smoky grey sky, and the streams of people are like ants moving up to sweetness.

'Are you coming?' I ask Steppan. 'You need to join the ensemble for Chimes,' I say. 'You can follow my solfege. It might help you learn.'

The boy shrugs. 'Can't,' he says. 'My father might wake and not know where I am. He wanders off.'

I leave the two of them and join one of the ant trails of people. When I reach the crown of the hill, it is full already, but I find a space out of arm's reach of any of the other citizens. Mud shows through the grass like thinning hair on a bald head.

Tingle of anticipation in my thumbs and in my own skull. Smell of pepper. Then a run of bright notes pierces through the white smoked sky. It's so loud it pitches into us, through all heads. And every man, woman, child or prentiss comes still and bright-eyed and rings clear to their own tone like a mettle tuning fork struck sharp and clean and held up to the heavens for all to hear.

Burberry

In the under, there is togetherness. We are linked by cooee and by the sightlines of the tunnels and by the magnetic shadow of the Lady. It is now, now, after practice in my quarters when the black rushes in like panic. It washes through the storehouse and I imagine Clare and Abel and Brennan and Lucien floating silent in the night, cocooned in their own hammocks, suspended in the black. I can't feel where my body begins and ends. Do I still have legs? Arms? Fingers? What if I forgot them?

The pain in my arm pulses in a rhythm that must be my heart. Breathe into it, hum a snatch of melody underbreath. I ran the empty streets back to Dog Isle after Chimes, followed the tune turned inside out though I hardly needed it – the river is the tonic of all tunes and my body swings back to it like the needle of a compass. I entered the storehouse. Down at the end, Abel had the viol low on his collarbone and his head cocked to one side. Lucien was teaching him a tune. The look on Abel's face all eager and young – his hair standing up from his head and his bow arm too high above the wrist as always.

It gets darker and darker. At last all is black apart from the small circle of my candle. I know the panic as well as I know my breath. Fear that the dark will take me whole and swallow me without a blink. Fear it'll leave nothing, not even my name. There's another urge also. It tugs against that need for remembering and says, *Let go, open up to the dark, let the clean order of Chimes take you.*

When I came through the door, I was still half winded from the run and they turned for a moment but hardly saw me, their faces all candlelit and calm. The tune they were playing was sad. After a while Abel had it by heart and they played the thing right through so that Lucien's voice was free to weave around and I listened in spite of myself. I listened for a while and the melody took me to a place I didn't know, somewhere with pale fluted ceilings and golden light. Now in my quarters, the thought comes that Lucien was singing for my ears especially. That there was some message in the tune for me. I know this to be folly. I take the bag in my hands.

In the depths of the roughcloth, none of the shapes has any meaning. They're just things I reach for like a strandpicker in thamesmuck. When my hand takes hold of the right one, a picture will flash up true as a bright note, clear as an unmudded stream. I don't know how it works. Maybe the object comes first; then the memory follows. Or maybe I choose the memory and my hand finds the right object to match. I do one each night only. And I can't take it with me into the morning.

I search through. I grip thick cloth, a heavy garment. The unravelled edge of a leather buckle. Up into the flickering light it comes. An old burberry. The colour of a dirty parcel. Enormous and the lining frayed and sleeves dipped deep in mud. A voice comes in my head. *The arrival in London*, it says, *what was it like?*

A rushing in my ears then, a lightening. The sounds of the river fade and the dark drives upward and I feel myself swing suspended up and out and away from the storehouse and down . . .

I am standing alone on a roadside in the rain.

Everywhere is mud. My whole body is heavy with sleep and with sadness. I look down. On my feet are farmshoes of rope and roughcloth, and they are covered with thick crusts of mud. A roughcloth bag bumps at my leg.

The fields around me are lines of grey along the horizon as I wait. I have been standing forever when a horse and cart at last come to a stop and the horse takes its brief breather to snort and fill the air with steam.

The rain is so heavy the horse's coat is almost black, the feathers round his feet strung out in whips of mud. The carter sitting in the back there gestures 'get up' and I get up into the cart presto. When I'm sat in the back midst the wool bales, the carter passes me an old burberry.

'Thank you,' I sign. He shrugs and flicks the reins. He shrugs once and then two times more, not out of choice. The look of his muscles dancing makes me sick to my stomach. Because I know that clutch somehow, in my own body. An echo of hands that are gripping and fighting. Trying to hold on.

The road stretches ahead of us and there is a lesson in it, if I was in the mood to learn. It holds no pressed shape, whether that's of raindrop or footfall or hoofprint. The road is a river, always the same and always changing and I must go ahead on it—

I come into the flickering light of the storehouse with an abrupt break. Something has pulled me out – a sound, or the new silence after a sound has been cut off. I train my ears like we do in the under. Bare calls from the river, half human, half animal. The sounds of a body turning against a blanket in sleep.

'Who's there?' I whisper to the silence.

There is no reply.

I get up and hold the candle to cast light into the corners of my quarters, but there is nothing except the tail of a wind that lifts the edge of the roughcloth curtain. And a feeling that is empty and hard. A question that sounds in my mind.

Arrival, I think, and am afraid. *There is no before, no after,* says Onestory. Which makes 'arrival' blasphony. Yet my mind snags and catches on the word like it's a splinter.

Matins

Darkness and silence. Somewhere in the deep black above me a blurred light. It reaches its fingers down and I swim up toward it. Then from underneath a tug at my legs. Something clings, tries to pull me back. Panic rushes in like water and I kick sharp. Kick hard until I am free and then push up presto to the surface, hungry for air, for light.

And I am awake.

Lie still and listen. Hardbitten half-echo of coldness. Foursquare solid walls to each side and the march of the wooden roof beams above, black with old oil. Creak of hammock as I sway. The light in the curtained room is grey and blurred, and down below is a river of sleep without the hardness of a yesterday to push off. But something has come up. Wrapped tight round my legs like wrack or weed brought to the surface. A dull brown garment, a coat, streaks of mud all over as if it's been long buried and dug up. And there's a sharp pain in my left arm.

In the half-light I pull my arm round to see. There is a dark, watery map of dried blood across the top of the shirtsleeve. I lift the frayed shirt gently and unwrap the cotton wrapped below. Lento, easing it where the layers are stuck. The last piece of cloth has dried to the skin in a rusted badge and I grip the edge and jerk it up and the pain comes. The lips of the cut are puckered and dark. All around the wound is numb, and fresh blood oozes at the ragged edge. I press the dirty cloth back down on it and too quick, too close memory breaks into the rhythm of the day and a picture of *Clare and me in the under . . .*

Clare down in the muck, wedging her tyre iron into the river's belly and levering up an object without shape. Holding it gripped loose in the cage of her fingers. The words hanging between us, silver and dangerous. 'Someone asking questions,' she says, 'like downsounding. Singing.' And then, sharper than threat or puzzlement, the bite of her anger. The arrival in London, what was it like?

I shake my head to clear it. *Clare knelt in thamesmud, her wet hands raised toward me.* Night is for remembering, I think. 'Bodymemory trumps objectmemory,' I say out loud. And body-memory says, *Join the others.*

There is no sound from beyond the curtain. Earlier than usual. I pull them aside noiseless as I can. Out in the storehouse, the door to the balcony is open. Through it, from the east, the light is just beginning. The clouds all covered in red, and the red covering the river. With the tight throb of my arm and the strangeness of the morning, I hunker at the end of the storehouse, back to the wall.

To my side, on an old plank propped on two blocks of concrete, are the things Clare has mudlarked from the river. Each day in the mud of the strand her hands go down and the objects come up, obedient as dogs to the whistle. She mudlarks them; she cleans them; then she lays them out on this shelf. I never give a least thought to these things, but today as I crouch in the cold, I look.

At one end is a red tin with old code and a picture of a strange white-haired man on it, coughing into a handkerchief. Then what must be a child's toy, a creature with a face neither dog nor cat, knitted in brown wool with arms and legs hanging loose at the joints.

Next an empty cloth bag with a picture of a tooth broidered into it, stitches so cleverly done that they set my own teeth aching. Then a set of silverish rounds like thin wheels smelted from mettle with some forgotten skill. In spokes like knives or rays of the sun. Old code on them. HYUNDAI. VAUXHALL. RENAULT.

A small hunting knife on a leather cord, a near match for the one I keep at my ankle. A handful of buttons – para, horn, mettle.

What are they? And whose? A long, lazy mettle spring that arcs over itself. A small woodframed picture of a woman and a tiny baby with secrets in their eyes and gold circles atop their heads. I step closer. Mother and child. Clare and I standing on the strand. *But you had parents*, says a voice that sounds like mine. *Do you remember them?*

I stand and I look at the oddments. They are fished from the river and spread out any which way like a market stall and I wonder what would happen if I were to take them in hand. What if I shifted them out of their still places and into different ones? What if I put them in a line that started in one place and moved to another?

I reach out toward the woodframed portrait as if to touch it and there is a gasping thump deep in my gut where the air should be. I bend double, half retching. Breathe lento and it passes and after a while I straighten. All that's left behind is a shameful feeling deep in me. Like something I've swallowed down in secret so as to keep close, away from the light. The objects are flat again and without promise. Unlinked and unmeaning. Rubbish that should have stayed dead and buried.

A noise behind me. A shiver at my back.

'What are you doing, Simon?'

For a second I wonder if Lucien has been listening to my very thoughts he is that still. I step away from the shelves.

'Nothing.'

'Something interesting in Clare's treasure?' says Lucien.

He must have been out on the balcony for water already. I look again through the gap and to the sky above the river, which is streaked red like burning.

'I wouldn't call it treasure,' I say. The feeling of breathlessness comes again.

'What would you call it?'

I wipe my hands on the legs of my jeans. Onestory must come soon, I think. And not soon enough. I am hungry for it. I stare hard back at Lucien.

'What does it matter what I call it? It's nothing. Junk.'

He gives me a long, blind look; then he moves toward the cookstove and slaps the blades of his hands hard against his thighs as if to clean them. Ding and clink as he takes the empty kettle from its place over the cookstove. He was not on the balcony for water.

'Are you taking over the gardening from Abel?' I ask.

'I beg your pardon?' His eyes flare. 'What do you mean?'

I have aimed in the dark, but I have hit something. 'Mud on your hands,' I say. 'Perhaps you were weeding the tomatoes?'

'No,' he says. And he passes the kettle to me. His voice is cool and distant as ever, but there is something new in it. A mild and distant pleasure, like I've finally learnt a tricky bit of rhythm.

I walk to the balcony door and slide it fully open to the burning light. It is not like burning, after all, I think, but blood. Sometimes a picture comes up in its own time from somewhere down below. And so it is that in front of my eyes where I should see the reddened sky, I see a white cloth with blood on it in streaks. Not the bandage from my arm this morning but a garment, fine linen. I shake my head to clear it and I walk out into the day. A bubble on the surface is all. A bubble and a voice inside that emerges, then is lost, reclaimed by the speaking air.

Before Onestory, it's only Lucien who does not sit. He walks the room with his long stride. He stands at one moment with his head cocked, already intent; then he starts the walk again. I'm almost to the bottom of my tea where the dark bits swirl on the mottled enamel when he stops subito. He stands with his back to us for a while, then swings clear of his thought and strides into the middle of the room.

Light in his sightless eyes and a hard smile on his face. He scissors at the knees and drops to a crouch, then holds up his arms to ask silence, though not a one of us is talking. The look on his face is full of craft and secret. The look that says, *I have something I am going to share with you, and it is magnificent.* His chest is bare. His fingers are long and pale. He bounces on the balls of his feet.

'Good morning, men and lady,' says Lucien in a stately drawl. 'Are you ready for the day?' Same as always, we draw together.

'What is your name?' he asks Clare, who is sitting to my right.

'My name is Clare,' she says.

Lucien's blind gaze moves on. 'What is your name?'

Brennan's voice hard and tight like a drumbeat. 'My name is Brennan.' He shifts his weight, cracks his knuckles.

'What is your name?' Lucien gentles as he comes to Abel.

'My name is Abel.'

Then to me, same question, careful and courteous, like he's asking an especial favour.

'What is your name?' he asks.

'My name is Simon.'

He winks.

I stare at him. A wink is not part of the ritual. A wink is new and therefore wrong. But there is not enough time to puzzle it because it is nearly Chimes.

After the run Clare leaves for the strand. It's a while before I can catch her. I hasten a few steps to fall into her rhythm. She avoids my eyes.

The run was tacet. Clare and I followed the first of the two strange, twisting melodies. Ours moved straight into the fourth chord and pushed on presto, skipping and meandering and returning almost completely on itself before branching straight out in a modulation to the dominant. From there it ran straight in clean, long strides, predictable but lovely. Clear as a bell, edging up towards the final cadence and the downward motif with the plaintive minor seventh. The Lady's interval. And there was a good-sized nugget, not fully pure, but not bad, about 0.85. But no buzz between us as is usual, the charge of its finding unshared. After the run I consulted the pain in my arm again, had the same bright flash of memory. It does not let me alone. So I followed her.

After a while of digging I whistle low underbreath to snag Clare's attention. She turns. Her light brown eyes flat as riverstones.

'Hey,' I say, and she says, 'Hey,' back. Keeps walking. No slight, though. No anger as I'd thought.

I try to find the words. The daily ones don't fit what I want to ask.

'Clare,' I say, 'you know what you told me yesterday?'

She turns her face. Its planes are so familiar, somehow managing to be both still and defiant at once. Her lower lip is pushed out stubborn and her eyes squinted as in thought.

'Not sure what you're speaking of,' she says. She turns and swings the iron in her hand with a flick and she's already looking ahead for the next spot in the mud. Then she's down on her knees in it, and brings forth today's treasure, which is a flat mettle board with a cracked glass face and a long para-covered cord trailing from it. I see the luck of discovery in her face. I step forward and there is the suck of mud on my feet and somehow it is urgent that she remember.

'You said Lucien was in my room. That he asked something about my memories.'

'I don't know.' She smooths muck from the broken glass like she's soothing it. 'Doesn't sound like something I'd say, does it?'

Then I do something I hadn't planned. I reach out and grab her wrist hard at the narrow bone.

'It doesn't *sound* like you; it *was* you. You heard it and you asked me and I made a memory of it. Why did you let it go already?'

She pulls away. Her eyes are very fierce and sharp in her sharp-chinned face and part of me is afraid of her and what the thoughts are beneath those eyes.

'Leave it, Simon.'

'No.'

'Well, I don't know what you're speaking of, so you don't have any choice.' She raises her chin like a dare and shakes her wrist as if she's trying to shed any trace of my grip.

'Is this stuff more important to you? You're so ready to leave everything else behind?'

As soon as I say it I am sorry, because Clare is my friend and I don't want to cause her pain.

She has straightened.

'I want to understand,' I say, though it's not clear to me what I am trying to understand. I start again. 'Your arms,' I say, and again am useless to say anything further. At night in the hammock, the shutters hold back any of the light of the moon and the river. The darkness dissolves it all. The storehouse, the sky, the river, all of the pact, until you're just hanging in a silence that goes on, will go on, forever. And you're falling. I think of Clare falling again and again through that bottomless dark.

'You think I don't know it's rubbish?' she says. 'You think I don't ask myself for more every time?' She presses the point of the tyre iron against her leg. 'You're no different from me with your broken things, so don't come proffer your pity here.'

I step back, wrap my arms against myself in the cold. I push down on the covered wound and I think of the raised white lines walking down Clare's arm.

Then I hear footsteps behind me and I see Brennan's shadow stretch long in the strand. There is something in its bearing of a favour to ask.

I look to Clare, but she is intent already, bent at the waist and digging. She walks on and I let her go.

In the Crosshouse Yard

Once you get over the broken entrance gates at Bow, the burial grounds are thick and full of life. Today I find the overgrown lush tangle a relief somehow. Plants with their leaves held up like hands, ones with huge coloured flowers like trompets. All among the trees and vines big white stones growing up crooked like teeth.

We walk among them. Some of the stones are in shapes made to look like they're not stone at all but cloth, or leaves, or an open book. Some are made to look like creatures with breasts like a girl and strange parts branched out behind. I notice these everywhere today. Figures with muscled branching growths on their backs that even though made of stone, look full of light and air. I stop for a while and stare. Most of the stones have old code on them, moss-covered and meaningless.

What I know and would prefer not to is that they're memories of dead people. Not ones they owned themselves, like Clare's oddments, but each a memory of the *person*, out in public for all to see. Public memories all in the open, so many gathered in one place. It makes me feel sick to think of it, and that people would wish to stroll through the dead like entertainment for a leisure hour.

Brennan stood beside me on the strand as I watched Clare go, black paracord dripping muck from the strange old electrickery she'd mudlarked. As soon as I turned to him anger flooded up. Rich, like a relief to find something that I could finally do.

'I've got to check the snares at Ropemakers,' he said.

'Yeah? And what the hell has that to do with me?'

'I can't remember all of the tune.'

Brennan bashful for once, shamed that I have kept it better when Lucien gave the tune to him in particular after Onestory.

But both of the snares at the wooded edges of Ropemakers Fields were empty. The green itself was flat and clean and empty too, and no sounds in the air. The thought of that lingers with me like a taste or a colour that I have no words for. Something off-key about it. We followed the Cut to the east and to the graves instead. Left the browngreen of the river for the dull, flat grey of the streets, and there was the small kick in my insides of leaving terri-tory, as always. A sick, weakened tug that makes me want to retch a little. But some way from market day and no meat in the store-house for supper.

Brennan swears now.

'What's wrong?'

'Sing the first phrase again?'

I repeat the phrase and he follows on from there. The first cadence closes by a slim white-barked tree between two fallen mossed gravestones. Each of the pair has a small, fat rabbit in it, not at all aware of its fate. Brennan holds them soft, gives each neck a sharp turn.

With some coaching, Brennan remembers the phrase to the next two and it takes us along a path and down some overgrown cobbled steps and into a clearing free of graves. In the middle is an old crosshouse, its roof burnt black and gapped. All around on the stubbled ground are the hunched bodies of memorylost. The sound as we walk of them crooning to each other in half-words, scraps of melody with no meaning. And another sound. That of legs and arms pulled in tight to the body's keeping again and again. At odds with tarp or roughcloth. The sound is familiar.

I see the picture in my head of Ropemakers Fields, the green flat space silent and empty. I click my fingers as I do when I'm trying to call up a rhythm. That field, stripped of bodies. Doesn't it usually look much the same as the view in front of me now? Clusters of bodies, tarps and blankets bundled. People all densely packed together. Seeking desperately whatever comfort bodies give when you've no other form of meaning. And that sound, the jerking of limbs. That sound with some underneath meaning I am too deaf to hear. That is usually at Ropemakers too.

Brennan tugs on my shoulder. He pulls me from the path and behind the trunk of a large tree. I follow him into a crouch in the dirt. Then I follow his gaze.

Standing at the edge of the clearing, northeast of where we're crouched, is a tall man in white robes and a brown travelling cloak. We lean close to the tree trunk and watch him. Over the brown cloak is slung the silver transverse flute that tells he's a member of the Order. It glints in the light as he moves. His back is crooked, one shoulder slightly higher than the other, and it gives a swaggered threat to his stride.

As we watch, he circles through the clearing. He moves through the memorylost with some reluctance, as if loath to be so near. The thin figures step aside with a shambling, shy confusion as he goes. Some keep their heads down, and some follow with vacant eyes. The member of the Order turns from side to side. Occasionally he steps forward and then stops, his head cocked. He pauses like this several times as we wait still in the shadows.

Then the tall man is walking towards us. Long strides and soon enough I can see the grey in his close-curled hair. For a moment I believe he is coming for Brennan and me. But then he halts at a tree near the edge of the clearing. A woman is sitting there, unmoving. Hands resting flat and palm upward on her thighs. Her hair is long and her clothes ragged, and on her face is a blissed-out look quite different from the others' daze. For a moment I think she is a moony. But she has no eyeband. Next to her is a girl about Abel's age, her hair shaved so close you can see a cluster of crescent-shaped white scars through the stubble. She's as calm as her mother, leaned into her shoulder like that and with eyes shut.

As I watch past the tree trunk, the member holds his right hand just above the height of their heads, and he caresses the air in a smooth wave up and down like it's riding a current that flows over them both. The wave of his hands returns and crests again over the daughter.

His gestures are familiar. They are familiar to me because I see them every day. When Lucien's standing in the under and waiting for the tune, he does the same. Listening, divining the Lady's tide. Yet, this man's movements are taut with anger. And, subito, some invisible wave breaks inside of him and he steps forward and pulls an object from his belt. Silver moving in his hand. A blade. From where I crouch I see him grip the woman's shoulder with one hand. With the other he slashes upward in a single fluid thrust. The woman looks up at him, her mouth an O as he holds up the shirt he has slit from her back and shakes it. Drops it on the ground before her in disgust.

Then he turns and he looks straight up. The sun flashes across his dark paraspecs and the whole of his body is poised and held. For a long moment he stares right where we're hidden. I hold my breath. Brennan tenses, as if ready to move, and I grip his shoulder hard as I can. Fear moves through me. Deep and chill.

At last the member turns away and whatever threat there was is broken. He moves on, past the stragglers and round the crosshouse. Brennan slumps beside and we sit there and I watch the wind make the trees flex and breathe. The man has dropped his strange errand and gone back to wherever he came from. Neither of us moves.

Then a sound comes out of the silence and the shuffling of the memorylost. It is a harsh scraping and it comes from inside the crosshouse. It is the sound of something hard being drawn over something rough. Arcs of it, each as long as an arm and with the full weight of a body behind. *Raaaaaaasp. Raaaaaaasp.* After that, a flurry of shorter scratches, like an animal struggling to free itself from something.

Brennan is rigid beside me. The sounds stop. Two beats more and the robed figure emerges from the crosshouse and disappears

63

into the tangle of green of the park. When he's out of earshot for certain, we rise without speaking. We cross the clearing and enter the small stone house.

The interior is gutted. Old rubble covers the dirt floor, and lines of black bloom along its walls. Circles of soot from many different fires, their various rings like the tidelines the river pushes up the bank and there forgets. The stone room smells of human dirt and broken things.

'What was he doing?' I say out loud.

'Don't ask me,' says Brennan.

'Have you ever seen a member of the Order outside the market?'

Brennan shrugs again.

'He looked like he was prospecting for the Lady,' I say.

'Why in hell would he do that?'

I don't know. He's right. Members of the Order don't look for it. They pay us to do the dirty work in the under. Or rather they pay the dealers, who pay us. It would make no sense for him to prospect here anyway. The Lady lives in the river.

It's only when we leave the crosshouse that I see the member's true leaving. We missed it when we entered because our eyes were blinded in the sudden dark. Scratched in deep across the broad back wall are two long sets of five horizontal lines, shapes trapped inside them like creatures in a cage.

I stand and stare for a while before my mind finds a way to explain what I'm seeing. Because it's not often you see music written down, is it? And when you do, it's on paper or parchment, not a wall. I can't read the strange up-and-down dance of the notes, or grasp what meaning it is they protect. But even I can see that the stave is scratched in vicious and deep, with the force of anger. The song is a threat.

Before I know what I am doing, I reach into my bag and untwist the package of oatcakes left from the morning's run, smooth out the greased paper. I burn a twig until there's a good end to it. Then I scratch with its black onto the paper.

It takes a good long while to get the whole tune down. The notes won't stay still in their grids. While I do it, Brennan stands by looking down at me. He waits tacet, every now and again picking a stone up from the dirt, weighing it in his hands, tossing it across the clearing. For all the world as if it's what we do each time we come to Bow. Though I am almost certain that I have never seen a thing like this before.

We sing our way back to the strand, at last, Brennan carrying the rabbits slung across his neck in a collar of fur. The light is fading. I stand and watch and breathe a bit as the river runs. Its path is hollow, rising up and rising down, nothing to stop it filling. It's a greedy thing, running both wide and deep. It's that unneeding way of it that tells you how old it is. The same look in Lucien's eyes and in other blank things.

Woodblock

It is dark and cold in the storehouse. In my quarters, there is a burberry lying on the floor under the hammock. I kick it toward the wall. Then I take out my memory bag. Its smell of linseed oil and damprot and a taint of woolfat from who knows where. I try to empty my head of thought and tune, but the roughcloth curtains are no shelter and the noises are strange. A creak in the wall beam as Clare or Abel turns in their hammock. A dry cough from Brennan's quarters behind. A fox barks once out on the race.

I rub my palms together, listen to my breath. Try to find a still space in my head away from the pull of questions, but I can't. I think about the three wrong notes that the last two days have sounded: the memory of Clare's questions that throbs even now on my arm; the empty, silent field at Ropemakers; and the member's message on the wall at Bow. Accidentals without meaning, or sign of some deeper shift or modulation I cannot read? And whose mistake is it, the awful jarred noise they make – mine, or someone else's?

I push my hands into the mouth of the bag. Edges, surfaces, fabrics. Roughcloth, wood, paper. Nothing speaks. I push through the silent memories until I touch the bottom of the bag and feel something hard and flat pushed inside the corner. I fish it up out of the canvas and into the candlelight. A flat, square piece of wood with unsanded edges and a smooth, cool surface, the size of my hand. There is a pencil drawing on paper stuck to one side and varnished over so thick it looks to be floating above the wood. The picture is a portrait of two people – a man and a woman – drawn in blunt pencil lines gone over and over so they are doubled and tripled in places. The many lines make it look like the two people in the portrait are moving. Vibrating. Shaking. And I go down . . .

I am standing in front of a house with a red door. The house sits in the middle of a large garden, and there are fields behind that stretch into haze. I open the door and walk in.

The hall corridor is filled with light that filters through corrugated parasheeting. I walk down the hallway and into the kitchen. My mother is kneading bread dough at the oak table. She pulls the dough flat with the base of her hands and then folds it over and turns it and stretches it again. She hums while she does it, and the low tune is one that I recognise. I know she has taught it to me, but what are the words that go with it? She sees me and she smiles.

Then the light changes and I'm standing in front of the door to my parents' room.

All is still and I don't want to go through the door, but I must. I enter into the smell of lavender and cut bulbs. My mother lying in the tall bed, her body under the white coverlet so small.

I go and kneel beside the bed next to her and she tries to smile, but her body does not let her. It wants to stretch and grip and pull. Her neck is tight, and there are bars of muscle at her throat.

Her eyes leave again. They go from mine up to the ceiling. Her whole body goes stiff. The shapes of her legs rise under the white coverlet, as if they are floating up in water. Her fingers spread and claw while I stand there and I cannot move. I watch the spasms go through her. Her chin pulls up to the ceiling and her forehead casts back toward the wall and I neither move nor speak. I sit by her side with my hand in hers, pushing against it, trying to straighten her fighting grip.

'I'm sorry, Simon,' she says. 'It's too late.'

Then she says something. She says it through pale lips and I can't hear, but I know that it is something about the song, the one she was singing earlier. Earlier in the day? No, earlier in the memory.

'The ravens are flying, Netty,' she says. Then she says the last word again to me. 'Netty.' And though I don't know what that means, I understand the look in her eyes. It's fear. Not for herself, but for me. I am looking at her and my heart is fading, and I know subito that I do not want to carry this fear with me. I want to pull my hand out of her harsh grip and run out into the fields. I am angry at the burden of her death, at the burden of a memory that her word is asking me to follow. I don't know what the word means, but I know it holds a hard task. A risk.

My mother struggles to raise herself on her elbows, to hold her head above the water of the illness. She wants to speak again, but her lips cannot do their work and against my body's impulse I lean towards her to catch the last notes that fall outward into that silence—

Something breaks in that is not part of it. A figure in the room where it shouldn't be and where I am standing *looking down at my mother's bed*. I push it away, but it comes again, insistent. The picture becomes smaller, breaks into pieces. *Dust through corrugated parasheets. Bread dough stretched flat and turned a half-circle. The white-on-white pattern of a coverlet. My mother's hands.* A hand on my shoulder, shaking, and I am between memory and present for several heartbeats.

The space I emerge into is spoiled and old – cold, flickering. I am sitting on the wooden floorboards of the storehouse. The flickering is the light of the candle, which has shrunk down to a pool of wax on its earthenware saucer, just the wick floating. I am holding a piece of wood in my hands. Shake my head and the air parts around it, chambered in wood, muffled in roughcloth.

The light moves. A candle disturbed by air. A voice has crept back into the storehouse with me. It comes out of the dark with the voice the dark has given it.

'Tell me, Simon,' it says. 'The arrival in London, what was it like?'

I spin round. And he is here. Standing tall against the curtain so that it tightens my breath and pushes the blood down my arms. Lucien in my quarters. And subito I know that he has been standing watching a long while.

'What are you doing?' I hiss. I don't want the others to hear. What I feel is a mix of anger and shame. Some other feeling I don't recognise. Something like biting round my heart.

'That is where we start.'

And there's a blur. Lucien's voice in two places at once. What Clare remembered and what I now see.

'You've been here before,' I say.

'We don't have time for this, Simon.'

'What do you mean?'

'I thought we had gone past it.' His face is cold, with a starry glint.

'The arrival in London is mud,' he says. Before I can stop him, he steps past me, grabs the memory bag. He pulls open the drawstring and empties out the contents.

My memories lying on the floor. Out in the open. The wrongness of it in my joints and bones. I shake my head like I can refuse it and I push Lucien to one side and go to my knees to start gathering back the objects.

Not looking at them, but pictures come anyway, through my fingers. I grab open my bag presto, shove the memories in, feel them fall from me. Arms sweep across the floor like I'm trying to swim. Memories at the tips of my fingers.

Then from the tangle of remaining things I don't want to see Lucien pulls something. The burberry from this morning streaked with mud. He pushes it into my hands.

69

'It's yours, Simon,' is what he says. 'Why the hell don't you claim it?'

Before I can drop it into the bag, the picture comes into my head. Hard and clear. A wide highway of mud with rainholes drilled. A heavy sky. *Fields like lines of grey along the horizon.*

Then memory comes at me and it is like being shoved under-water. Cold water in my lungs, breaking into my nose. Cold, dark water pushing behind my eyes as if from somewhere inside of me. My body is heavy because I am moving in the wrong element. The ground looks stable and solid. I should be down there, I think.

I think vaguely, This is what it must be like for him, to be blind, to hear only.

And in the moment before everything goes black, I see Lucien watching. His eyes are searching for something inside me I don't know is there. They are pale and cold, but they are not without sympathy.

Matins

I wake. The pact wakes. We sound Onestory. I run in the under with Clare. A fight between strandpickers in the mud. A half-toll after None, down in the strand by Green Witch, two pickers working the same stretch. They are dressed in the same dark green roughcloth, their odd bounty of tin and token and old blue stickwrap bags tied and strapped to them every whichway. At Vespers comes Chimes and we hear it on the strand. In the storehouse, we practise round the cookstove.

I wake. The pact wakes. We sound Onestory. I run in the under with Clare. We take five ounces, and then from the snares at Embankment Gardens I take two rabbits and a squirrel. The skin on my upper left arm itches like it has something pressing to say. There is smoke on the river after Vespers. Thick and sweet and heavy like incense. At Vespers comes Chimes and we hear it on the strand. I rid my mind of questions and wait for the circle of chords to take me.

I wake. The pact wakes. We sound Onestory. I run in the under with Clare.

We're at the end of a run and on our way back with the Pale when I hear the cooee. Wistful and lonely sounding, a repeated falling minor third like the playground songs that children sing. My neck bristles for there's nothing lost or lorn about those notes. Their meaning is scum in the tunnels: poliss. I turn to Clare and she hisses under her breath, her eyes wide and white in the lowlight. She has heard too. The whistle again closer already and then, poco a poco, I hear the footfalls that bring them.

There are at least three running, by the sound of their far-off tread. I am frozen for a second. Run, or go tacet and wait? Cut stick, or hope like hell they're moving down here for another reason? In the dark, I push through what pictures come thin and breathless for guidance. None of any other run-in with the poliss. It's forbidden to hold the Lady except with intent to trade. The law says it and it leaves a hole to get in or out by wide open. There is nothing to stop the poliss breaking us here, pulling some easy Pale, selling it on.

In the dark, the footfalls come again, nearer now, and there is no time to seek out reasons as the footsteps are coming in our direction. I pitch myself forward. Clare is behind me and we run headlong, tacet as we can though the walls ring loud in our flight. Behind us, the footfalls are heavy. I whisper the melody underbreath as I run. I do not want to be taken. My fear is not of a beating but of a dark box with no window far from the river and I search desperate for a crack in the tune, a hidden cranny to follow off the main wide tributaries. Something that they will not be privy to. There are three of them, and it is clear they know the tunnels almost as well as we do, and they are faster.

We follow the path that we came on. I turn the melody inside out as we run. I hold to it even through the cold clamour of my heartbeat. After the second cadence we stop. For a while there is nothing in the tunnel but the ragged duet of our breath. I look for the white of Clare's eyes.

'Do you think we've lost them?' I ask.

Clare doesn't reply; she is listening still. I turn my ear in the same direction and I hear what I do not wish to – the dull tread of boots. About the same distance off as before. Again I hear the low murmuring and for a moment I don't understand. Why idle in the under if they could take us? And then I realise they are in no hurry. We are leading them to the entrance, our amphitheatre.

I see then what I have to do.

'Here,' I say. I loose the Lady to her in a short lob. 'You go tacet. Take the Pale. I'll lead them off. I'll meet you at the storehouse.'

Clare nods mute and is off with silent footfall before I can speak again.

I wait for five beats and then I pull the small whistle from round my neck. I put it to my lips and blow our comeallye, as high and taunting as I can make it. Strange to hear the tune, innermost and close as a name, skewed in the harsh, baiting echo. I fight the need to run. I wait two beats more past what I think I need to and then I move off. Presto, forte.

Like some miracle, the path to take is picked out clear in my head, lit by panic. I pull them round in an intricate woven circle. Every few cadences I force myself to stop and send out the come-allye again. I push out in shallow darts from the circle to seem like I'm trying to shake them off.

I pull them up and down, through all the main stormwater drains with their nice clear echoes, until I hear the shallow sound of running water. For a moment I forget my fear in the small glow of pride. I have kept my bearings. It is the sound of the culvert, the border of our territory with Earl's Sluice. I pause for good measure; then I send out the comeallye for the last time, sharp and high so it will cut deep into the ears of the poliss who are following as well as into the tunnels of our rival pact. Then I wait.

I wait for the sounds that I know are coming. Keep my eyes fixed hard on the flickering light of the culvert where it gives into the grey. A wild yell to my right and I breathe and I do not move. Bootfalls come closer on my other side as I stand stockstill, trying to hear into and through the deafening thud that's inside me. Then clanging sticks to the ceiling, and a tall, barechested figure comes teeth bared down the tunnel with cohorts mad behind. Their faces in wide grimaces of joy to see a Five Rover solo on their legitimate run. Like I've given them a splendid gift. I wait, pray some rune I didn't even know I knew. I hear the footfall to my left at the same moment, and just then the coshes and upswung

73

arms and thick uniformed bodies round the tunnelcorner. And it's like it's all gone lento for a few beats almost peaceful and just at the moment they're nearly on me I ready myself and bend my knees and push out, dive out, into the tunnelmouth of the culvert and the dark, cold rushing.

Cold of water goes all through me. Sounds echo oddly behind and the current carries me down the sluice, so strong I can't get my head up, and then I'm full in the Thames. The hard, dark water pushing at my back and I go with the tide that sweeps me down, half drowned, until I am spat back out on the muck of the strand, my chest heaving against any order of mine and a shivering cold so deep inside me I can barely stand.

Black spots float in my vision. Some last energy bestowed by god knows what and I manage to pull myself up to the strand and half walk, half crawl over the narrow road and into the nearest park. Using silence and elbows, I get in close to the huddle of memorylost round a firelit mettle rubbish bin. I warm myself and wait there until the shivering has stopped and my clothes are damp only. And all the while my brain is trying to work. Poliss in the under is wrong. And there was something else too. Some other break from the daily rhythm over the last thrennoch. Through the grey of forgetting I try to chase it. Something wrong. Something to do with Lucien. Something to do with my memories. Some connection between them like a constellation of dischord, a burr round which the fumbled notes cluster.

I do not know what to do. Though the pact will no doubt think me taken by the poliss, I am not ready to return to the storehouse. So I walk and I think and I try to understand.

The leftover buildings that I pass are empty and blank-eyed. The floors left above hang empty, like cages. The arch of the bridge with the layers of faded posters. A looted ground-floor shop that still has the sign for a pothecary on the window. The wall of that building there with graffiti in a messy spray of faded

74

red paint, last message from a person long gone. I've passed this all many times, I know, and I am also happening on it for the first time today.

After a while I have walked as far as Tower Bridge.

I sit then, in the shadow of the abutment, at the bottom of a set of steps so that my feet rest on rivermud. I put my head between my knees. Every few minutes I feel the thrust or shove of a stranger pushing past, home to their family, home to food and Vespers. I have to get back to the storehouse, but I cannot move.

I take a fistful of thamesmud in my hands as I sit. Sieve it through my fingers until all that is left behind is a single river-stone, dry and gritted and without life. And it speaks to me, or tries to speak, sitting in my palm there like a token of something long forgotten. I raise my head and lean back and I look west to the enormous sprawling ruin. Behind the bridge, untouched and keeping its own memory of Allbreaking, blocks of pale stone lie where they have fallen. Vines all over the broken walls. Two pale towers still mostly whole rise up out of the rubble.

Between the bent blue mettle of the bridge and the river. There, with its half-arch reflected like a mouth gulping at the river's green water, a half-moon opening. Between river and city, between water and air. There are letters of white code painted across it that speak in letters I cannot read. ENTRY TO THE TRAITORS' GATE, they say.

And something rises up. Bubbles to the surface. A picture.

I'm lying on my back. Pain in my temple and skull. Head in the water and light flickering through.

Someone in ragged jeans stands over me. A thickset boy of prentiss age with brown hair. Behind him, someone tall and lean with pale eyes and curled hair. And with the picture come the notes of a song, simple and clear. *In the quiet times of power.* I hear the notes unfold in front of me, and as they go past, I snatch them.

And then it's Chimes.

75

I stride through the darkening streets past the tripropes and the gatehouse of rusted cranes, past the rest of them sitting in the storehouse with instruments held and their faces turned toward me tacet in shock and relief and I go straight to my quarters.

Candle by snuffed candle, the dark comes. Sitting there with my back against the wall, I finger the riverstone I took on the strand. *The arrival in London?* I go to the shelf where I keep my memory bag. Next to it is a block of hardwood with a pencil sketch of two figures. Next to that is a bundled-up garment streaked in mud. I stand there and look at these two things I have left out in the shallows like a message for myself. I stand there and I finger the riverstone and I see myself flat on my back with my head in the water and I hear the song creeping by me on the waters.

Oddments in thamesmud, these memories. Unlinked and unmeaning. And then I put them together in a line.

The arrival in London? the voice asks. I sweep through the debris in my head. Do it like Harry's hand does to clear shell and stone. Empty so that the pictures can rise. I see myself standing in mud on a long road. What road was it? What was I doing there? I was leaving the farm I had grown up on. Why? What happened to my parents?

I feel the grip of my mother's hand, shaking. I see her worsen with the shaking. I see her speak to me in the pause of the spasms.

I see myself travelling to London alone. No, not alone. With a carter, on the back of a cart. He gives me his burberry and I go into the noisy streets. I was looking for someone, something, but I couldn't find it. Then Chimes came and everything was stripped clean and quiet.

And I heard the silence of the Lady and I went, for the first time, down to the river. To the strand. Then my head knocked half through by the blow of a thrown stone. Down by the ruins of the tower, Brennan threw a stone that hit me. With my head in the river I heard a song.

The first time I laid eyes on Lucien he stood, pale and blind, with the light in his hair. Then the edge of his mouth twitched up. Half-grin, half-smirk.

And then he said something else, under his breath and to me alone.

'That song,' he said. 'It's worth your life in these parts.'

I didn't understand what he meant. I didn't say anything, just kept my eyes empty like I know how to do. And he waited, examined me somehow, though without sight. Then the moment passed and the edge returned to his voice.

'Forgive Brennan,' he said. 'He is very protective of our territory.'

The voice in my head is Lucien's. The questions are Lucien's. The song is how he chose me. It is where his questions started and the place to which they always circle back.

The darkness that has kept me covered for so long pulls back. In the half-light that is not yet understanding, I stand up. And finally, finally I walk out to the balcony where Lucien is waiting for me.

The moonlight falls on his face. When his voice comes, it is as clear as Chimes.

'The arrival in London,' he asks, 'what was it like?'

'I was standing alone on the roadside in the rain,' I say.

The words seem to come from someone else, or some bit of me I can't touch or feel. Like bodymemory from a missing leg or finger. 'I was waiting for somebody to come along the road and give me a ride to London. I waited for a long time before a carter stopped. He handed me his burberry and I put it on, and we went into the city.'

'Good. Where were you waiting?'

Saltflats in the horizon. Flat fields. A farmhouse with a red door.

'Outside of London. Essex.'

77

Lucien is doing something with his hands, twisting a bit of leather cord. He knots it and threads it between his palms. Then he does something complicated and quick with his fingers so that the cord stretches between his open hands like a noose.

'Why were you leaving the farm?'

I pause. A white shape moves up in me. I don't want to look at it, but I have to.

'They died. Both of them. My mother first.'

'What did they die from?'

'First my mother's hands started to shake. It wasn't bad at first; she could still work. She could do solfege at Chimes, make bread. Then it got worse. She could hardly hold a pencil.' My voice fades. I stare at my own hands until they blur in front of my eyes.

'After that she couldn't walk and had to stay in bed. Then she could hardly talk. Then she found it hard to breathe.' I try to keep my voice calm. I rub my eyes. 'She died, and then my father. I don't remember his death. It must have been soon after.'

And they were buried twice. Once in the ground, once in my memory. My heart hurts. What had I felt before in that spot? Numbness. Hard and lifeless like a dry riverstone.

'I am sorry, Simon,' Lucien says. He pulls the cord from his hands so that he can sign the mourning cadence of the formal solfege.

Then he looks at me harder, measuring.

'Simon,' Lucien says, 'after your arrival in London, how did you find us? How did you find the pact?'

'I didn't find you. You found *me*. I heard the Lady, and I went down to the river. I was trying to find where the silence was coming from. Then Brennan bloody well knocked me out.'

Lucien laughs. 'Brennan saw you. If I remember right, he said, "There's some Walbrook scum on our turn, right in broad daylight." Before I could stop him, he threw the stone. He hit you and you fell into the water and stayed there. I thought he might've killed you. When we got closer, he saw what you were wearing.

Farmclothes. So we knew you weren't Walbrook. Not Effra or Neckinger either. You weren't even some prentiss who'd stolen a leisure hour for mudlarking. It wasn't chance or mistake had brought you to the Pale. You heard the Lady and you went straight to her.'

'But you didn't ask me to join the pact because of my hearing,' I say.

To put the memories down like this in a line that starts in one place and moves to another, to know that they live outside me in Lucien's keeping – not just hoarded in a memory bag. It rings through me that thought, like his voice does. 'It was the song that came to me when I was head down in the river. You recognised it and warned me against singing it.'

'Yes. That's right.'

'Well, what does it mean?'

He shakes his head lento. 'That's what I need you to tell me. Can you sing it?'

'No.' But as I say it, words come into my head.

'*In the quiet days of power*,' I say. All at once I am certain. 'That's how it starts.' Then I stop. 'I don't know what comes next.'

'Take your time,' says Lucien.

I close my eyes. Why was I coming into London, and what did it have to do with the song? Pictures float up and pull apart and come together again. Then at last I see a picture of my mother standing next to me. We are working. I feel the rhythm of it in my hands, a grip and twist like kneading bread. Then my mother singing.

I listen. I wait.

Nothing comes. I close my eyes again. I hear a rhythm first and then nonsense syllables that roll in my mouth.

'*Gwil-lum Hu-ginn Ce-dric Thor*,' I say.

Lucien looks at me, wondering.

I hold my hands in front of me and study them. The echo of the movement is in the muscle. Grip and twist. Easy and sharp. What were we doing?

And subito I have the answer and as soon as I do, I see that it could not be anything else. Not kneading bread. Breaking bulbs. A clean break and the smell of white sap. A drawing of an animal with a hooked beak, wings spread. *Wings.*

Seven ravens in the tower, I think.

'*Seven ravens in the tower,*' I say out loud.

I look at Lucien. His eyes are bright. Then I say the whole thing out without stopping.

> '*In the quiet days of power,*
> *seven ravens in the tower.*
> *When you clip the raven's wing,*
> *then the bird begins to sing.*
> *When you break the raven's beak,*
> *then the bird begins to speak.*
> *When the Chimes fill up the sky,*
> *then the ravens start to fly.*
> *Gwillum, Huginn, Cedric, Thor,*
> *Odin, Hardy, nevermore.*
> *Never ravens in the tree*
> *till Muninn can fly home to me.*'

Lucien's face glows in the half-light. He places his hand on my shoulder so I feel the weight of it right down my back. 'Thank you, Simon,' he says in a low voice, and there is nothing of joke in it.

'I don't understand,' I say. 'What does it mean?'

'Do you trust me, Simon?'

I look at him. In the under, we follow Lucien. Follow him like blind faith. In the under, when the map flares up around like a fire with the door open and the arms of the tunnels reach out, it's all you have. A following that's almost like falling. And once you've felt it, nothing else has much pull anymore. Why would it? What else opens up your veins like that, pulls the sky in, fish-hooks the stars into such brightness?

I nod.

'Then listen. I don't know what the song means. I know the tune and I know its threat. But I need you to remember what your mother told you about it.'

I stare at him. He has slipped the leather cord between his hands and I watch the patterns he is making, triangles moving and being cut in half and then in half again. His hands muddy, like he has just dug something out of the earth.

I realise that there is something else he needs to know.

'We saw a member of the Order in the burial-ground cross-house, Brennan and I, when we went to sing the snares.'

His hands halt with the pattern of crisscrossed cords between them. 'What night was this?'

I think hard, count back. 'A thrennoch ago, I think.'

'Not at Ropemakers, at Bow?'

'Yes. Ropemakers was empty, no snares, no people, which I thought was strange. He was walking among the memorylost. He . . .' I try to see it again, the movements he made. 'He looked like he was prospecting for Pale. He listened to the air around the memorylost. Then he disappeared out of the yard and back into the crosshouse. We heard something scratching on stone.'

'And then?'

'After he was gone, we checked the crosshouse. We wanted to see what he was doing. What made the sound.'

'And?'

I describe what the member scratched in the wall at the entrance. The staves the length of a broad armspan. Then I pause, turn presto and leave the balcony. On the shelf behind my hammock, the folded paper is sitting where I left it. When I hand it to Lucien he says nothing. I watch as he opens the paper. He shades his brow and squints hard and then he traces the deeply lined scratches. After a while his pale eyes flinch and then flare. I have not asked him if he is able to read music. For some reason I do not need to.

'It's formal,' he says. 'A kind of fugue.'

I wait for him to say more.

'An old form. What used to be called a *ricercar*. Which means "to search out". The first few notes are a name. Then the last part means *forze*, or "power". The way it's put together is what makes the message.' He pauses. 'We will have to move presto now. We need to know all that you can remember about your mother. We need to know more about what the song means. We don't have much time. Every spare moment you have, try if you can to remember. I will downsound it with you.'

'Yes,' I say. I wait, but Lucien is tacet, still in thought.

'Well?' I ask.

'Well what?'

'What does the message mean?'

There is something unspoken in his pause and he looks straight at me, testing, waiting.

'There are a couple of ways you could read it. But in the vernacular the simplest reading is: *Lucien, we will find you.*'

Wandle in the Under

Today we start off at a quick jog. Though everything underneath and above it has changed, the rhythm of the day stays the same. I wake. The pact wakes. We sound Onestory. We run in the under. The tune is bright and cocky at first, moving stepwise up the tonic chord into the large tunnelmouth to our direct north. It's a stormwater drain, but a large one, quite dry.

We run easy, barely crouching, side by side. The echo of our splashing feet in the tile tunnel keeps us company. Sometimes the splashing seems to be coming from ahead of us, and sometimes from behind. And then I'd swear that I hear a third lot of footfalls, speeding and slowing, as if trying to get us to lose our pace. Strange sounds are part of the under. Sometimes you see strange things too. Glowing patches moving with us as we run, floating across the path. Maybe it's gas burning off. Maybe the spirits of pactrunners who've died down here.

The tune takes us further down the tunnel, deep into the heart of the map. Its beat fits to our jogging rhythm. I hear it thumping in my blood too. Then the tunnel starts to bend and we both hear the modulation to the fourth chord coming in mind's ear. The modulation that spins around the home key and shows us which tunnel to take. It's an easy path. The first tunnelmouth that looms up ahead is the one that fits our cadence. Due west. Without a word, we both veer off the main tunnel and enter its dark mouth.

Narrower, now. The calm, clean echo of the tiles changes into a harsh clang. It's mettle, filled with the sharp note of rust, a strident, bright smell that pitches us on faster. The melody fills the tunnel right up and takes on an orange ferrous darkness and ringing speed. Try not to trip over your own feet as they outpace you.

Clare takes the lead, shifts us through some tricky cross rhythms and time changes. It's jaunty, full of darting offbeat flurries. After five bars of the same four-four time, there is a quick near-blind corner and then the path doubles back awhile. Then it breaks into a triplet rhythm, three-eight, for about the same distance. Each version of the tune darts out into another tunnel juncture.

We are breathing presto when we reach the final spurt of the first subject. From there, it's into a drawn-out, restful melody with long strides all heading northwest. Clare sets our pace at a rolling trot. I put my hands to the walls and feel rough concrete then slim wiring along it, at about the level of my head. It's a comms tunnel.

The lines of wire, someone said, I don't remember who, used to be how sound travelled. I don't understand this, as they are not tight stretched like cello or viol strings, but slack and covered in stickwrap.

After a while we're coming near to where Lucien sang the Lady's cadence. I start to listen for her as we run, wait for the telltale drops of silence, the silver shiver.

When her silence speaks out, I pull on Clare's shirt to get her to stop.

Lento steps and then the usual flash of surprise as her silver fills my mind with quiet blindness. I extend my hand in the dark ahead of me. The water is cold, and leaves and wads of stickwrap and mulched paper swim past as I try to sluice tacet through the muck. And there she is. A smooth, gnarled round and the silver bright in my ear. My fingers close on the nugget and I lift it clear of the water.

We retrace the tune and are heading clear south back to the tonic and the amphitheatre when I hear it. A high cry, cut off sharp. I stop short and Clare, a few metres ahead, wheels. In the few seconds as the echo dies, I take its bearings. We stand and wait for the sound to come again, but it does not.

'I think that was Abel,' Clare says. The fear in her voice makes my stomach and throat feel like they're made of cold water.

The cry came from one of the large tunnels to the east. If I am right with my bearings, it is one of the ones with two times a man's headroom and echoed mettle tracks. We need the straightest path there.

I force the map up in my head and look for it. I peer through the darkness and its half-lit, ghosted strands. And at last I think I have the route.

With Clare behind, I run back down the gutters of the path we came in on, ignoring all the turnings until we reach a wide brick mouth. It's a dry stormwater drain, and a long straight run with the brick walls circling overhead. If I'm right, it will open into a service tunnel that will take us down to the tracks.

We sprint down the bricked way. I feel the sweat in my eyes. But after only a few beats of straight run I can see the tunnel's end, sealed in brick. I curse. We come to the bricked face and slow to a walk and I draw breath. On the left wall is a blue mettle door.

It opens onto a short corridor and a curving mettle staircase. Rust under the yellow paint. At the bottom of the stair, another heavier door and I breathe relief as I know we are in the right place and it opens. We slide out at ground level, into a wide, high tunnel. Dark rusted mettle rails run under our feet.

Four or five beats from us, on the wide grey expanse of the concrete platform above, three figures are struggling. They push and turn in a strange sort of dance. Two are tall pactrunners with legs bound in black stickwrap. The third is Abel.

Abel fights silent. He spits and bites and kicks. The tallest, a thin-faced, dark-haired guy, is trying to hold his arms back while the other searches him. As we watch, Abel's knee makes contact with the searcher's stomach.

'Fucking leave trying to hold him and just get him down.' And the dark-haired one punches Abel in the face.

Clare flinches. I reach to my ankle and pull my knife. Light is coming into the station from behind us, where the tunnel emerges at ground level. But we're standing in shadows and invisible. They must be Wandle. Why they're in our territory I have no idea. The worse for them.

Things move lento. I pull Clare back into the stairwell, then up one flight of steps. The door to the platform is warped, but we shoulder it together in one push that scrapes harsh on the concrete.

I run with my hunting knife held close to my body, Clare with a full-throated scream, lips back and teeth bared. We're across the platform before they can turn. Clare jumps the short one and I land a fist to the other's head, my punch loaded with the knife handle. I feel the jolt through my arm and teeth.

He stumbles. Drops to hands and knees. I go in for the kick, but before I can connect with his ribs, he pushes up and grabs my foot. I hop on the other, kick back hard. My kick connects with shoulder, but he scuttles back and gets up with a sneer. Then he leans low and comes forward with slow sweeps of his arms, just out of reach of the knife.

I see how much bigger he is, as he bounces from foot to foot with a leer. His hair is black with dirt and oil, and his rattish face is grained with it. I flex my fingers against the knife handle, try to imagine the feel of it meeting another person's body. It can't be too much different from rabbit or squirrel, is what I think.

Between Ratface and me Abel lies still on the grey concrete. To my right, Clare and the other runner. Clare tight on his back, knees gripping his waist. Her forearm across his neck, and he's pulling at it, trying to throw her off. She can't hold him for long. If we want to get Abel clear, I need to get the tall runner down.

I move forward, holding the knife in a hammer-grip still, testing it against the air. The runner backs off, but his face is mocking. He's watching my eyes, not the knife. He doesn't think I've got the stones to use it.

As if to show he's right, I hunch my shoulders. I let the tension go out of my neck and I drop my knife arm. I spit into the dust in front of my feet. Then I feint to my left. As he lunges forward to grab me, I twist down under his arms and behind, close enough to get my arm over his shoulder and my knife blade up under his neck. It speaks cold and hard against his jawline and he goes very still.

'OK, OK, OK,' he says. 'OK.'

'Tell your friend to let Clare go.'

The other runner is throwing himself against the wall to loosen Clare, who's clamped to his back. I tighten my grip on the knife and Ratface calls. Clare's runner turns, sees me with the knife and straightens, releasing his grip on Clare's arm.

Clare slumps off, falls to her knees. She scrambles over to Abel. The runner who held her stands straight and still. He looks from me to the knife to the eyes of his leader. There's a long gash down his face from Clare's fingernails. None of us move, apart from Clare, who is feeling Abel's ribs and face, listening to his breath.

My heart is beating in my ears and I feel sick. I shift my grip and adjust the pressure against the runner's jaw. My other elbow is tight against his ribs, letting him know what will happen if he tries to twist me off. I don't remember when I have been so close to another person. He smells of the sweet rot of clothes that have dried damp.

I throw a sharp whistle through my teeth. 'You!' I jerk my head at the one who still stands there bleeding. 'Get down onto the tracks.'

Clare's runner walks to the edge of the platform, executes a neat jump and lands on the rusted rails. Mice scatter.

What I am holding is a puzzle. How will we get away without them coming after us? Even if Abel can walk, we'll be slow. The thought of putting one of them out of action doesn't appeal. I take a breath, but before I can give my next order, there's a shift in the sound on the platform.

From the edge of the tunnel where the dark bleeds out into the early light, a figure comes at a light jog. Hands lifting and skating along the air in his coming, and I swear I hear him humming underbreath too. Lucien.

He vaults up to the platform and stops a way from Clare. On the tracks at a few beats' distance behind is Brennan. The runner I'm holding goes rigid for a second as he sees Lucien. Down on the tracks, the other runner has turned too. Then he looks back and I see Ratface shake his head once, lento. I clip his ear with the knife handle.

The next thing I hear is Lucien's low chuckle.

'Two, Simon?' he asks, though I have no doubt he can hear them in mind's ear clearer than I can see them in the half-light.

'Yes. Wandle. They had Abel.'

'Gentlemen,' begins Lucien, looking direct from Clare's runner on the platform to the one in front of me. 'Gentlemen of Wandle. You're in our territory.'

Down on the tracks, Clare's runner walks closer to the edge of the platform where Lucien stands.

'It won't be your territory for much longer,' he says. 'Not if they have anything to do with it.' And he reaches to the pocket on the side of his jeans.

'Hey,' I yell, and tighten my grip on the knife.

With his spare air, Ratface shouts his friend a warning, '*Jakes.*'

But Jakes doesn't hear. He swaggers insolently close to the platform.

In a quick few steps Lucien is crouched beside him. His hand snakes out and he has Jakes by the T-shirt, pulled close under his throat. He grabs the runner's hand in his fist and removes what's crumpled in it. Then Lucien leans his head close to the runner and whispers something. A dark second passes. I cannot hear what is said, but I see the runner buckle. His legs weaken and he sways and I notice in shock that he is almost crying.

Lucien pushes him back gently. I let out my breath as he stumbles and falls loose on the tracks.

Lucien unbends and looks straight at me.

'Under the Green Witch parallel, the territory is open. We leave you, Wandle runners, to prospect there. We typically have more than we need, so we can afford to be generous. However, it would be worth your while to keep in bounds.' Then he nods to me.

I let go the runner I've been holding and shove him forward with my foot. He takes a step and then looks back, as if checking he's done what he was supposed to do.

'Get out,' says Lucien, reasonably.

Ratface jumps to the tracks where Clare's runner is still sitting on his arse. Then he roughly grabs him, pulls him to his feet, propels him forward. The fallen runner stumbles, as if some life or fight has been taken from him. They push off down the tunnel, into the dark. We are left alone in silence.

Lucien sings the melody for the quickest way back to Five Rover. Brennan takes Abel on his back and Clare walks beside, stroking Abel's forehead now and again and murmuring to herself in disgust. I'm last. I cast a look back over the platform. I try to think how long we've gone without any territory dispute. Why was it worth Wandle's while to enter our run?

Clare lies Abel down by the cookstove and tries to get some sweet milky tea into his mouth, though most of it dribbles back out. One of his eyes is swollen shut, and a bruise spreads down the side of his face. His eyes move under the lids. Lento, like he's in no hurry to surface. And I see he needs a push to come up. Or something to reach down and hook him.

I leave the storehouse and run toward the vendors at the edges of the Cut. I run it with my footfalls hard and echoing on the flat concrete. The tunes bristle sharp with banter and haggle among the stalls and carts and blankets. A man with a tall trolley crammed with bottles stands some way down the line of them. Next to him there's a large pot boiling on a sterno ring that wafts clouds of hot gin steam, heady with sugar and lemon. *Rum, sweetwine, porter, brandy*, goes the man's song. *Sweetwine, ginpunch, brandy, rum.* I fish the tokens from my pocket in exchange for a small, flat bottle of his brandy. 'Careful of the kick,' he says, and his braying follows me down the canal.

The swig I take on the way back burns salted fire down the back of my throat and makes my eyes run. 'Strong enough to bring anyone back from the dead' is what I say to Clare when I hand it to her.

Later, through the curtains, I hear the muffled sound of Abel coughing, then a low murmuring until all is tacet except the rhythm of Lucien pacing. He did not speak to me when I came in, but his voice is somehow still in my head. *Do you trust me?* he asks, and the weight of his hand on my shoulder. *Every spare moment you have, try if you can to remember.* I hold my memory bag, let my fingers move over the objects. Silent textures slip through my hands without snag or speech. And then I come to rest on a piece of cloth with a frayed edge. I fetch it up.

Roughcloth. Hardy, for farm use. The colour faded. Something thrums inside me and I know I have chosen right because I smell the smell of sunheated parasheeting, the peppery perfume of daffs and a green and brown warmth and I go down . . .

Dappled sun through parasheeting.

Smell of earth, of green things, of sap and leafmould.

I'm standing in the forcinghouse where the hard, driving sun makes flowers open before their time and I'm holding the rotted wood handle of a trowel. I've been weeding irises in the near fields with the journeymen and it has broken. I've come in here to find another.

Along the walls are shelves that hold tools and supplies. Balls of twine, cardboard boxes filled with old seed packets, leather gloves that still hold the shape of hands, poly seeding punnets that fit one inside the other in tall steeples. But for the life of me I can't see a single trowel.

I have been standing for several breaths before I see my mother. She is stripping and splitting bulbs at the workbench at the other side of the forcinghouse.

'Hello, love,' she says. 'Why don't you leave the weeding for a bit and give me a hand with this.'

I walk over to her through the sunshine that's coming through the leaves that grow up the para panels. She passes me a short, blunt knife. There is a tremor in her hand and she tries to disguise it by gripping her fingers tight into a fist and releasing them by her side. With her left hand she pushes a trug of clumped bulbs toward me. When her hands are moving, I cannot see the shaking. Is it still there, in the joints? I make myself ignore the thought.

There is something familiar about where we are standing and what we are doing, the light, the smell, the rhythm of our hands. We have been here before, standing in the same positions.

'There are things you'll need to know when I am gone, Simon. Some of them important.' As if she's stepping out for a while to visit a sick neighbour or to the next village to swap seeds.

'What do you mean, when you're gone? Where are you going?' I turn to look at her.

'Keep working,' she says. 'Keep splitting the bulbs while I talk.'

After she's satisfied that I'm doing so, she continues. 'You've noticed the shaking,' she says. 'You know, don't you, that it will keep coming, that it will get worse. After a while I won't be able to work.'

'Then I'll do the work,' I say. 'You don't need to worry about it.'

She doesn't answer. Waits a bit.

'You keep your memories in the green bag. The one in your room?' she asks.

I am uncomfortable talking about that. I slide a fingernail under a clod of mud, twist the knotted bulb so that it breaks in two. The split is clean and white. I wash the two new bulbs in the bleach bucket and put them into the wet paper. 'Yes,' I say eventually.

'That is good. You should keep them with you always.' She turns to me. 'Simon, when you choose a memory, what happens?'

'What do you mean?'

'In your mind. What happens?'

What happens when I put food in my mouth? I taste it. What happens when I hold a memory? I see it.

'I see it,' I say. 'The pictures come into my mind. They stay for a while, then they go. What do you mean?'

'You know not everybody can do that, don't you?'

I look at her, disbelieving. 'Why would anybody make memories at all, then?'

'It's not an easy thing to explain. What people can and can't recall. How they do it. It's a bit like the mudflats.' She looks at me, then, like she's fixing something in with the drill of her grey eyes. 'When the water lies at the far edge of the sky. At its edges the two elements are blended. Forgetting and remembering are like that. It's hard to tell one from the other at times. But, yes, you're right. Some people never make objectmemories.

'And those who do make physical objects, most don't see memory in them at all. They keep them for comfort. Or there's a bare shadow in them of what happened. If you don't know any different, a shadow is probably enough. Of course, there are a few like you who can see them clear, as if they are happening. Then there are those like me.'

'What can you do?'

She holds her hands out from her so we both see the current that plays over them. Thumb and smallest finger oscillating in the air like she's playing an octave trill on an invisible klavier.

'I can see memories,' she says, 'that others have made.'

I am silent. The idea is impossible.

There is a sound at the end of the forcinghouse and we turn at

92

the same moment. Standing at the door is a man, his expression scared. He sees me and draws back, pushes the bag that's slung across his shoulder behind him.

'It's all right,' my mother says. 'You can come in. This is my son.' She turns back to me. 'It's your choice, Simon. You are old enough to decide.'

The man comes closer. I recognise him. It's Johannes, who teaches rudiments and solfege at the local school. I raise my hand in the notes for greeting and he carves out the response. So crisp and clear I can't help feeling the implied correction of my slumped tones.

'What do you have, Johannes?' my mother asks.

'My son is leaving the village,' he says. 'He will be prentissed to one of the instrument makers in London.' He comes forward and the pride is evident on his face. I know Charles. He came up in my year. A skilled lutenist. And a bully.

'I have many memories of him, of course. But this is our final dinner.' He holds out a coiled mettle lute string. 'I want to remember it particularly. We played a duet that he wrote for the occasion.' He hums a phrase and places the string on the bench in front of my mother.

'Thank you for bringing this. I will keep it. Would you like to be told of it again?'

He nods. 'Tell it to me next time at the market. Then I'll decide when after.'

He leaves, and my mother places the memory on a piece of roughcloth.

It's a while before I can speak. Everything I thought I knew about my mother is shifting, moving, modulating. 'Does anyone forget they've given them to you?'

'Yes. Most wish me to remind them, tell them the story of it again. But some are happy to forget as long as I keep the object-memory safe.'

She beckons to me. 'Over here, Simon. Come.' I walk nearer.

'My mother had the skill to keep others' memories too. It goes in families.' She looks at me, and her look is a question.

'It's illegal?'

'Yes, it is. And you will have to understand the danger. But isn't it better to know what you can do? Then at least it is your choice.'

She is asking me to touch it. 'I'm not sure,' I say.

Then there is another noise, this time sharp and loud. My father is standing a few feet inside the door. A basket hangs loose in his hands. On the dirt floor, the bulbs it held are scattered askance and rolling in misshapen half-circles. My mother spreads her arms wide. It is an unthinking movement and for a moment I wonder whether she is shielding what she is doing from his vision, or whether it is my father who is the one that must be protected.

If you did not know him, you might not hear the anger as he forms his words careful and precise. I can feel the cold coming from across the room and I draw back.

'You gave me your word,' he says to my mother.

'What did I say?' she asks.

'Don't play those tricks.'

'I said I would not take them to London anymore. I didn't say I would no longer keep them. I can't refuse to take them. I can't turn people away.'

'What you said is that you would look to your safety so we could bring up our son. You said Simon would stay clear of it. Do you want him to be hunted down and tortured? Killed?' The muscles around his mouth work even after he stops speaking. His hands clench, unclench. I am afraid, though not sure what I am afraid of. When I was young, he would carry me across the fields and I thought nothing could come for me, not even down out of the sky.

My mother speaks piano. 'We don't have the right to choose for Simon if he has the gift.'

Mouth crooked like it's broken. Everything out of line. 'Don't have the right? What rights are left? He is my son and I might *forget everything else, but I won't forget that. I won't let him do this.'*

He takes my arm and pulls me to the bench where my mother steps aside. He bends me over the bench with his weight at my back so my face is close to the memory. So close I'm almost touching it with my chin. I stare at the string. Threads tuft off the yellow cotton at its tail where it once wound onto the peg of the instrument.

'Look at it, Simon. Look close,' he says. 'Do you see it? Other people's pain? Other people's happiness?' He pulls me back up toward him and puts his hands up to my cheeks. 'You are not going to die for that,' he says. And then he punches me in the stomach.

The floor is cold and the nails' smooth heads touch like mouths on my bare feet. The echo of my father's punch is raw and empty in the centre of my belly, and a part of me feels like crying. I walk to the balcony, open the door and lean out. It is empty, only the tomato plants climbing their way slowly upward in the silver light. At Lucien's quarters, I stand still for a while. My heart is loud. I am certain that I have forgotten something. I should not disturb him. I clear my throat, enough that he would hear. I wait. Five long breaths. Then, in one movement, I soundlessly pull aside the curtain.

It is bare, empty. There is no shelf. No memory bag. No candles. His hammock is folded neatly on the ground next to a grey wool blanket the same as the one in my quarters. Lucien has gone.

I go back to my quarters, pull a jacket from the small bundle of clothes that makes my pillow. I dip a waterpouch in the parabucket. I take my knife from my ankle and slip it through my belt so that I can feel the cold of it lying against my stomach. Then I slip the bolt out smooth, push down the latch and try to open the door as silent as I can.

Nothing is moving out on the race. I stay close to the storehouses, slide past lento and pause at the rubble of the row past ours, where one section of the side wall has been destroyed. The wind comes off the river and blows between the emptied buildings, giving birth to fast new currents.

Then, down the far end, just before the cranes, I see a figure weaving. It moves forward lento, and every few steps it stops.

Even while standing it sways back and forth and has to hold its arms out in a curious way. Just before the first broken bridge, the figure clips down to its knees and empties its stomach into the water there, hunched over and all out of tune.

Lucien's walk is from the top of his head down, his neck pitched straight as a plumbline, like a keen vibration. This is just some poor sick soul who's wandered into our territory by mistake. There is nothing I can do for them except offer some water, perhaps point them out past the race and back to one of the parks or crosshouse yards. The crumpled shape is visible only as darkness in the surrounding faint moonwhite and I pat my knife. Just because someone is so sick they're vomiting their guts into the river, isn't to say they won't have some strength left for a fight.

Yet something keeps me pressed against the brick for longer. A thought like a note off-key. In the greying light I see in my mind the path the intruder would have followed. Along the towpath, then up Liver Street steps, then through the alley between the bank and the old dockland museum. As soon as I have the path in my head, I see fretlines of fine cord running across the turning alley and the flights of steps. Nothing that would do you harm, just enough for a nasty trip, a face full of gravel.

Snares and triplines invisible on the grey concrete. The morning spent putting them into bodymemory: running, bending, lifting feet and jumping. It had been a game, Clare the best at it and quickest, like a fox.

No stranger would have had a chance making it down the narrowest part of the steps without being tripped or snagged.

Definitely not one this sick. When this thought comes to me, I understand that the person spitting on the race is not a stranger at all. I push myself quick from against the storehouse wall and move toward Lucien.

He's pale, even paler than usual, his back stiff and flexing and his face in a sweat and grimace when I reach him. He's in a hunch gone sideways, and his knees are half drawn up under, and I feel sick myself in my stomach and don't know what to do. First thing is wrap the jacket over his back, as he's wearing no shirt and his skin is wet and cold as if he's just come up from the river. I wipe vomit off his pale cheek. I try to put his arms into the jacket sleeves, but he is too stiff and he says through teeth rigidly together, 'Leave it.'

So I just drape the jacket and lean over him and lie my arms over his arms so that there's some warmth between us. And wait. My heart beats flatly onto his back and I have a shifting feeling of dread, as I know there are many things I should be doing, but I can't think of any of them. It's him who decides and says what will happen with people, not me.

I wait in the night, holding him. Above us, the stars swing past lento. A long time goes and only stops when Lucien tips his head to one side and shakes it sharp, like he's clearing water out of his ears. It's a rough movement, but it takes control of muscles and bones and how they move together. I lean out enough to see his face. Afraid of looking. I have been here before, and if I have to go back, it won't be in the same way. I see in my mind a person getting ready to enter dark water, drawing up all of the breath, taking everything from the world outside that he can fit within himself, sealing it tight against the plunge.

Lucien is very still now, but his eyes are moving smoothly. He's looking up and down and to the sides in a way that seems like he's testing them. He blinks: lento, lento, then presto. Then he shakes himself and shakes my arm off his shoulders. He rolls and rises enough on his knees to look at me, and his eyes hold their gaze without fixing. He smiles.

My own face is locked with cold and not moving, and I shuffle myself backwards, my palms on the rough concrete, looking at him, and sit there.

Now that I've had fear and dread and sickness, what comes is anger. 'What the hell's going on?' I say to him, as if it is his fault. 'You're sick.'

But I stop as I do not want to speak like this with my voice raised. I lift my shoulders in a useless sort of shrug that signals, 'I'll be silent.' I'm tired. The feeling of dread still rising up under my ribs, under my throat.

'You have to help me. I can't walk right.' He gestures to his legs. His forehead is pale and wet; the words cost him some thin sweat. 'I can't go back to the storehouse. There's space in there.' He points to the building outside of which I'd waited.

He's taller than me, but he's light, and even with his legs dragging, we're across the race quickly. In the shadow of the building, I let him slump down again, and I push the boards back as he instructs and get him through.

Inside the empty storehouse, the lower floor is much smaller than ours. Divided in two, and the stairway is intact, though there are gaps in the ceiling. It's near black, but there's just enough light to see. Lucien points to the corner without saying anything. In it is a long, low wooden box. I lift the lid and feel there's a mess of paper inside. By touch I learn also of three new candles and a box of lights.

Once I've lit one, I see that the chest further contains a folded wool blanket, a clean shirt, a small cloth bag and a half-loaf of black bread wrapped in clear stickwrap. I take another of the candles, the bread, the shirt and the blanket, and bring this back to the wall where Lucien is still slumped inside the draped jacket. His eyes are closed, and the sweat stands on his face, but his muscles seem to have stopped their dance. I light the other candle from the first.

This time when I bend his arms to get them inside the clean shirt and then into the jacket sleeves, he lets me, and just smiles with his familiar look of mild amusement. His eyes flutter up a bit, and when he speaks, it is his usual voice, clear and mocking.

'You know, I often wonder what's going on in your mind. Even tonight, I can't find the answer to it.'

He reaches out and grabs his outflung right leg at the calf and pulls it in. I watch carefully. He has some muscle control in his legs. I rip a hunk off the crumbly loaf and hand it to him, but he places it aside on the floor.

'Simon's someone who is always watching and waiting. I know that. But why does he see what the others don't? Why is he always in the right place to see these things?'

There is in his eyes, if I'm not wrong, a kind of apology. I'm not meant to answer any of these questions. They are like his careful movements, a kind of testing, finding the place where he and I fit again. So I just wait, which as he's noted, I'm good at doing. I eat some of the bread.

'I went to your quarters . . .' I say, finally. I can tell he is listening though his eyes are closed and he doesn't move, 'because you didn't come as you usually do.' This makes him open his eyes.

'Where did we get to last night?' he asks.

I stand up. It is not the time for him to ask questions.

'What did you take from the Wandle runner? What were they doing on our run?'

Lucien looks up. 'I didn't know you saw that.'

'Yes. You took something from round his neck. What was it?'

Lucien looks away. 'They must have known Abel was Five Rover. Though none of us sing the comeallye when we're running.'

'What do you mean?' But in my head I hear a fragment of the threat left by the member at Bow and I know already what he is going to say.

'Wandle weren't pushing into our territory. They weren't after the Pale. A single piece of Lady wasn't worth the risk. They were looking for me.'

Lucien puts his hands into his pocket and draws out a piece of paper.

In the candlelight, it is hard to see clear, but on the thick surface is a hasty sketch done in ink with a steady hand and a good eye. A young man with curled hair that peels back from a high forehead. A long, thin nose. It's a good likeness.

Next to the drawing in a different hand is written the symbol for two hundred tokens, more money than we could take in a month of trades.

'I need to know, Lucien. You need to tell me now. Why does the Order want you?'

When Lucien shakes his head, I forge on. 'Where did you go? When I came to your quarters, I thought you had left us.' The other question is unspoken. I can't ask it of him. I couldn't ask it of my parents. *What is the sickness? How long . . . ?*

I had meant to stay calm. Calm like he could pass out of existence as they did and I would forget him. But my voice does not obey. It shakes. I close my eyes and curse it.

I am halfway across the floor, just out of the candles' intersecting circles of light, when he rises to his feet.

'Simon,' he says, into the darkness where I'm standing, watching. He can't see me, because for him the light has slipped a covering over the room's depths. 'Simon?'

'Yes?' I say.

'I'm not sick. Not in the way you think. I'm not dying of it.'

While he is blind in the light, I let myself turn back to him. He is pulling himself together, bit by bit. After seeing him by the inlet, I wouldn't have thought it possible, but he is becoming Lucien again. All the parts of him have come back, so that when he stands, it's alive like an alert chord. His neck is rising and lengthening in the usual way when he speaks, and his milky eyes are wry and straight-staring.

The relief is strange. It makes me feel giddy, light-headed.

This time he says it, not just with his eyes. 'I'm sorry. You weren't meant to see.'

His legs are straight under him and there is nothing to tell you he has been rigored. I can see the pale fret on his face as he turns toward the shadows I stand in. A door in my chest opens with an unfamiliar happiness. In my arms, there is an echo of his nearness, what it felt like to hold him.

His voice is quiet when it comes again. 'I'll answer your questions, but you must let me ask first. Sit down.'

I shake my head. Not to the questions, but because I don't want to move from where I'm standing in the shadow. I need some distance between us. I want to keep out of his eyes for now, while my face finds some way to arrange itself again. The happiness is new to me, and so is the fear.

'Simon, the arrival in London, what was it like?' His voice in the shadows.

My response is immediate. I don't even need to think now.

'The arrival in London was mud. It was nether year. I came in along the east A-road. A carter who was going to market picked me up about five miles from Romford. The rain was so heavy it drove holes in the mud.'

He pushes me backward along the line of the story. 'Why did you come to London?'

'I came to London because my parents died. And I needed to find . . .' I look for the answer for a while, but it's a blur still. 'I needed to find something. Or someone. I don't know. My parents had a farm. We sold bulbs, flower bulbs – tulip and daffydill and iris.'

'What did your parents die of?'

I look at Lucien. I see his stiff legs and I see the shape of my mother's legs rising under the white cover. The farmer's neck twitches and jerks on the road to London. The boy in the crosshouse yard – what was his name again? Steppan. I see Steppan's father's legs and arms pull into spasm . . .

'My mother died of a sickness that looked the same as yours,' I say. 'So when you think it's the right time, I'd be grateful if you tell me what it is. If you're just going to ask about my memories, though, you should ask what I remembered tonight.'

Lucien looks up. 'Was it about your mother?'

'Yes. We were standing in the forcinghouse, splitting bulbs. She bound the memory with that.' And I tell him then what my mother told me.

'Good,' he says. 'Good,' as I speak. When I tell him about her skill, his face opens and his concentration is clear to me even in the dark. I describe Johannes giving her the memory. I tell him about the lute string in its silver coil and he nods and nods again. I tell him that she asked me to touch it. I don't tell him what she said about a family gift.

'Simon,' he says. His voice is close. Warm, like he is standing still next to me. 'This is well remembered. This is important – do you know that? It is right at the middle of things.'

Then I tell him what my father did.

'He hit you?' asks Lucien. 'Because he didn't want you touching others' memories?'

'Yes. He said I might be killed for it.' I look at him. 'Who would do that?'

Lucien looks at me, as if waiting. Then he leans back against the wall.

'You can hold a picture of what happened for a day or two before it fades. And you make objects that let you bring the memory back, the ones you think are important. You touch them and go down. Do it one by one, object by object. What you cannot do so easy is to thread them together so that one connects to the other. Without help, anyway.' He shakes his head. 'Do you think that is usual?' he asks. 'No, forget that question. Do you think that is right?'

'What do you mean?'

'Do you know what steals your memories?'

I look at him. Because it is a strange question, one that has no answer and many answers. The river of sleep takes memories down into the murk and silt. Night and the darkness take them. Waking takes them, or our own sadness. Or maybe it's that forgetting is like a spore or blight inside each memory itself, and the two cannot ever be separated.

'Chimes steals memories,' says Lucien. 'You know that.'

I stand there and I look at him for a long while. I hear the words in my head and I imagine the music cutting through the sky, as it does. Pushing us down. Its vast perfection stripping all the small and broken pieces that give us meaning and returning them in order and harmony. And I don't feel anything. What should I feel? Anger, pity, grief? Is that what they've taken from me, then? I want to ask him. Or is it just something missing inside myself?

'Chimes steals memories,' I say.

'Yes. Or you could put it another way and say it's the Order who does it, which is also correct. Simon, who knew your mother's skill?'

'I don't know.'

'Were there others like her?'

'I don't know.'

'There must have been, because your father knew that what she was doing was dangerous. Think.'

I think. 'That is all he said. That people had been tortured, killed for it. But something my mother said . . . I think she took memories to London. I don't know the reason why.'

Lucien nods. 'And you travelled to London too, and we don't know the reason for that either. But there was one or you would have stayed on the farm, where you would have kept what body-memory you had from the bulb farming. I think the two reasons are one and the same. Your mother's skill is bigger than her, and it's bigger than us, and if we follow it, that is where the song's meaning is.'

He straightens further against the storehouse wall. 'It's near Matins. We should be getting back.'

'You haven't answered my questions,' I say. 'About how you recognised the song. And about your sickness.' When I use the word, some of the panic comes back.

'Do you trust me, Simon?'

The same question. The same answer. I nod.

'Tomorrow I'll show you what I know, and we will try to fit the two together. Then you can decide how you wish to act hereafter. Tomorrow,' he says. 'Can you wait a bit longer?'

Hereafter, I think. A backwards-looking word for time that is still to come. In itself a blasphony. *Before Chimes*, a voice says in my head, *there would have been a time for such a word*. A tripleted rhythm driving upward in my mind. *Tomorrow and tomorrow and tomorrow.*

'Can you walk?' I ask. Which is a way of saying, 'I can wait. I will be there in time ahead. I will be there for you hereafter.'

'I think so.' He rises into a crouch and his legs are still stiff, but they flex. He grips my arm so tight it hurts. Then he shakes his legs and I see the stiffness drop away. It is Lucien again, and as we walk back through the night to the storehouse, it is Lucien's usual walk. I feel his presence next to me in the night without looking.

Inside the storehouse, all is quiet. The others are sleeping. Lucien disappears into his quarters with no word or sign.

I stand in the middle, by the cookstove, which is still warm. I want to go out to the balcony to look at the river, but I don't risk the boards' creak.

My hammock is still strung. I long to lie down in it and into darkness. But in my mind Lucien stands in candle circles, tall and pale, his spine flickering live like a flame itself. I see myself standing out of his sight and for once knowing one thing he does not. He cannot see my face, or he would know.

Is there solfege for the word of what I feel? There are hand

104

movements for harmony, accord, consonance. Could it be told in music by the longing in a scale? The urge of the seventh to rise to its octave, the fourth to its dominant? I think of an urgent minor key, of dissonance resolving into sweetness, but it doesn't really get close to the feeling. Those things are in it, but it is more complicated, less ordered, harder to understand. I walk the two beats up and down my quarters over and over.

I want work, something to learn or do. If I do something, let it be for him, I think. Let there be a discipline. Try to remember, then.

Tonight I have no patience for the currents of chance and luck that might bring the right memory to my hands. I close my eyes and I take hold of my memory bag and turn it upside down.

After a while I open my eyes. What I see is a collection of junk. Strange objects: a shell, a spoon, a paralighter, a muddy burberry, a dog collar. An old leather-bound scorebook. A block of wood with pencil-drawn figures. A scrap of paper ripped down one side. A bar of chocolate, a heavy, rusted mettle lock. I tap a dull rhythm. I try to empty my head, clear and silent but full of waiting, like a crosshouse hall just after an orkestra has finished tuning. I think of my mother and what she was doing and how little I must have known her. Then I reach for the bound score. It is old and from it rises the smell of bleach and dirt. I reach out and open it.

It is not a score at all. Crawling down the pages are the ugly, alien black shapes of code.

I turn the pages. Interleaved within the old parchment, yellowing and brittle, are paper cuttings. They are all in old code too and I have to force myself to look at its dark, angry tangle. I try to study the old signs for meaning, but there are no patterns that I can see, no rhythm. I turn pages presto. *Analysis of Specific Allegations with Respect to Acoustic Weapons. Whole-body Vibration and the Human Nervous System.* Each page and a different cutting of code in its tight black columns. *The Blind Leading the Blind: Convergent*

105

Evolution in the Origins of Specialised Hearing. The Potential Effects of Anthropogenic Noise on Birdlife.

All meaningless and I hold the old book by its spine and flick and a burst of colour comes up out of the denseness of code. A picture. A drawing tinted with skill in old ochre and plant dyes. The picture is of a fat man with a long white beard. He holds a sword in one hand, and above him is the sun, growing high in the sky like a strange flower. On each of his shoulders is a winged creature. They cling to the cloth of his cloak with sharp claws like they are clinging on to life. And at the same time a rushing feeling in my ears and I go down . . .

My mother's voice. Sun, warm through parasheeting. We are in the forcinghouse again. In front of me, piles of knotted bulbs have been pushed to the edges of an earth-covered table and the smell of bleach is strong in the air.

'Simon,' my mother says. 'Come.'

Before me, she sweeps a clean space on the earth-covered table. Then she reaches under the workbench and draws out a tall red mettle tin. Her hands are shaking so hard she can barely hold the knife she uses to twist the lid. She drops it once, and I step forward to help, but she pushes me back. At last the lid comes off with a reluctant sucking sound. She lifts clear a flat object wrapped in clean blue roughcloth, unwraps it.

A book. Bound in leather like a score. She places it on the bench, and holding one hand with the other for steadiness, she opens it.

From where I look over her shoulder I see that the page is covered with strange black shapes of code. I breathe in sharp.

'Written words,' she says, as if she's lonely for them. 'Coded ideas. Nobody understands them now.'

'What were they for?' I ask.

'Code was a way of keeping thoughts still. Of helping them stay in formation. Everybody used to understand it, and they could write in it too. It meant that you could return to the ideas when you wanted. Code is a kind of memory.' She strokes the pages and it's as if the tremor in her hands calms a little. 'My mother gave this to me, and now it's yours.'

She flicks past yellow interleaved pages for a while, and then she nods and I look. It is a picture of a fat man with a beard and two strange creatures clawing tight to his shoulder.

I lean over close so I can see the grain of the colour on the thick pages.

'What are they?'

'Birds,' she says.

'What?' I say. It is a word I have never heard before.

'Birds. They died out. These were the ones called ravens.'

She begins to sing.

'In the quiet days of power,
seven ravens in the tower.
When you clip the raven's wing,
then the bird begins to sing.
When you break the raven's beak,
then the bird begins to speak.
When the Chimes fill up the sky,
then the ravens start to fly.
Gwillum, Huginn, Cedric, Thor,
Odin, Hardy, nevermore.
Never ravens in the tree
till Muninn can fly home to me.'

The song is mournful. It does not make sense. When she finishes, she asks, 'Do you understand?'

'No,' I say.

'Listen,' and she sings it again. 'The meaning is simple,' she says. 'It stays simple so we remember. When Chimes came, the birds died. When the birds died, words died. When words died, memory died.

'Gwillum, Huginn, Cedric, Thor. Those are the names the song lists.' She turns the page of the book carefully. 'Gwillum, Huginn, Cedric, Thor, Odin, Hardy, Muninn . . . There were seven of them, and they lived in a tower in the city of London. But two of the ravens were more important than the others. Huginn and Muninn. Huginn – that's the word for an idea, a word picture in your head, something that flies in from outside. Muninn is different. The most important of all. Muninn is another way of saying memory.

'Before Chimes, the ravens flew all over the world together. Free to fly and haunt and free to look and to understand what they saw. But however far they travelled, they would always return home. Muninn often the last of all, they say, because memory had the furthest distances to travel. Then one day they didn't come back: Muninn was lost. And with Muninn, human memory, and written words. Ravensguild want to bring Muninn back.' My mother closes the book. Then she thinks for a second and hands the book to me.

'For memory,' she says.

I take it, hold it hard. I empty my mind, and using all my will, I tell the memory to stay in it. I bind it hard with our movements, my confusion, the smell of the forcinghouse, my mother's words.

'You see others' memories,' I say. 'You keep them and you help the person to remember.'

'Yes. But some memories are more important than others,' she says. 'Because some memories belong to more than just one person. Like the story of Huginn and Muninn. Some memories tell us about who we are. They need to be kept safe so that things can change for all of us.'

All of us. I see the village square, the market place, the old crosshouse, the new assembly hall. I can see nothing bigger than that.

'What do you mean?' I ask.

My mother studies me, as if measuring how much I will under-
stand. 'The world stretches far beyond this farm, Simon, and
beyond the Citadel also. We have forgotten to think of ourselves
in this way.'

'What happens to those memories?'

'I pass them on to someone with more skill than me, with more
vision than me. Someone who will keep them for longer. I give
them to a woman in London, and she passes them on to someone
else, and in this way the network grows strong and the memories
stay alive.'

'What is Ravensguild?' The name has a strange taste in my
mouth, like copper. Like mettle and blood mixed. 'Who is
Ravensguild?'

'We are,' says my mother. With difficulty she rewraps the book
in the cloth, places it back in the tin and uses the handle of the
knife to hammer the lid back on. Then she puts the tin back under
the workbench. Amid the other trugs and pots, it becomes invis-
ible, hidden.

She turns to me and her look is either a challenge or an invita-
tion, I can't be sure.

'You are,' she says.

The Dead Room

Trade at Barrow

I wake some time before Matins. I wake with the taste of copper in my mouth, like I've been sucking on old mettle. And with the echo of Lucien's arm over my shoulder as I helped him to cross the race. There are other things I newly wake with. A sadness that is different altogether from the cloudy sediment dread bears up. It is dark and solo. I can't see the bottom of it. And another thing I don't recognise, a kind of hunger to grab another person and press them as deep into knowing as I've gone.

Up until now I've been stuck in a dark room that I thought was the whole world. Now there are doors in the room, and the doors lead into new rooms. How far back does it go? What is in the centre?

Then I let myself think of Lucien. I see myself waiting on the race. Lucien hunched in sickness. The both of us standing in another storehouse – the secret twin to ours. I feel his weight on me. And that thought sends light into my arms and fingers. I lie still, letting things settle as they will.

Out in the storehouse, I can hear the others moving. The coiny clink of the kettle, the scrape of the cookstove ashes. Abel whistling a tune known only to himself, holding some half-buried song of his own past.

I push aside the roughcloth curtains and let them fall behind me. All is as it ever was. Clare cuts bread at the counter, measures tea and spice. Brennan skewers bread on the toasting forks. Everything the same.

But the way I see it is different. I see the fine layer of dust across the surfaces, and I see the patterns on the wood. For the first time I see the storehouse in one glance and it is narrow. Even the thick, rough, oil-stained walls feel thin somehow, hardly a shield from the outside world. I shiver. The pact has changed too. We are not one whole, held together by breath and song, but five people, all afraid, all alone.

Abel is young, too young even for a prentisship. Brennan moves with a kind of pushed-down anger that is hardening and going sharp. Clare is too thin. I see all this as if for the first time. And I see the scars on Clare's forearm. Faint white raised lines walk along under the fair hair. She pours spiced tea and her sleeve rides up and I see fresh cuts, red and pained-looking, scored like a stave, like the notches on the door panel, too neat for accident. Cuts that fade from red to pink to white. Cuts to keep memory, to measure time. Pity moves in me. I look away.

Lucien comes from the balcony, stops at the door and counts notches. Is he different also? Has he changed? Yes, I think. I wait for something to tell me what the distance is between us now, but all I learn is a jangling note. Fear, but fear with a sharp edge. Not dull or murky but bright and pressing. Is that what I've gained? Lucien sits. His body the same and different. His wrists and forearms clear and real. The jangling fear is mixed with something else. The happiness begins again inside me and signals in a white flash across some border to the happiness of last night. The two join together and make a new territory, a completely different key, white searching notes. A door opening. Hereafter.

I look for a signal from Lucien, but there is none.

'By my count today is a day for trade,' he says. 'So trade it is. We will go together to the market at Barrow.' He hums the tune that reminds us of the path from the storehouse, the vast crosshouse of South Walk a flourish of stern minor notes.

'Good,' says Clare. 'We cooked the last rabbit yesternoch.' And Lucien nods, grave and absentminded.

I stand still at the edge of my quarters. He can't be serious. The Order are looking for him. There is a prize of two hundred tokens set for him. And he talks of going into the city to trade?

'Simon,' Lucien calls over his shoulder to where I am standing. A different voice, his old voice. Imperious and distant. 'Join us, if you please. Onestory commences.'

And as if the measure is inside him, the Carillon sounds for ensemble. The pact gathers round in a sung chord. We are a guild. A world. Small, fragmented, afraid, perhaps – but we come together in the downsounding as one.

Down the race, past the cranes and onto the river. Abel not yet well enough to join us and our footfalls sound hobbled and absent without his tread. By Limehouse Caisson, Clare crouches in the muck where it's brown and cold and agleam, dips her hands to the river like she wishes she could go right in. Brennan and I walk on. Lucien, up ahead, bites at the air to taste it and see where the wind's coming from.

Once he's had his fill of morning air, he starts off at a pace that tells us follow, and so we do. And I see that he is leading us some-where else, not straight to market, but to Harry.

Harry's been on the river forever. Always under one of the bridges, though you can never guess which. I try to catch up to Lucien, fall into step beside him without it seeming forced or unusual to the others, who are running behind. But Lucien moves presto under the bridges, always a few beats ahead until we're at last into the lea of Cannon Street. And there he is, Harry, swad-dled in roughcloth, his beard threaded with shell and weed. Just up from the half-wash of the river, where he can sift and sort the pebbles he uses for his forecasts. His trolley is pushed up between the rotted struts of the bridge, and inside are the blue stickwrap bags where he ports his memories. He has his little kettle and sterno on to boil thameswater for tea. It smells of tide and leaves.

Lucien has the pact wait out on the strand, but he hooks his finger at me to come with him. 'What are you doing?' I ask piano, underbreath. He says nothing.

The air under the bridge is thick with woodrot. We crouch on the sand and pebbles, and Lucien shows Harry his palms, so I follow suit. Lucien hums a greeting piano and reaches in his knap for a pouch of drum, which he unrolls from its stickwrap and proffers. He does it as if he's ignoring Harry, as if it were by accident we are there at all. Harry murmurs and mutters like an old housebound dog, sore because you're able to get up and come and go when you want.

It's dark enough that Lucien can see a bit in the hood of the bridge. The stones are brown and green like the river made all the colour emerge. It all returns to the river anyway – stonegrey, greybrown, mudbrown, stonegreen. Water moving slow there, and time too.

'All's well?' Lucien asks.

'All's well. All's well,' Harry mutters, clears his throat, looks up. 'Wandle on the move between Mill Wall and Five Rover yesternoch, I hear,' he says. He grins at us. 'Trust you met them?' He comes forward for the baccy, only the flame of the sputtering blue sterno between him and us. There is a handful of white and orangey pebbles tinkered in his mettle cup and he shakes it. Holds it up to his ear as if it's speaking to him.

'Yes,' says Lucien. His voice is impatient. 'Harry, will you read the weather for us?' he asks. 'Drum for a forecast?' He points at the pouch.

There is a hesitation in my throat. Why is he asking Harry to read the weather? How can we learn anything from the old weatherman?

But Harry is happy enough to oblige. He goes down on his haunches. He takes the cup and jangles it with his left hand while the old fingers of his right clear away a smooth place in the sand in front of us. He pushes away pebbles and branches and the few shells until there's a space that's sanded flat. In his mouth he mutters, then scatters the pebble runes.

Runes land on the cleared sand. Harry cries out. Then before we can move, he sweeps a hand through the pattern of pebbles.

'What is it?' asks Lucien, presto and sharp. 'What do you see there?'

Harry on his arse. Fallen backward as if pushed in the chest. He scrabbles crabwise in the sand on his palms away from Lucien. Something incanted under his breath over and over. A fragment of Onestory, the refrain we repeat each morning.

'*The Order gives us harmony. The Order gives us the Carillon.*' Harry says it over and over like a child consoling itself.

Lucien takes a few steps so he's again close to Harry, who sits blankfaced and breathing presto so his chest pants up and down.

'What did you see, Harry?' asks Lucien with his quiet voice, the one you can't refuse to answer. His hand on Harry's shoulder white at the knuckles.

The fear on Harry's face weakens. He plucks at Lucien's ragged jeans and looks pained. His voice takes on a whine, like a warped reed. 'I can't say it. *Blasphony*. Dischord. I can't say it, Lucien.'

Lucien leans in closer. He has a question at the ready. Lucien the questioner, I think. I lean in too.

Harry shakes his head quick again. A mutter. A rune. A half-answer.

'There's a girl. Not of the city. Not of the city, you know. And she's waiting.'

Harry rights himself from his fallen crouch and goes to sit in front of his kettle, unfolds the drum and sticks a wad in his mouth. Chews for a while, then spits.

Lucien looks at me and I can't read his eyes. He straightens up from his crouch and pulls me too. I look back at Clare. A girl not of the city. The words say something and nothing. And I see that even now, in the newly opened room of what I remember, there are closed doors and hidden things.

'Thanks, Harry,' says Lucien.

We clear the bridge, and Lucien blinks in the light, and we're all walking two abreast again. In my uncertainty, what I feel is distaste for the old weatherman with his filthy jacket and stranded hair and his smell of salt and piss and mud. 'Why thank Harry?' I ask. 'Harry ruins more runes than he tells.'

And Lucien shakes his head and hits his hands once, twice against his legs to rid them of dirt.

It's not much further to Barrow. We walk triangled in the city for strength, unlike the two-file along the river or under, which is for longhear and narrowness, cooee and length. Lucien takes the lead. He can't see much in the city light, even with paraspecs, but he's cocksure and jaunty anyway. His sharp shoulderblades back like wings, and his head seems to rise on his neck. His curls are clear in the light. My heart goes up at that moment – a lift as I follow.

As we near South Walk Bridge, I grab the chance to take my place again next to him. The others fall into pairs behind. He ignores me as we run, but we pull ahead of the others a little. I say to him, piano as I can, 'You can't go in the market, Lucien. They're going to be there to take you. If Wandle know, others will too.'

Nothing to show he has heard. The grey light flints off his dark paraspecs. He is listening for the footfalls around him, the distances from buildings, the plumbline of the river, myriad other infrasounds I can't fathom.

'I know,' he says. 'But we need the money. You can do the trade for me. It isn't hard.'

He hears my protest before it emerges from my throat and he cuts it off with a gesture of his lifted hand. He lifts the pouch of Pale from round his neck and puts it over my head. Silence stops my argument.

'Find a low-level dealer. Ellis, or the girl who fences for the Fleet runners. Umelia. Someone without brass. Not connected.' He sings me their tradesongs. 'We've got five debased nuggets between six and three ounces each and two smaller pieces of pure. Worth about thirty tokens together. Don't get rid of it for more than twenty-five, but no less than twenty either. Try not to draw attention to yourself. I'll meet you at the storehouse after Chimes.'

There is no discussion. Lucien pulls away so we are in single file for the bridge. He weaves us round a group of threshers who come along the bridge with bundles of rye on their backs. Their grey clothes blend them with the streets, and they're chatting among themselves in their odd farm speech, not interested in us.

There's a glimmer of gold in the whiteclouded sky and we enter the first of the market streets. Lucien disappears into the crowds of tinkers, threshers, vendors and buyers. None of the others notice. Or if they do, they do not say.

The noise hits as we enter. The frenzied din that is the opposite of the calm order of Chimes. A cloth seller sings, '*Finecloth, roughcloth, wool, silk, linen*,' a flowing warp and weft of notes. Behind him, the potter sings of ochre and saltglaze, of platters and pots and beermugs. Twisting between is the drawn-out, coaxing whistle of a vendor who crafts memories, good-quality, purpose-made, built to last.

We walk past the butchery stall in the dark caverns under the railbridge, with its warped steel and few remaining planks of soapy wood. He sells whole rabbit and pig. Neat red parcels of smallgoods drip on his clean white paper. Tails of shining sausages hang in their casings like a strange curtain behind, and he sings their provenance in a florid patter. Cow and deer is a laugh. More like dogs scrounging around the workshop sawdust, and a presto despatch into sausage heaven.

'No one here yet,' says Clare. She is bouncing on the balls of her feet, tense and fast. Her sharp teeth bare in her face, and river-wet hair tangled down her back so she looks like a small fierce animal.

We each of us listen for signs of another pact, or some other clue that will lead us to the dealers. I whistle the comeallye as Lucien would. A subtle announcement of our presence to the soundfabric of the market, a signal to the pact to focus. They gather round me, their expressions open. I hand out our last tokens and split them off to scout bargains.

I walk by myself into the heart of the market. There is the smell of chestnuts, and the weird, dark scent of fresh-dyed wool. Under the arches, cooking smoke clouds the exit, and people are standing half in, half out on the street. The smells hit me hard today and are not quite pleasant. The noise is strange too. As well as the din of the guildtunes and vending songs, there are all sorts of odd echoes, clatters and hums. I take the north arcade, towards the artefact vendors.

Pacts are conspicuous. We are ragged and skinny, and we smell of the river. I catch the scent – mud and tea and green and dark – among the chestnut smoke and it makes a keening feel rise in me that helps me move faster. I walk past arches where families group around their livelihood. Bunches of woody asparagus, pig pickle, knitted blankets. They draw back a little. It's fear of the unknown. Pactrunners are not easy to pigeonhole like prentisses, who have their guildsigns stitched on their chests and their clear place in the order.

I nearly bump into a cluster of moonies crosslegged at the entrance to the artefacts hall. There in a circle in their ragged white robes they rock forward and back with the high blank trance in their white-banded faces. As I pass, they make the sign in front of their faces: five-fingered starbursts where their eyes would be, and in front of their closed lips, speaking their dumb sacrifice in the only way they can.

They hear me coming and the leader's hand darts out for the begging saucer of measly tokens and pulls it in under his cloak. They shuffle back under the green-painted wood arch, their hands starbursting their surrender. They make me angry. So deep in thrall to Chimes that they hold any other sense to be blasphony. A hot feeling like shame and I hiss as I pass them like the kids do, and spit to my side to get rid of the white cloud of salt that's in my mouth.

And all the while I'm listening for a disturbance, a shift in the fabric, someone communicating they're there by their absence, their silence. It's illegal to carry the Lady except for trade. And as steady a current as the river, the channels of trade carry the Lady back up to the Order, to the Citadel. I keep Lucien's face in my mind like a beacon.

All my senses are prickling and I walk on the very toes of my thin plimsolls, into the artefacts hall. The vendor and his prentiss there with a bunch of old electricks nobody has any use for. Only a dark-haired woman with a cloth board covered in spoons and jewellery is doing any trade. I am losing my focus and stop, allow myself to become invisible again.

He's there. I can feel him waiting in the shadows about ten beats away before I see him. Nondescript. He's wearing grey travelling clothes and he's humming. It's only if you're listening for it that you hear the Lady's interval in the tune.

He hasn't heard or seen me, which is good. Trade goes better when you take the lead. I walk forward nonchalant, as if to inspect some of the electricks, until I'm standing direct in front of the dealer. This is how it's done. No eyes, not until the end. I whistle the common tradesong, a comeallye that all the pacts know, rough and a bit crude, but effective. '*You need. You want. You need. We've got*,' is what it says.

Around it I weave a few teases from our own comeallye. Not enough to give anything away but enough of a reminder that ours is the best run of the river. And in there too there's the silvery interval, an answer to the dealer's casual hum, and really the most important of all. The advertisement of our wares, the Pale Lady.

Ignoring me with disdain, the dealer continues humming to himself. But this is all part of the ritual. I know that he's heard me because his melody shifts and beckons. And though I don't remember his face, I know his song. Ellis uses a simple blue tune on the five-note scale that dealers favour. But he can't seem to keep a weariness out of it. He's uncomfortable – he thinks this work is beneath him, he's past prentiss age, and he's worried he's missed a safer line of work.

Then, like that, the courtship is over. 'How much do you have?' Ellis asks, underbreath. I turn to see that he has pushed himself upright from the wall and stands with eyes eager. He has recognised me, but he seems confused. 'Five Rover? Are you here alone?'

I ignore the question. 'I've got five measures of solid,' I say. 'Two smaller pure nuggets.' He is looking for Lucien, I think, and I tense.

'Let's see,' he says, gesturing with impatience.

I glare blankly ahead. I need to take control. He wouldn't hurry Lucien. I pull the pouch from my T-shirt and unloose it. Ellis reaches under his travelling cloak and offers a small wooden tray. I brush it clear of imaginary specks, blow in it twice. Then I balance the wooden tray with its blue field of velvet carefully and place each piece of palladium we've found this eightnoch. The pieces glow quietly. They seem hungry, each pulse taking in a gulp of silence. It's like the feeling of water entering your ears – a bubble of air, a glotted stop.

Ellis doesn't make any attempt to take the tray, just stands tacet. His hand plays over the ore as if he's caressing the glow itself. The gesture reminds me of the moonies' starburst eyeburst hands, and I hear a note of warning in my head: *Get the trade done and get away.*

Then Ellis looks from the Lady and into the far corner of the artefacts hall. My stomach hitches. 'Hey,' I hiss. 'Do you want to deal or not? I can take this elsewhere, you know.'

Ellis shakes his head. I look past him. Who is standing there where I cannot see?

My heart starts up and I rake pieces of Pale.

'That's fine. Store's shut. Moving on.'

Ellis snaps into focus. 'No, no, no.' He puts a hand over mine, turns it, studies the nugget.

'The quality of the three-ounce nugget is pretty low. The others are median,' he says, speaking presto. 'The smaller are superfine, but they're only a few grammes each. I'll take the lot from you for forty tokens.'

I cough. Lucien said not to drive for more than twenty-five. Everything in me is saying to take the tokens and run. But I need to move careful. Like when you're clearing snares. No sudden movements. 'It's not much debased,' I say, keeping my voice calm. 'I'd put it at 0.85 pure. And it's rare to find nuggets that size now. They go for more if they're whole like that. Forty-five, for all.'

'Yes, then. Done.' Ellis's voice is clipped, scared.

I hold the tray and shift back and forth. He counts the tokens, leafing them out lento, and he takes a step nearer for the exchange. And then it's been going on too long. I reach for the money presto and just as I do it, his hand shoots up and closes round my wrist. His grip cold but hard, and I feel the strength of his arm like a bar of mettle. Quick as a flash I bring my other arm up and I flick the tray high into the air. The Lady carves silver arcs of silence into the air so they seem to hang above us for a moment, and in that moment I twist out of his grip, turn heels, run.

I pull the whistle from my neck as I sprint down the hall. Blow a cooee for the others as I go. The crowds fold round me and I don't look back to see if Ellis, or whoever gave him orders, is following. I pound it down through the market, people turning to watch me go, whooping and egging me on. It's not till I get to the vegetable vendors at the entrance that I let myself stop, listen, breathe. Echoes of the Lady play through the market. I don't wait to find whether it's getting closer.

When I'm down by the railbridge with lungs and ears straining, I cooee again and at last there's footfall behind me. White faces of Clare and Brennan. We beat back to Dog Isle presto, jogging all the way.

The white of the day has some pink in it as we enter the race, and the storehouse is there like an old friend waiting. We get inside and close up the door. Brennan hefts the heavy mettle bolt into place and it falls with a straining creak.

No one speaks as they lift market goods from their packs. To me, their movements seem wrong, behind the beat. My head is racing onward. Where is Lucien? Clare lifts out two rabbits, a string of sausages, pig's dripping. Brennan unpacks white loaves, walnuts, sacks of flour, a stickwrap bag of apples, bunches of herbs, carrots, potatoes.

We say nothing and we pack the things away into their places in the kitchen so that everything is square.

Night comes with no Lucien. I think of what he told me last night about Chimes taking memory. But if it does and is thus to be dreaded, why does he follow it so close with us, carving out Onestory each day? And his solfege for the changing chords of Vespers. How is it so clear and accurate that it's like he sees the music almost before it comes?

Vespers sounds and we stay in the storehouse. I don't know what else to do. I lead the solfege and the others follow. I am angry at the ease of their acceptance, the way a change slips in and they think it normal, their lack of questions. How long would it take to forget him? It makes me feel sick.

After the last chord has faded, the pact unfurl their legs and arms and bodies from their crouching bracing positions. A feeling in me like a bruise. I can see it in Clare's eyes too. She rubs at them and presses them deep in their sockets – as if an ache will heal an ache. I look at them and wonder what has been lost.

As night comes in, Brennan begins to get edgy. No one is speaking. The time we would practise passes, but nobody moves. Clare won't make eye contact with me and she goes to the cupboard and brings back four candles. She passes them round and we hold them, the dark sheltering round the light, which moves with our breath. If you keep staring at the flame, you see many colours. Red, orange, blue. Wet wood in the fire makes it green. The smell binds us to all the nights that went before, that will come. How many will there be?

Clare moves again, this time to fetch a blanket from her quarters and return to the fire. One by one we all follow suit. Do they know we have never done this before? That the vigil is not part of our routine, not part of bodymemory? I feel lonely and I miss the close body blindness of being one with the rest. The smell of damp heated wool is salt-humid and homely. Everyone's hair is mottled by the fire, shined in it. Clare makes pictures with the shadows of her hands. After a while she turns to me. She scratches her arm through her shirt.

'Where is he, Simon?' she asks. And the others turn their faces also, quiet, expectant. A fear so grave it can't be put into words and can only emerge in their expression as blank trust.

I don't have anything else to tell them except the truth.

'I don't know,' I say.

In the Under

I wake subito and I am swinging in the darkness. Something has moved. Lucien is standing over me.

'Where did you go?' I whisper. 'I didn't know what to tell the pact.'

'I was in the under. I have to show you something. The last piece of the puzzle.'

'The last piece?'

It doesn't feel like the last piece to me. In my mind, whatever puzzle Lucien is making is half missing, half scattered. The pieces that are turned right way up seem to come from completely different pictures. I pull myself out of the hammock.

'I promise to explain. I couldn't show you before now.'

I stand there, waiting for more information, but it doesn't come.

'Bring your memories with you,' says Lucien, and picks up my roughcloth bag and pushes it into my hands.

I am silent. I follow.

The night smells of fever and smoke from fires around the city. There's a dull fog hanging close to the river.

We pass tacet under the huge shadows of the cranes. They stand there, judging perhaps. We jog down the empty race and the direction is the same as ever. We are heading east. East to Five Rover.

I follow two steps behind Lucien, through the cold dark. I want to be in my hammock, under the woolsmelling blanket. I want to wake into the same morning as always. The one where I watch

Clare heat milk in the copper pan. The one where I help Abel turn the black earth in the polytubs ready for bulb planting. Where I walk the embankment at None and watch the long white sky up to Paul's get pink. But instead, Lucien and I are out in this hard-edged morning. Later and earlier than ever.

'Simon, what is the Lady?' Lucien's voice is piano in the cold air.

'The Lady is mettle,' I say.

'She's mettle, yes. But why is she so precious to the Order?'

'Because palladium gets the clearest tones for the Carillon,' I say.

Lucien leads us down the steps, taking them two at a time.

'Doesn't it strike you that they might have finished building the Carillon by now?' We edge round the triprope and down to the strand. 'What if there was another reason the Order needed palladium?'

'Like what?'

'Tell me again. What is the Lady?'

I sigh, prepare to start again from the beginning.

'Let me put it another way,' Lucien interrupts. 'What is the Lady to you? When we're in the under, how do you hear her?'

'I don't hear her,' I say. 'I hear what's not there. The Lady is silence,' I say. As soon as I say her, I see her. *Calm and balm.* Pulses of quiet in the rivermud.

'Yes,' says Lucien. 'The Lady is music, but she is also silence. Remember that.'

We enter in the same place as usual. One second the night sky above, the sounds of the sleeping city extending farther than I can hear. The next, the world stretches as high only as the dome of brick and just the whisper of tunnels ahead.

The run starts straight away. No pause to set our tonic, to sing the comeallye and get bearings. Lucien takes one of the large tunnels that lead off the stormwater catchment, and he leads fast.

For a while I try to keep the map up in my head. We enter the stormwater and splash through several bends. We're still close to the surface and there are thick glass tiles in the ceiling that let some light in, enough to see the patterned brick. Then a ladder of mettle rungs and a new tunnelmouth and a drier, echoing tunnel that pulls north. And the dark presses its hands on me. From where it's been sitting tacet for so long, panic gets up, sets up knocking. And with that, I am blind. I must trust Lucien.

We run a long time, following twists and turns. Taking the different terrains of the under – mettle, drybrick, bilgewater, tile. Through tunnels tall and arched and ones tight and narrow as being born. We run until we are many miles from our territory.

Then in the middle of a clear straightaway, I hear Lucien stop. I hear his hands patting tunnelbrick and his whistle orient me to his whereabouts. Then he disappears into a tiny tunnelmouth. Through it where I follow there's grit and concrete dust and it smells like cut bone or hair, something bodily and aloof but not unpleasant. Thin pipes run along the sides of the walls and press against my arms as we move through. Sparks of light cross my blinded vision.

I try to breathe shallow, save myself lungfuls of dust. But as we go, the dust gets thicker. Grit, then chunks of rubble, then broken pieces of concrete under my hands. Raw and snagging and a tear at my nails with a warm liquid trickle down my palms, though I can't see the blackness my blood adds to the dark. Soon so little space that I cannot push aside the rubble as I crawl. My jeans tear at the knees.

Then, ahead, the sound of something heavy breaking and falling. I jump. The back of my skull hits domed tunnelmouth and I bite my tongue, the pain as bright as a flare in the black. And I am reminded that I have a body still. That I'm more than just a crawling, forgotten piece of darkness.

A cascade of smaller broken sounds further off, breaking and falling lento in the silence. In the dizzy groundlessness, the crash could have come from above me or even below. I wait until all sounds have stopped and I listen for Lucien's presence. Nothing. The immense weight of the city above presses down on me.

Subito I am tired, so tired, and I want to lie down in the dust and concrete grit and rest. But from below then comes the comeallye, Lucien's whistle. I feel forward with my hands. There is barely any crawlspace between the rubble and the roof. But I stomach it, pull forward with my forearms, feel the tug and snag of rock on shirt and skin. And my head meets wall. The way ahead finishes like a cut-off breath. I lie there for a while, roll from back to stomach so the tunnelmouth is a bare few breaths from my face. Then I feel a current of cool air play across one hand.

Halfway down the rubble slope, in the wall of the tunnel, I find a small jagged hole broken in the brick. I work my legs back so my head is level with it and I whistle the first few bars of the comeallye and Lucien's whistle floats back up. No other way but head first. I push the rubble clear of the gap and then worm my way backward so I can get my head and arms through. My shoulders barely fit. I stretch out far as I can and my hands swipe air.

'Push through,' says Lucien's voice below. No traction behind, my feet scuffing in the cramped tunnel. Then one plimsoll finds solid wall and I push through until I'm half suspended. 'Further,' he says. I stretch and the bricks round the hole break a bit and my balance shifts. Down below, there is nothing, only panic and a drop without measure. Then Lucien's hand grips mine.

'Give me your weight,' he says.

I push back again behind me, pray he's strong enough to take it, and kick free. Then Lucien is gripping me by the chest and I'm half over his back and falling for a moment. Then I'm down and my feet on flat ground and I'm standing close to him, both of us breathing hard.

Something is different. In the air is a low and constant ringing, silver and steady. The Lady tells her presence in drops of silence.

But this silence is a constant flow, sure and so loud it's deafening. My whole body echoes to it. I start to speak, but Lucien is already off. The space lengthens as we run, a long tunnel that leads ahead wide and curving. Underfoot are narrow mettle tracks, shoulder-width apart, big enough for a trolley or a jigger. The silver silence seems to fill the tunnel, flowing down the tracks to me.

On the next turning, something strange happens. Like a magic trick, the silver ringing disappears. Normal echoes of brick and mettle, and the matter-of-fact light tread of Lucien's feet ahead. I shake my head, as if this might clear my ears. I keep following. Large, wide tunnels, brick and tile, by their echo. Left, left, left, right. We are returning in the same direction. With the final turn and another five beats, it is back. A sustained, silent peal. I feel light-headed.

The great current is now running perpendicular to us. As I listen, it seems to grow stronger: a full stream, a torrent that will pull us along. After a while Lucien stops and I can hear him breathing in the dark. I hang back, piano, listening to the pattern his halting breath makes in this vast, grand ringing. I wait for him and listen. I let the peals of silver settle over me.

His voice comes to me through the dark, as it always does.

'Simon?'

He knows that I am here. He hears me as clear as I would see him in daylight.

'Yes,' I say. I try to say it without expression, without panic. I doubt that I succeed.

'Can you hear it?' he asks. His voice has the familiar excitement in it, and my heart rises up as it always does.

'It's . . . it's vast,' I say, finally. 'I don't understand what it is.'

'I have to show you. You won't believe it otherwise.' He moves forward again slowly until he is about ten beats ahead. He hums soft and then places his hands against the side of the tunnel. The sound of this is hollow and resonant. I can hear him grip something, and then the noise of a short, violent pull. Mettle creaks and strains heavily, and then the tunnel is filled with a different light, a pale glow. In the glow I see Lucien's profile, with the curled hair pushed back high off his forehead. He turns to me and his eyes are reflected in the light like a cat's.

'This way,' he says, calm, and then he disappears into the door in the side of the tunnel.

I stand there alone. The door stands just ajar and the milky light appears to be flowing from it. The door is thick and made of mettle. Circular bolt heads ring the edges of the door, cruel and ornamental at the same time. In the pulsing glow, I see where they are bleeding dark red rust. The colour sounds something in me and I hesitate. But there is no choice. I hold the levered handle tight and swing the door open and hear its underwater creak. I draw a breath and hold it deep, seal it tight inside me. And then I step inside.

When I open my eyes, I am surrounded with an intense, silver-white glow. It is the most beautiful thing I have ever seen, and Lucien was right. I would not have believed him if he had told me. We are standing in a vast tunnel. Its roof arcs high over our heads, and the walls are wider than my arms, stretched out full. The tunnel is made of pure palladium. Its glow is blinding. I feel its pulse rolling over me in steady waves, pure peals of resonant silence. My whole body is dripping with silver, humming with it. The resonance seems to begin inside me, in the bones behind my ears, and run down my spine and out to the tips of my fingers. I feel as if my spine is a candle and there's a white clear flame emerging from the very top of my head.

I am grinning mad and huge, and I turn to Lucien, who is standing close, and he is grinning too, his smile wide and hilarious. The space around my lungs and where my heart is beating is opening up, stretching. I think of the picture in my mother's book, those creatures with their dark wings stretching too, until they're full of light and air. The strangest thing of all is that I can feel my parents there, in the tunnel. Their faces come into my mind without effort. I see the two of them alone, standing in the field next to one of the parahouses. They are healthy and young, and their faces are calm. The silvery space opens somewhere inside my throat and middle, and of all things I realise that I am going to cry. Standing in a tunnel under the river somewhere – who knows where?

Lucien is several feet ahead of me in the tunnel, walking with his stately lope, and reaching his arms out towards the tunnel's sides as if he wants to pull the light in to him.

Then something changes. It starts slow, somewhere down in my feet. A sense of unease. Nothing has altered around me. The silver glow is as milky and clear and beautiful. There is no sound in the thronging silence. Nothing has moved or shifted in the tunnel. I start walking in the same direction that Lucien is going in, and I have the sense that I am moving impossibly slow, as if through silted murky water. Nothing there. But round my ankles a feeling of coil and release, coil and release. The feeling moves up from my feet to my knees and hips, and rises then up my spine, where moments before I'd felt the light coming through.

How to describe it, except as the opposite of the opening, lengthening feel of the Pale. It's as if my joints are shutting, seizing, refusing. My whole body is saying no. I form the word with my lips as the black current reaches my hands and they seize and grip and try to push against something that isn't there.

There's pressure under my ribs, around my heart. The creature that had opened its wings within my chest now has my insides trapped tight in its claws. And then I no longer seem able to walk. I try to put my hands up to break my fall, but I land hard on the flat of my knees in the silver tunnel. The glow is still playing piano around me, like something cruel, as I retch and feel my back curl, without my control, inward and prone.

'Lucien,' I say, or try to say, or just think. 'Lucien. What have you done?'

The next thing is my arms being pulled from where they're

curled under me, hugged in around my ribcage. Pulled out in front of my head. Pain in the shoulder joint. Hard, pointed pain, not the dry, refusing pain that has taken up everything else. I try to lift my head up to swear at him, but I am pathetic. I have no strength. Lucien pulls my two crumpled, useless arms together so he can grab both and then there's nothing, followed by a painful wrench that has his whole weight behind it. He's dragging me. I feel my forehead bump over the pitted silver. We are moving in slow jerks down the corridor. From time to time I hear Lucien go to his knees. Then his feet at my sides as he rearranges his grip on my wrists.

The claws inside my chest are strong and tight. They have stalked bone by bone up my back and gripped my brain there. My brain is both terribly big and terribly small at the same time. It shakes hollow like a walnut and it grows and pushes fleshily at my skull. At some point I throw up whatever is in my stomach, and then I feel Lucien tip my head and shoulders with the edge of his para-covered foot to avoid the mess as he pulls me through.

As he does it, I blink. And then I blink again because my brain has not obeyed this instruction. And then I try to spit to clear my throat so I can scream. Because my eyes are open and I cannot see. I am blind.

The Dead Room

I come to in darkness. It is cold. I don't know where I am. I blink, but the dark with my eyes open is the same as the dark with them closed. I am lying on a hard surface and every bone and muscle in me aches and pulls. I try to focus my hearing, but my brain is bruised, seems no longer the right size for my skull.

Then I try to make a sound, any sound, to hear my bearings. All that comes out is a dry sort of moan. The noise should be loud enough to get some hold on the size of the room, but there is nothing. It is completely silent. I try to hear beyond or underneath the silence, but it is dead, closed, shut. And then there is too much pain in my head and I give up.

Off behind me is the sudden sound of loud, violent retching. Lucien. Because of the deadness of the room, I cannot tell where he is. I lie still, as I have no choice but to do, and gradually things come back. I remember the running river of silver. I remember a tunnel made of pure. I remember happiness and harmony beating right through me from head to foot. I remember my parents, shining and healthy. And then, from foot to head, I remember the creep of the sickness that is still inside me, that remains as a brittle twitch in my joints and the horror feeling of something pressing on my ribs.

I understand then. Lucien has brought me here. Lucien has exposed me to something that has made me sick – sick like my parents, like Steppan's father, like he himself the other night.

I test my limbs. My arms move slightly, but they are tense and tight, caught in the numb grip. I cannot move my legs at all. I can feel them, though I almost wish I couldn't, as the pain is worst there, like ice. I lie still and try not to think.

After a long time the ache of pressure inside my chest and ears eases a bit. I try to concentrate again, to focus my energy enough to move. Begin at my chest, let my thought move down my arm, trying to remember its network of muscle and bone, to will it back into being.

'Wait.' And the falling feel of a memory trick jolts me. This is how it always starts. Lucien's voice speaking to me out of the dark, sounding me through the questions – always detached, always a step ahead. The voice that knows more than I do always. More even about my own story. But that means something else too, I realise. If someone knows all there is to know about you, isn't that a kind of forgiveness?

'It's easier if you wait until some of the feeling comes back. You're going to be all right. You've had the worst of it.'

I shape the one word that I have in my head and somehow push it past my lips with the hope he will understand.

'Eyes.'

I can hear him shuffle toward me, maybe on his knees. Then I feel cold fingers on my face. The fingertips of two hands touch just at my cheekbones, just under my eye sockets. I try to flinch away. The touch moves on to my eyelids and then to my chin and forehead. Then there is a cool, distant feeling, almost unrelated to me, where I think my hands are. I feel movement as Lucien picks them up and places them on my chest. Both of them lie over my heart, and I can feel their outline and relief.

'There shouldn't be any lasting damage to your eyes. You'll start to regain sight soon. But it's dark in here. Hold on.' I hear rustling and Lucien's hands pat at my shoulders. 'Do you have the lighter, the one your father gave you?' he asks.

I hiss an approximate 'yes'.

'Can I get it?' he asks.

I hiss again and feel him tug my shoulders to remove the pack. I want to tell him it's in the outside pocket, but he finds it presto and I hear the rolling burr-bite of the wheel and see the blue para in my mind. The flint sparks and I strain to see through the dark.

'Anything?'

There is only blackness.

I muster a grunt and then wait to hear the wheel bite again. Still just blackness. Grainy, world-ending, silent dark. This time Lucien waits without speaking. I feel the touch under my eyes again, and the cool pressure on my forehead and chin, and a small segment of melody that I do not know.

'Come back, Simon,' Lucien says, and he strikes the flint a third time and I see it haloed in the black, a small, dull orange glow of flame.

I try to lift my head. I want to tell Lucien that he has to let the light burn, that it is very, very important to do so. I have never felt so alone, not even on my first arrival in London. But the light flicks off and I am blind again. Helpless.

Then he begins to talk.

'It wasn't meant to go like that, Simon. Please believe me. I knew it was a risk bringing you here, but the wind was from the south all day and I didn't think it would change.'

He pauses, waits, as if he's listening for a response. Then he whistles. It's a few notes from the start of our usual comeallye, and it sends a jolt of homesickness through me. But the notes behave strangely. They enter the room and then they stop. Each note stands dry and separate and dead. There's no resonance at all. Nothing like the silver hush that comes off the Pale Lady. This is as if sound had ceased to exist altogether, even while it's occurring. The silence climbs right into your ears, packs them full like wool, or something even drier: cotton, sand, dust.

So many questions that I can't put them in order, so I start with the most obvious.

'Where are we?'

'In the under, near to Batter Sea. The pipe I rescued you from just now runs straight, roughly east to west. If you imagine the scar is the centre of the wheel, there used to be a series of pipes that moved off it like spokes. We were in one of those. As far as I can tell, the scar must have been the site of a forge, where the pressure was generated. They must have needed a huge amount of power to get the airflow.'

None of it makes any sense.

'You mean the scar from Allbreaking? Where the weapon of dischord was destroyed?'

'Yes, I do. But it wasn't destroyed. Not completely. We're inside what's left of it.'

Onestory gives you meaning. It helps you understand what it means to live in the time of the Order, and it helps you understand your place. This must be why Lucien always sounded it with us, I think, even knowing what he did. It helps you keep going ahead. But we follow it like we do the weather. It's always there and it's always coming, but it's also distant. When you spend most of your life in the under, the weather doesn't make much matter anyway.

And now, somehow, the time we're living and the time of Onestory have come hard up against each other. As if Onestory has erupted right out of our downsounding and into the night. Here is the weapon that destroyed cities, that brought down Parliament and London Bridge, that put the Thames into a standing wave. It is here and now and real and not just song. And we are sitting inside it.

My breathing gets calmer after a while. I hold up my hands and I can see them clear at last. The knuckles a raw, violent pink. There's no pain yet because they are not yet fully part of me.

Again there is silence, and then Lucien's voice, chanting. Sounding.

> 'Mettle in the river, out of breaking's harm.
> Calm and consolation.
> Bright and balm.

'All we know of the Lady is what Onestory tells us. We know that she came from Allbreaking, when the weapon of dischord was destroyed. But how? That is a mystery. After Allbreaking there she was: mettle in the river. *Out of dischord's ashes, harmony will rise.* Tell me, Simon. What have you just seen?'

'A tunnel of palladium.' I pause. 'Are you saying the weapon of dischord was made out of the Lady?'

'Yes,' says Lucien. He looks at me lento, waiting for me to make the next step. 'We are harvesting pieces of the old weapon, the first weapon.'

I stop for a second, as there is something wrong with what Lucien said. There is only one weapon in Onestory.

He moves closer to me and his voice is hard in my ear.

'The tunnel is not a tunnel, but a pipe. The wind in it was enough to make it sound, though at a far lower volume. And that's what made you sick for a while. The weapon was a vast instrument, made out of palladium.'

I blink presto, testing my eyes, unwilling to understand.

'The weapon was a Carillon,' he says. 'Or you could put it another way. The Carillon is a weapon.'

I struggle. I am still shaking from the fear of blindness. I think of everything that I have learnt of the Order, through Lucien and through my memories. But even knowing that, I'd believed, deep down, in the part of my own spine that rings to the chords of Chimes, that the Carillon was driven by harmony and beauty. I cannot grasp that it might be meant to hurt.

'Look,' says Lucien, and he holds up my lighter again. The walls are made from highly carved white tiles, their grooves deepened by shadow. The tiles' hollowed trenches create intricate, orderly patterns, swoops and curves and curlicues. Where the light moves, it looks as though the shapes are growing and receding.

'I can't hear anything. It's completely dead.'

'Exactly.' He flicks the light and we're back in dark. 'The Lady is a conductor. She is used to make the pipes of the Carillon. But

138

the reason the Order needs her is twofold. In the Citadel, she is also used to insulate. She can convert sound into silence, or soften the effects of sound.

'If your hearing was perfect, you would hear a web of silver lines running right along the tiles, twining through them. So fine they're almost not there. They are threads of the Lady, running through the walls. Throughout the Citadel there is soundproofing like this.' He snaps the flame to again so his face is illuminated. 'In the city, it's illegal to hold the Lady except to trade. This is why. If citizens learnt of this, they might use her to protect themselves from Chimes.'

'How do you know?' I ask. I look at his fierce, hooded, unseeing eyes. Lucien springs fully formed out of the Thames. Lucien emerges clean and pale, untouched by Chimes. Lucien leads us with his miracle hearing under the city, to the Lady each time.

'Lucien, you need to tell me who you are.'

He looks at me, steady. 'I think you know.'

'You're of the Order.'

He nods.

I don't know what to do next. We are sitting in an abandoned corridor under the Thames, next to the true weapon of Onestory. And Lucien is a member of the Order.

'You're beginning to look feeble.' Lucien finds the supplies I packed at the beginning of the night and unwraps the sandwiches. 'Here, eat.' Then I hear the lighter strike again and the yellow glow of a candle comes.

I obey. The goat's cheese is sharp, and the bread is nutty, and it surprises me that it tastes so good. I wait for a while before I speak again.

'Tell me,' I say again. And he does.

'You must doubt it could have any good in it, Simon, but when I was young, it was only that way.'

'Why did you leave? How did you come to London?'

'First you have to understand some things.' Lucien draws a

breath, lets it go. 'In the Order, if you're born without sight, it's a sign that you have a gift for hearing. I was born like that, and I was born into music, and I never asked why or what it meant. I just felt lucky. I had another language I could think in effortlessly, one that opened up the world in truth and beauty. I knew that I would never run out of it, you see.

'Not everyone who's born blind becomes a member of the elect. You have to want it. But I did. It was like a light shining right through everything. The magisters began to treat me differently, give me space, ask my opinion about chord progressions or a complicated piece of rhythmic notation. I remember one particular day when it felt that everything I was learning was part of some bigger pattern. I was walking through the gardens and everything was music – leaves, trees, clouds. I was very happy. There was never a time that I didn't expect to become one of the elect.'

'The elect?'

'All children born in the Citadel join the Orkestrum. That's where you learn to play and understand and write music. The Orkestrum trains musicians for its own ensembles and orkestras, and some of those who go out into the cities to teach, or they become scholars and attendants. Each year a handful of students are chosen to be prentissed to composition for the Carillon. Then from that group, every ten years or so, a magister is selected. The magisters are the highest of the high, the most skilled. At the top of them all is the magister musicae. He is the one who organises the compositions for Vespers, composes the festival masses.

'I felt certain that I would become a magister. I was very proud when I was selected from the Orkestrum to become a novice, but it wasn't a surprise. I had been working towards it all my life. The week before we were to be ordained, all the novices spent time in solo meditation in their cells. We were each given a phrase from a Bach sonata to use as the theme for a new fugue. The best composition would be played at Vespers – a great honour.

'It was autumn. When we weren't working on the composition, we were meditating, practising. I remember the leaves changing and feeling as though my life was about to begin. Then somehow one night my mother managed to get in, past the attendants, and she woke me.

'She told me that I was not going to be ordained after all, that I would leave the Citadel and travel to London. I was desperately angry. I didn't understand. Then she told me she had learnt that the Carillon was harmful to people outside the Citadel. She told me that it was a weapon, like the one that caused Allbreaking. She gave me this.'

Lucien comes near to me again; he pulls something from his pocket and unfolds it. It is a square of cream linen.

A meandering blue line runs across the square in a rough downward slope from left to right. I look closer. It is made of tiny precise stitches that stand high enough above the cloth to be read by fingertip.

'She came from the outside, you see,' Lucien says. 'She joined the Order young, through audition. Her family were broiderers in Oxford, employed by the Order to sew the magisters' vestments. When she entered, she brought her attendant, Martha, with her.'

At both ends of the fine blue line, a bell is broidered in silvered mettle thread. The first bell is large, with cream lines radiating from it as if to show that it's speaking. At the bottom of the tributary that connects them, the smaller bell is stitched through with black lines of breaking.

I close my eyes. Open them again. 'The line.' I point to it, careful not to touch the cloth. 'That's the river.'

Lucien nods.

'The top bell is the Carillon, in the Citadel. The other is the weapon. Here.'

'Yes. She made the memory for me to take. She said that only someone from within the Citadel would be able to find it, that it would take a combination of good hearing and memory.'

'But how did she know about it?'

'There must have been a rumour. My father was high in the Order. Not a magister but a scholar, someone who travelled for research and to conduct auditions for the Orkestrum. He could have known.'

I think about what Lucien's mother did. Going against everything she knew, sending a son alone to the city with its dirt and its struggle and without protection from Chimes.

'My mother's attendant rode with me to London. It's only when I left the Citadel that I learnt there was no proofing outside. I tried to understand how the Order could allow it. For a while I tried to find a reason. Maybe they believed memory was unimportant. I knew magisters in the Order who lived inside music alone, whose lives went by without any events worth remembering. Maybe they believed life without memory was better, simpler.

'But then I saw the other cost, the shaking. The pain. Chimesickness. And I knew that there wasn't any explanation. The Order saw the Carillon's toll and did nothing to stop it.

'Because of the weapon's soundproofing, it's very well hidden. I've been looking for it since I arrived. A very long while before I caught even a small glimpse. Then I had to start again and again, night after night, approaching always from the same angle. Working out the route that would take me closer.'

'What about the pact?' I ask.

'I needed to eat and I couldn't get a prentisship, looking like I did. So I started to trade palladium. I got into a fair few fights before I carved out some territory, but my hearing gave me an advantage. So, I began to trade and the pact grew up by itself. First Brennan, then Abel, then you, then Clare.'

I think about Clare joining the pact, but I still don't have a memory of it. And then I try to fit together the two parts.

'You recognised the song from what your mother told you?' I ask.

'Yes. She told me there was a group who opposed the Order.

She thought I would be able to find others who could help me. But I didn't have any other clues. And just the melody of the song at that, no words. When I heard you sing it whole on the strand, I knew that I needed you to join the pact. I needed your memories.'

I listen to the bare refusing silence of the walls, the breathless dark. Then to Lucien's presence, his body bending forward in question. It feels like days since my last memory, the codebook and my mother's explanation. *I needed you*, is what he said.

'It's a guildsong,' I say. 'For a guild that tried to keep memory.'

Lucien is still, unmoving, listening.

'My mother told me about a time before Chimes.' I feel the bite of the blasphony. The biggest one of them all. 'Before Chimes they could write down words so that the ideas stayed in formation. That's what code was. Everyone knew how to write and read in it. But when Chimes came, no one could keep the words still anymore. And at the same time as the words died, birds died too. And memory flew away.'

I look again at the shapes behind my eyes, trying to see if I have it correct.

'The name of the group is Ravensguild. Gwillum, Huginn, Cedric, Thor, Odin, Hardy, Muninn, they're all names of ravens. My mother said the guild had spread across the country.' I think of the word. 'Like a web, a network. All of them like my mother, people who could see others' memories. They were trying to preserve memories and also put them together, so that people would understand what had happened. She chose the key ones and took them to someone else.

'I think she meant they had to preserve memories that would tell the truth about the Order. Because the song isn't just about time before and time *now*, is it? It's about time hereafter. They had a plan for how to make things change. *Never ravens in the tree till Muninn can fly home to me.* The most important of the ravens is Muninn, which is another way of saying memory. When

Muninn comes back, memory returns. In order for them to come back, Chimes must stop.'

The meaning of what I have just said strikes me in the stomach.

'That's why it's not safe to sing in front of the Order,' says Lucien, wry. I laugh. I have been holding my breath inside myself for who knows how long. The candles flicker.

'So, they're afraid of what you know,' I say, and Lucien nods. 'And they're afraid of what you could do. But if you're such a threat, why didn't they look for you when you left the Citadel?'

'According to them, I died. That is what my mother planned. They must have buried something.'

'Then why are they looking for you now?'

'I'm not sure. An eightnoch ago I got word that there was danger. We need to act presto. By now Wandle will have reported back – the Order will know our run.'

'What do you mean, you got word? Your mother contacted you?'

'Yes.'

'How?'

'You can answer that,' he says.

I shake my head. 'No.'

'Go on,' says Lucien. 'You can.'

Though I want to refuse, the urge to remember is like a hand now at my back, pushing me. It comes smooth and it comes in a line. Yesternoch was the fight with the Wandle runner, Lucien chimesick on the race. Two days back was poliss in the under. Three days before there was the smell of burning incense on the morning air. Four days was a fight among the strandpickers. I cast back further. It begins to come harder. My brain dry like there's not enough air for it. Our daily rhythms blend together. I look for detail, anything that will keep a day separate.

Five days, there was the member of the Order in the burial grounds at Bow.

Six days back was when Clare asked me about Lucien, and I made the memory of that in my skin.

Seven . . . 'Seven was the rabbit stew that Clare made,' I say. I see the pot hanging from the mettle tripod over the flame and the warm light on Clare's forehead as she stirs.

'Eight is . . .' I stop. My mind is only blankness, white as seawake. I wait and nothing comes. Eight is nothing.

'Eight is . . .' I say, and I can't ignore my sense of failure. I see a mirrorsmooth stretch of sand uncovered by the water at low tide, with the patterns of water on it. And I see the clear space of a sky without cloud, opening and blue.

And just as my brain refuses and closes, there's a jerk from somewhere else, violent and sudden. And a bubble rises from under the seawake, dark, and I can't stop it. A picture of a white shirt with red on it in streaks.

'Eight is the dead girl.'

There is silence from Lucien. Only the sound of the two of us breathing. And in the dark where there had been nothing previous, there's now a picture.

How could I have forgotten it? How hard would it have been to have made a memory? Guilt is a blurry feeling – like forgetting. It makes you want something solid and sharp.

I tell it.

'We were down in the tunnel near Mill Wall. Abel found a big piece of Pale. You were the only one who hadn't returned from the run. And when you did come, you were dragging something behind you.

'She had blood on her clothes,' I continue. I can't read Lucien's expression. It's strange that what is buried deepest comes up clearest. I can see it all in front of me. 'They weren't from the city, the clothes that is. They weren't roughcloth or wool. They were fine. Linen, I think.'

I pause, keep going. 'We did our best to clean her up. I washed her face and her hair. We gave her Brennan's shirt. We waited all day in the under until it was dark and we wouldn't be seen. Then we put her on a board and pushed her out onto the river.'

It had been dark. Abel had sung a weird melody in his high-pitched, halting voice.

I look straight at Lucien, waiting for an explanation.

While Abel and Brennan had gone to find a plank or piece of fencing to lie her on, it was Lucien and I who had cleaned her.

I ripped a wide band off the frayed hem of my T-shirt and poured some water over it from Lucien's canteen. First I cleaned her face, and then her hands. With the last of the water I had tried to wash some of the debris from her long red hair.

It should have been stranger and harder than it was, but the girl looked alive, especially in the low light. I cleaned her neck, and then quickly, not looking, I unbuttoned the bloodied shirt, and we slid Brennan's cleaner one under her.

And that was when Lucien did what he did. He reached his hand past mine, where I was beginning to do up the buttons of Brennan's shirt, and he took the girl's old shirt. He held it up first, as if looking at the blood. Then he bit the hem and ripped it right down. The seam was doubled. A placket sewn in between. Out of it he took a small leather pouch, weighed it on his hand tacet, and when I protested, cut me off with his eyes.

The picture of that look is as clear to me as if it were happening now.

'You stole that girl's memory,' I say at last.

'I didn't steal it, Simon.'

I look at him in disbelief. 'I was there. I know what I saw.'

'I didn't steal it, Simon. She came from the Citadel. She was bringing it to me.'

His voice is urgent and direct. He holds something out toward me in his hand. 'It was a message from my mother.'

My stomach hitches.

A small leather pouch with a long knotted cord. The leather is smeared in earth. Up by the drawstring some fine stitching in a different colour. A couple of bars of music, the five-line stave stitched on in deep blue thread, and notes threaded onto it in pinks and greens and reds.

'You buried it in the paratubs on the balcony,' I say. 'Why?'

Lucien shakes the pouch and lets the object inside slip onto his palm. 'So you didn't hear it.'

It is a ring made of the Lady. I've never seen her crafted into ornament in this way, although I know she was used for jewellery in the time of dischord. The ring is large and in the setting is a deep blue stone. It's the colour of eventide sky in early spring – so deep it's near black. It's worked very fine. I've not seen anything so fine made of mettle of any kind. The claws that hold the stone in its place on the base of the ring are shaped like leaves, knotted with thin vines. The detail is precise. You can see the veins on the leaves, and small thorns on the bramble.

'The ring is my mother's,' says Lucien. 'So I know she smuggled it out to me as a sign.'

Then Lucien tilts the ring under the light and I see that under the flat base of the stone is a small notch of mettle. He uses his fingernail to push it down until it sits flush and there is a soft, neat sound and the base of the ring clicks open.

There is something dark inside the ring's hollowed, flat space. Lucien picks it up and holds it out to me. A small worn coin of copper mixed, going by the slight silent pulse as he removes it, with a small amount of the Lady. There is a picture sunk into it. The picture is of a raven, the same I saw in my mother's book. A bird with a cruel hooked open beak. Wings that outstretch and hold it in the air. A small eye like a bead. Clawed feet that trail behind.

'This is their guildmedal.'

'Yes.'

'I don't understand, then. Your mother *was* a member.'

'No,' says Lucien. 'Not my mother. The person who came with her when she entered the Order. Martha.'

'What do we do now?' I ask Lucien.

He pauses. 'We need to know who your mother took the memories to in London.'

I nod. I sit up and rub my forehead. 'I don't know if I found them,' I say.

'Try,' he says. 'It's the only connection to Ravensguild we have.'

So I sit there and I search through my mind. The picture of the forcinghouse, the smell and the sounds of our talk. I see the bright blurred edges of the memories I have already uncovered, but nothing else. I shake my head.

'Think harder,' says Lucien. 'When she was sick. What then? You are kneeling beside her bed. She is lying under the white coverlet.'

The picture forms. I see my mother's hands gripping mine.

'She had to wait for the pauses to speak,' I say. *The shapes of her legs rise under the white coverlet.*

'The pauses?'

'Between the spasms. When she was dying.'

Lucien is silent. 'What did she say?' he asks after a while.

'She told me that it was too late,' I say.

'Too late for what?'

Too late for what?

What if she had meant that it was too late to tell me anything more about the song, or about what I should do next?

'I was angry,' I say to Lucien. 'If you can believe that. She was dying and I was angry with her. I thought she was leaving me with nothing, just this meaningless thread I was meant to follow.' Lucien is silent, holds me in the empty gaze of his eyes.

I force myself back into that room. I go into it. I see my mother's hand gripping mine. A single word, but not even a word, just a rhythm, syllables dropped from a height and breaking. Press my ear at the door of memory and listen. Syllables dropped from a height into something hot, hissing, spitting.

I look at Lucien and suddenly I know exactly what the word is.

'Netty,' I say. 'That's what she said. Then she said, "The ravens are flying, Netty."'

I see it again, as if it were happening in front of me. My mother struggles to raise herself on her elbows, to hold her head above the illness. A spasm comes and she arches back. Some large hand takes and stretches her, then squeezes her small.

There was something else. Her final words are not words at all, but half sung, the notes falling away from her and into the room. A humdrum, homely tune. A tune that has in it the sound of food cooking, water bubbling.

'She gave me a tradesong to help me find her.'

'Simon,' says Lucien, and he says it with such sudden warmth that I feel a current of light run through me from the very top of my head.

'And did you?' Lucien asks.

Blue tarp and faded light and the sound of her voice like that of something shutting. I feel a shiver through me. I found her and she refused to help me.

'Yes,' I say. 'Yes, I did.'

'Can you find her again?'

I nod. 'I think so.'

'So, we find her. We learn more about these memories. Then we travel to the Citadel. We must get within the walls and we must destroy the instrument.'

His voice is improbably confident and clear, as if describing a new place to set snares, rather than the impossible act of breaking Chimes. And I feel the creeping arms of the Lady reaching down to me from somewhere far away. And the deafening silence presses down heavier on my ribcage.

'How will we get into the Citadel?' I say.

'My mother will help us. And my sister too.'

'You have a sister?'

'Yes. She was two years behind me in the Orkestrum. A cellist. Far smarter than I ever was.' He looks at me and laughs at my disbelief. 'Why shouldn't I have a sister?' he asks.

Fully formed from out of the river, I think. Born pale each

149

morning, untouched by Chimes. Then I shake my head. 'Do you miss her?'

'Of course.' He looks at me as if seeing something new, measuring it. Then he moves back, pulls me to standing. 'We can't wait any longer.'

I nod. They're looking for Lucien, and where are we going? Straight into their stronghold.

'But we should go back to the storehouse first,' I say. 'For supplies at least.' I notice that my voice rises at the end.

'No. We need to go now.'

'And just leave the others?' I put my hand to my upper arm, press the pain that's still at the surface.

Lucien studies me, patient.

'In a few days they will have forgotten us, Simon.'

And I know that he is right.

Netty

We are in the eaves of the entrance to the Five Rover amphitheatre.
Lucien just inside the tunnelmouth. I am standing on the strand.

'Camden first,' I say. 'Then Covent Garden. If she's not there,
I'll go south to Barrow and then to Elephant and Castle.' I sing
Lucien the route I plan to take and he sings it back to me with a
few changes.

'Take the backstreets as much as possible. They'll be looking
for me foremost, but after the trade they may know what you look
like too.'

I wrinkle my brow for a beat and wonder what my description
might be. I have no clear idea of what I look like. I can't remember the last day fine enough to catch a steady glimpse in the
river. What I know is that I'm skinny, ragged. My clothes shout
pactrunner. It is possible, when I think of it, that I have my
mother's brown hair. My father's green eyes. But I think of
myself as nondescript, ready to fade in anyone's memory. Is this
what Lucien sees?

'OK,' I say. I repeat the bass line of the route so Lucien knows
that I've got it.

'And then what?' I ask. 'How will we travel to Oxford?'

'Just follow the tune,' says Lucien. 'We'll answer the other
questions as they come. And be careful.'

Netty is not at Camden market. I did not really expect it. I walk
through the crowds that gather thick around the foodstalls. It's
mostly prentisses, because Camden's streets are filled with music
printers, all needful of quick fingers for their heavy presses. They
produce the Order's official publications – teaching materials,

guildsong directories, primers for Onestory, special occasion Chimes and masses.

It's a young crowd in the market, muscling and hooting, dressed in the bright uniform of their trade. They group around the vendors selling vegetables and rice, hot meat pancakes, thick cacao blended with spices that will give strength to bodymemory. Music printers are well paid, and the prentisses are all strong, and the instruments they carry are rich and ornate. I stand out in my ragged jeans, my face streaked with sleeplessness and mud. I listen for neeps and tatties, but the homely tune does not come.

From Camden to Covent Garden. When I arrive, I walk through once presto and from habit I watch for a disturbance in the fabric of the market's music. I hear no pacts, no Lady, no trade. Just people buying food for their lunch, gossiping in duos and trios.

It is an older group of traders here. The clothiers of Jermyn Street. The prentisses of the instrument makers, who walk along in silence in their pale uniforms. I think for a moment of Johannes's son, Charles, and wonder if I would know him if I saw him.

I hear oysters, and pasties. I hear melted four cheeses on granary loaf with pickle. I hear foxwhelp apples by the bag, cider by the gallon. And then under the tunes I hear, like I've willed it into being, a threaded humdrum melody, bubbling and impatient. *Bangers and mash, neeps and tatties, bubbles and squeak.*

It is Netty.

I walk down, not too quick, not too slow. I see the blue tarp awning, the red-painted stools, the sterno plate, all even smaller than I remember. I see an older woman with greyflecked hair, her back to me, the strings of an apron tied in an angry knot. She times her patter with the spoon's stirring, the bubbling of the pan.

'Netty,' I say to the woman's back. She turns and she sees me.

Her face when she turns is arranged in a calm mask, only the watchful hooded eyes showing through. For a short second when she sees me, the mask drops and her face grows old and fragile in one half-beat. Her eyes fill with fear. But then before I blink, the flat dead look has come back.

'Who's asking?' she says, and turns back to the skillet.

I reach up and untie the tarp and let it drop behind me. I come in so close that I can feel the heat of the sterno raising the hairs on my bare arms.

'It is Sarah Wythern's son,' I say. 'But I am not asking.'

Netty turns lento and this time she lets herself stare. Her lips lift as if she might smile.

'How?' she asks, and the rest of her question is silence.

'How did I remember?' I say. I don't bother keeping the anger out. She is looking at my chest, has seen the lack of guildsign there. 'How is it I haven't lost my memory yet? How did I know to come back? None of it thanks to you.'

She nods without speaking. She doesn't take her eyes from me. I notice the slight tremor in her hands and feel a tinge of pity that she does not deserve.

'I joined a pact,' I say. 'I found my way back to the memory of our meeting.' I don't mention Lucien. 'You refused to help me. You knew who I was, but you let me go anyway, into the city. Though you knew it meant memoryloss for certain. You said you wanted a sign. Well, I've brought it with me now.'

She nods.

'Was it the song you wanted?'

She nods again. 'The song or the guildmedal.'

'My mother never gave me a guildmedal, but she gave me the song.' And I sing it.

Netty nods for the third time. Her old face with the hard eyes has crumpled, grown soft. The blankness has gone and in its place the weakness of an old hope allowed back in. But the hope has also strengthened the bitterness, like air feeding flame. It is a strange sight to see this story on her face. Neither expression wins.

'You look like her,' she says.

'I looked like her back then as well,' I say.

'Perhaps I should have helped you.'

'Perhaps you should have. But there's no point arguing that. You'll help me now.'

I will her to find some strength better than the brittle mask, better than bitterness. I sing the first two lines of the guildsong again, as if that might convince her.

'Sssh,' she says, and gestures in alarm to the world outside the tarp. 'I'll help. I'll help, but you must be quiet.'

Netty goes to the awning, checks outside. She ties the tarp again tight to the door poles. Then she pulls the two stools close and swings the countertop over on its hinge so it lies between us like a table.

'Sarah Wythern's son. Do you have a name of your own?' she asks.

'Simon.'

'Simon. Tell me, then, Simon.' She takes a breath like she's putting her shoulder to something. 'What do you know of Ravensguild?'

I don't look direct at her in case she changes her mind. I pull the memories in.

'I know they oppose the Order. They want to keep wordmemory. They know it is Chimes sends memory away and gives the shaking sickness. Their sign is the raven, which is a bird, which is an animal that died because of Chimes. And it has the meaning of memory. I know they work to share and record memories. We need to know who they are.'

'What was your mother's role, do you remember?'

'My mother had the gift of seeing others' memories. People came to her and brought memories they would forget otherwise. It was her task to remind them, to keep their memories alive.'

'Yes, admirable,' says Netty. 'But there was another task also, a different way she dealt in memory. Did she tell you of that?'

154

Something rankles in me. Netty talks as if all the fire is gone from the task and no heat even in the coal.

'Some memories were more important than others. My mother chose which ones and she passed them along. She sent them to you, didn't she? Then you passed them to the next and so on, so that the meaning would spread. And so those with better memory could put them together and help us remember and understand.'

Netty studies me.

'What do you think made certain memories important?'

'Those that were bigger than single stories. That told people something about themselves in this time, about where they were and why.'

She nods. 'They kept alive what Onestory left out. They told of the crimes of the Order, and the suffering of the people. These were the important memories. The ones that were meant to drive the rebellion. Those memories moved through the networks of people like your mother and me, to the strongest of Ravensguild.

'You surprised me, boy. I didn't expect to see you back here anytime before the next Allbreaking. But your mother was in the dark about many things. Things we had known in London for a long while.'

A sense that Netty is stretching her story for her own savour, that she is enjoying the taste of it and the knowledge she has over me.

'And what was that?'

'That Ravensguild is dead,' she says. 'It has been dying for a long while, but in our life we saw its final throes. When she died, your mother was one of very few who still transported memories to London. One by one the memory keepers had been picked off by the Order. The gift was depleted. If your mother had not come down with the shaking sickness, they would have come for her too.'

She looks over her shoulder to the market street. 'I have been waiting for them to take me, but either I am not enough threat or they have forgotten I am here.' She sounds almost disappointed. Like an overlooked guest waiting for an invitation.

Under my hands the woodgrain is dark with use. Elbow, knife handle, oil, sweat, shirtsleeve. The same table at which I sat to eat all those many months ago. Though how can I be the same person as him when so much has changed since and so much of myself shed? The only thing we seem to share is a name. If Netty is right, then my mother's sacrifice and pain were for nothing. And everything I have fought to remember is for nothing. For a moment it occurs to me that if she's right, then there's nothing to stop me going back to the storehouse. Tomorrow I could wake as usual in the hammock. Drink tea and sound Onestory and run in the under with Clare, match her pace, wait patient for the Lady's largesse.

'But it's not over, is it?' I say. 'If Ravensguild is no longer a threat to the Order, what's sending them out of the Citadel to find us? They may have left you alone to rot and forget, but what we know has them searching the city. They've sicced poliss and pacts on us. Don't tell me that they're no longer afraid.'

Netty goes behind her eyes.

'What do you mean, "we"?' she asks. 'Who is acting with you?'

'Somebody who was born to the Order and left it. Someone who knows the truth and who can remember it. Who can sing us back to the Citadel if need be.'

Still in deep like she's dredging up a thing long lost. Aggrieved to find herself back down on her hands and knees in that old mud. Then for a moment the hope behind her eyes fattens like it's found something new to feed on. She sings a fragment of a rune or tune I do not know. '*One to sing*,' she says. '*One to keep the plot. One forgetting. One forgot.*' I nod, as if to encourage her. Whatever nonsense this is, if she believes me, it will be to the better.

But it's as though the effort of remembering that snippet alone has exhausted her. She shakes her head and bodymemory pushes her face back into its bitter, flat mask. It is easier that way.

She leans forward. 'What you'll learn, Simon, is that people do not want to know the truth. You might think you are doing them a great favour to bring it to them. But even if you put it right on their doorstep, nobody will thank you for it. They'll throw it away. Throw it in your face. Most people prefer to forget.' She moves behind the counter. She mutters and it's a stuck note. It reminds me of Harry somehow. 'This has nothing to do with me at any rate. I left Ravensguild. After your mother died. After your father took his life. Too many deaths.'

I stand up. 'What did you say about my father?' I take the few steps across the stall. I grab her brittle shoulders in my hands and I shake. 'What the hell did you say?' I want to make her feel pain. I want to see something other than the flat, closed look on her face. Because the last picture I have of my father is him slumped at my mother's side where she lay under the white coverlet. His hand gripping hers tight enough to stop the shaking. And she is lying again. I shake her and my face is hot and the air is hot and it is me who needs to feel the pain. I am crying for it to come now, sharp and sure. Because I don't have any other footing. I don't remember his death. The only thing I hold in my body is the memory of his fist, and the cold of his anger.

Then after a while I see Netty and the look on her face. I drop her shoulders and step back. 'Who is left?' I say. 'You owe it to the people whose memories you took,' I say. 'Those memories were their lives. Who is left?'

'Keep your voice down,' says Netty.

I stare at her. She is scared. She looks back through the tarp again.

'Who is left?' I say, forte.

'Please. All of the memory keepers we used have died or been taken,' she says. 'I waited, but there has been no word of new keepers to replace them.'

I step closer again. She is holding something back. I see the glint of it in her eyes, and I want to see the fear in there again.

'Who is left?' My voice is so loud that I hear footfalls beyond the tarp come to a halt.

'Just one,' she says. 'She was my keeper, but she is mad. It has been years since I sent her anything.'

'Where is she?' I ask.

'In a place called Reading. Between here and the Citadel.'

'Sing it,' I order.

'Mary has gone mad. She will not help you.'

But before I leave her, Netty sings me the way to find the last memory keeper.

Upriver

Lily Bolero

We are on the towpath. Matins came and went, and Lucien and I walked through the early morning city, keeping to the empty backstreets. Just the occasional people up that early – bakers, coffee sellers, a few traders. Lucien had his dark paraspecs on and we moved quickly, curling past Euston, past Morning Town and through the old market to the first lock.

The stone of the path is cracked, and the bank leans over us on the side, covered in moss and small ferns. There's mist coming flat across the water. I walk in front, but it's Lucien setting the pace, a presto stride to eat up the distance and go unremarked by any watchers. At Primrose Hill we hear the lone notes of a muted French horn coming across the water and I see a bundled-up figure, short enough for a kid, standing at the bottom of one of the gardens whose lawns fold right down to the canal. The horn-player strolls back and forth, and the horn gets slowly flatter in the cold. The muffled arpeggios repeat over and over: major, minor, first inversion, second inversion. The morning light reflects off the chill pale gold of the instrument whenever the player turns. Nothing else moves, though, and we're past, listening to the notes stepping strange and relentless up and down.

More houses with lawns, each with a boatshed and jetty at the bottom, a dinghy, some mossy terracotta flowerpots, the habitual pair of para boots. Windchimes hang from one tree. A rope swing is knotted to another. In me, there's an ache of something that is missing. I do not think I have been down here before. These are homes – homes of the wealthy, the successful traders and the lauded instrument makers, those whose children go to the top schools, and maybe even audition for the Order. In the houses, both parents are alive, alive and getting their children out of bed for morning practice at first light, shoring away memory even before Chimes tolls for Onestory. The windows are tall and golden, and they look down on us as we walk past through the misty dark.

The waterway gets wider and the road above us higher and we can't be seen. Lucien moves us into a jog. We go past old cages with their signs and pictures of animals. One of the cages is arched high and has fine netting, and the branches of the trees inside are covered with chalky white splashes.

I can feel a headache coming. I need to stop, to wait and to think. I need to remember. The thought of leaving London is full of dread – dark water that rushes in to break connection. I am not ready for a journey. I whistle to get Lucien's attention. He wheels round, sharp.

'What?' His voice is harsh, but it is worry, not anger. I wait. 'What?' he asks again. He is not happy being in unfamiliar territory in the daylight. For a short while I feel sorry for him.

'I need to stop and wait for a time,' I say. And for some reason, this is awkward to say. 'I need to think. To remember.'

'I know a good place. Come with me.'

We walk further up the towpath and cross a road, and we're back on the canal. Old abandoned buildings grow high above us. Pipes break into the concrete walls, leaving rust on the concrete where the stormwater flows down.

After a while the canal widens again, and there is a broad tunnel in front of a low estate. We leave the path and walk upward past a fenced place with mettle towers inside. Signs hang on the mettle fencing, their code eroded. A picture survives, of red lightning striking a child's climbing figure. Lucien leads us between mettle rails that let us pass one at a time, and then round the side of the building with its empty windows. There's a thick hedge at the end of the overgrown lawn. Lucien gestures to me and I come up close.

'What is it?'

'Through here,' he says. 'Can you see anything?'

'I can't see a thing. There's a hedge.'

'No, beyond that. We need to go through.'

I get up close and use my elbows to make a small gap in the piney branches. Through it is a small grassy space that was once a kept garden. The bushes and trees are wild and overgrown with ivy and twining flowers. There's a small, open-roofed circle hut at one end. No one around.

'It's clear,' I say. 'How do we get through?'

'How do you think?' he says. 'Push.'

I do as I am told and suffer scratches to my face and hands, and then reach through to Lucien to grab my hands and follow me blind through the space I've made.

The garden is so overgrown that the trees have made a canopy. You can't see out and you can't see in. It is quiet and still and almost warm in the morning sun. A bee buzzes by the flowers. Lucien drops onto the grass and covers his eyes with his arms. 'We wait,' he says. I nod, invisible.

In the circle hut, there is a wood bench, soapy and splintered. I sit on the floorboards and lean back against it. My heart is beating shallow. The thoughts are shallow too. I am losing my place, and have in my body a need for darkness and depth.

I search back over the past days. I follow the path through the days and notches until I reach the dead girl; then I go forward again and what I land up next to is Clare on the strand. I press my fingers into the cut on my arm and I see myself standing next to her and I hear my own voice. *But you had parents*, I say. *Do you remember them?* I am angry at the arrogance of it. We were all born on the river and Clare was right. My broken things are no better than hers. I sit there in the sun and think about this for a while. How without mercy and without blame we have all of us been. And how careless to have misplaced so much.

I open my memory bag and search blind through the tangle. I

search until between my fingers I feel a pouch of roughcloth with something inside that is hard and brittle like kilned clay. I take it out and look at the undyed roughcloth. Then I reach in and remove what's inside the bag. A piece of old white pottery the size of my palm. A piece of a plate, I guess. Its surface cool and smooth, with one rough edge smoothed and browned by dirt and another where the break is clean and white and very sharp.

The rounded edge fits easy into the fleshy part of my palm, and when I hold it, the sharp edge faces away from me like a blade. And something shifts sides in my head and I am going down . . .

A wide green space. The sun above making a buzzing sound like a trapped fly. Like something burning in a pan. Where? Trees high all around, their arms all twisted and bent, lean over me as if listening. And flowers overgrown in beds.

The buzzing sound gets louder. The sun high and frayed above.

And the buzzing isn't from the sun at all. It's somehow inside me. Inside the memory. It says, Don't stop. Keep moving. *But I am tired. I have to sit down.*

Stretch my legs in front of me with their jeans full of holes. Wrap my arms tight round my ribs to keep the sting sharp and thereby keep awake, keep alive.

I'm tensed before I even know why. Then the voices are clear coming into the yard from around the crosshouse. I hear them before I see them. Singing. Laughter.

Men. Things move lento so I can look down and see my legs like they're not even mine. Jeans with holes that are ragged like the sun is in the sky. I use my hands to make my legs move; then I get into the trees by crawling.

They are there in the yard.

Two of them. Not the same men as before. I watch them walk. And I see they're not men at all. They are prentisses. But still I don't move from where I sit. Prentisses are a danger just as men are.

One wiry, one heavyset. The first one moving his hands in the air and singing too. He is looking around, speaking to the other. Both are coming closer to where I'm sitting.

There's pain in my arms, everywhere. The buzzing gets louder.

The two prentisses tread toward the trees where I am sitting. In the dirt in front of me is half an old plate. I grab it. Break it again so there's sharpness.

The first prentiss is walking to me through a window in the buzzing. Dark confounded eyes, staring. Neckbroke rabbit in his hands, looking at me like I'm something he's found caught in a snare. And sorry for it. But you can't trust anything in this world, not even kindness.

I hiss at them.

I hold out the only weapon I can find.

I push out, away from the pictures in my head. The thing I'm holding clatters hard on the floorboards. The sound makes me jump and it's that which shakes the pictures that cling around my head.

Sickness rises in me and I'm shaking. I force my head down between my knees, try to breathe, but it's like the ground has come up hard and pushed out the air. The memory is not mine but Clare's, and I have touched it, and somehow the pictures of her memory came into my head.

Things are swinging and I can't find the place where they stop. My memory. Clare's memory. I blink at the strangeness of it. How do I have it in my bag? And subito I see it again, but from outside not within, so it is my memory that flashes up not Clare's. I see her sitting there in the crosshouse behind Paul's where Brennan and I were singing the snares. So thin you could see the tendons in her face and shoulders and the rib bones through her T-shirt. And nothing in her eyes, though we could see the dark bruises on her, and blood on her shirt. She was terrified and it took me a while to realise that she thought we might hurt her. And though we held our hands out in front of us to show 'no threat', it didn't matter. She still came at us, her teeth bared, the half-broke plate held like a knife.

The broken piece was her memory of joining the pact. And she must have given it to me. When? And I saw it and I don't have time or desire to wonder at this right now.

I look close at the cut at the top of my arm. It is still painful.

'It's time,' she said when we were standing on the strand. How many days ago now? And she showed me how she measured it. I will find her a better way, I think.

'It's time, Simon,' says Lucien. He stands at the door of the open-roofed hut, in the sun.

The narrowboats in the canal mooring are shiny blacks and reds and greens, with polished brass and bright curtains. Along the wharf, people have risen into the morning. There are families sitting on the roofs of boats drinking tea from mugs. A few men paint and caulk the boats that stand on the jetty. A young couple leave their boat with tense strides and stand by a bench only a few feet away and begin to argue as if now they have left their home, they are all alone and no one is listening. Everybody around them is listening.

The narrowboat Lucien walks us to is at the farthest end of the mooring pool. The water round it is oily and grey, and the boat looks abandoned. It isn't polished to the high shine of the others – it's painted a thick black colour that is dusty and doesn't reflect the light. There are brass handles and portholes, but they are also dulled and dusty. The curtains are drawn at the portholes. The only thing that marks it as lived in is a teeming garden of pots that grows on the roof. Pots tiny and large, mettle and clay and para. In them are herbs and flowers, bushy shrubs and plants with small leaves like stones.

'Are you sure this is the right place?' I ask. Lucien hushes me with a hand gesture and knocks a trick rhythm onto one of the cabin portholes. Inside, the curtain pulls back a few inches. I see a quick glimpse of green eyes and sandy eyebrows before it twitches into place. There is movement inside, and after a few beats a man's head emerges from the cabin door and he's on the deck, pulling on a T-shirt.

He's older than us, a square and practical build, with quick fingers, a plain, energetic face and long hair tied back. The T-shirt has old code on it, and a picture of a skull with a lightning flash across it – an odd relic. His movements are precise as he jumps the short way to the path to stand in front of Lucien.

There is no exchange except the wad of tokens that the man sticks presto into the back pocket of his lean, faded jeans.

'So, you boys want a ride on the *Lily Bolero*, I hear?' he says, and for the first time smiles, which shifts his face from plain and square to handsomeness in a flash. 'I'm Callum.'

The boat's name is also that of a familiar jig, and as soon as I hear it, I know I won't be able to shake the music free. I sing the nonsense words under my breath in a bid to clear them. '*Lero Lero, Lily Bolero. Lily Bolero Lullen a Ba.*'

Callum looks into the cabin window again, waves inside. 'Hey, Jemima! We have guests. Come and show them around.'

Another face emerges from the cabin. It's a girl a bit older than us. She stands on the deck to survey us with a look of confident appraisal. She's not very tall, and she's wearing a pair of jeans that are cut off and frayed above the knee, a sloppy blue shirt, a heavy pair of lace-up boots and a man's green anorak, far too big. Her hair is dark brown and as long as the man's, and I wonder if he is her father, but I have a feeling he isn't.

'Hello,' she says, and her voice is different. Low and like there's something in her mouth. Then she signs in solfege to Callum. She doesn't sing, but her hands move so quick I miss half of it. Something about us, about pacts and pactrunners and how they're not to be trusted.

I break in, 'That's not true.'

Callum turns to me and Jemima breaks off, turns round also and sees my indignant face. She begins to laugh.

'She's only joking,' Callum says. And he signs it at the same time, which I find strange. Why use solfege as well as speech for something like that? Jemima is still laughing, a sound of pure humour. The joke is clearly at our expense, but it is so surprising to hear laughter that I cannot help but laugh also. I think I had forgotten what it sounded like.

'You've been misled about pactrunners,' I tell the girl. 'The guilds are always badmouthing us, but they need our trade as much as the Order does.' Something in me wants her to laugh again, to approve of us.

'She can't hear you,' Callum says.

I stop laughing.

'She's deaf,' he says.

Without thinking I look straight at Lucien. His face is as blank as mine and even paler than usual.

'I didn't know,' I say. 'I didn't know that was possible.'

'She lost her hearing when she was young,' Callum says, sharp.

I struggle to imagine it. What could it be like? Like living in a closed room for one's life. Cut off from joy and beauty and meaning.

But Jemima does not look despairing or trapped. Then I think of the Carillon and I wonder if she is able to keep her memories. Is deafness an escape? Perhaps the closed room of her mind is actually full of strange and complex pictures and objects. Perhaps the memories in her head are able to form a line that moves along those walls from start to finish. I look at Jemima and my pity disappears.

I expected the inside of the boat to be all dust and disrepair, but what Jemima shows us is a narrow galley and a scrubbed kitchen table, bolted to the floor. Everywhere things are hanging – lanterns, small sacks of sugar and flour and coffee, knotted ropes of onions and garlic. Small copper pots sway above the large sterno, its gas cylinder lashed firm to a roof beam. The floor of the other half of the cabin is covered in a thick, rich rug with shapes in gold and black and red. There is a curtain and behind it two beds are fitted to the rounded sides of the boat, neat roughcloth covers over them. Beyond that a wooden slatted double door, very low.

'That's our room,' says Jemima. 'You two are sleeping here.' She points to the bunks. She signs in solfege, slow so we can hear it. 'It's nice to have some company.'

'We will leave after Chimes,' Callum says. 'And travel at night. You two want to move tacet,' he says. 'We can do that. We also like to remain muted, *sotto voce*.' He signs to Jemima, who laughs again and nods.

'It's all quiet on the towpath now. No poliss. No sign of the Order. Narrowboaters have a good chain of call and response. Any movement and we'll hear it.' He signs to Jemima, speaking aloud too for my benefit. 'Why don't you take Simon for supplies, get some air. There are still a few tolls before Vespers.'

Jemima fetches two parabuckets and a large flat sack that she secures by straps to her back. I try to help her, but she shrugs me off and gestures me to follow. I look back to Lucien, but he has already disappeared behind the curtain into our new quarters.

It is strange to be walking beside somebody new, somebody not of the pact. Somebody whose bodymemory doesn't share the confines of the tunnels and the vagaries of the map. Jemima, I notice, wastes movements. She turns often from side to side, looking all around her. She stops often to inspect things I would have thought hardly worth notice – a branch that has fallen across the concrete path, a pattern of leaves scattered, a cloud that moves lento overhead. I'm so used to the steady pace of Clare's run and the silent measure of our shared task that I find several times I've outstripped Jemima and run ahead. Each time I expect an angry response. I see Clare with her quick kindle and her eyes sparking at me, but Jemima just smiles to herself as if she is looking at those pictures on the walls of her inward house. And each time I return like an overeager dog and take up her pace again.

I try to imagine what she sees in her world without music, without Chimes. I want to ask her where her happiness comes from. The trees are budding their new leaves and a thought comes into my head. They have a kind of rhythm in their upright trunks and their branches that start thick and then divide and get narrower and lighter and faster till they quiver in the air like breath past a clarionet reed. That is a rhythm you can see, not hear. Perhaps music happens elsewhere than in ears.

Jemima stops at a quiet corner of the canal and looks at the water and waits for a while, studying something that is invisible to me. Then she opens the flat bag. From inside she removes a mettle wheel from an old kid's bike. Over the bike wheel is fitted a woven stickwrap sack like the kind that carry flour.

She ties rope lengths to three parts of the wheel and picks a few stones to weight the bag. Then she throws the whole thing into the water. After a long wait in which I almost stoop to touch her shoulder and sign my question of 'What are you doing?' she pulls it up subito. There, silver in the sack, are two fish, longer than my hand. Her grin flashes up at me presto and her eyebrows go up as if to say, 'Yes? And what can *you* do?' She dumps the fish in another sack, ties the neck to one of the iron rings along the canalside and submerges it under the water. I am still watching without any words, intrigued.

'Dinner,' she signs. And then she points to a thick bush that grows along the canal path and hands me one of the buckets. 'Berries,' she says.

I leave her fishing and walk along the path. The bush is thick with brambles and, behind that, dense clutches of blackberries. I pick hundreds, enough to fill the bucket. My fingers are stained deep red and stinging. I think about Lucien. I think about what we are trying to do. I wonder if we will ever come back or if we are leaving London forever.

Running

We travel lento. Lucien usually sits on the deck hooded, listening for any sign of poliss or the Order. Callum listens too, for the coded messages of the narrowboaters up and downriver.

Two nights in he reports to us there's a tune doing the rounds. Poliss looking for two pactrunners who have made off with large quantities of Pale. Two of prentiss age and they are travelling by water. One tall with pale eyes; the other has brown hair. A prize rumoured.

'Three hundred tokens,' Callum says, 'is a lot of money. You should both stay below deck as much as possible until the tune fades.'

So we do, though it's close and cramped and I'm ready to go out of my skin with the itch to be in the tunnels.

To keep busy, Lucien tests my memory. We start with the day we're on. Lucien's voice, like in downsounding, leads me through the memories. Then back to the day before and the day before that. I wander through the strange events of the last eightnoch: finding Lucien on the race, the member of the Order in the crosshouse yard, poliss on the run, the discovery of the weapon. I reach six days, then seven, then eight. My head hurts, but it gets stronger each time. Then together we go back through my personal memories. My mother's death, leaving Essex, finding Netty, losing Netty, joining the pact, finding Netty again. All that I can I share with Lucien.

Like in the storehouse, Lucien makes small notches on the edge of his bunk each morning as we travel. On the third day on the water we start something new.

Lucien asks, 'How clear is your hold on the map?'

I look at him. In my mind's ear I see our storehouse and the path down Liver Street steps. I follow it down the strand to Five Rover and I place myself in the amphitheatre. Then I try to see the map as it spreads from there. I can't do it. My head is blank and empty. Panic starts in my hands, which go tight and gripped.

'I can't see it,' I say, and my voice too is tight held, knuckle white.

'Breathe,' says Lucien. 'Start slow.'

He sings then the tune of our amphitheatre, slow and circular with a slight dazzle of the Lady. I close my eyes and hear it, the fretted ceiling, the rust, the ferns, the silence of the tunnelmouths.

Then he sings the beginning of a simple run. A run that leaves the amphitheatre and moves in a circle of fifths. 'Wait,' I tell him.

Instead of trying to see the whole map lit up like the masterwork of some crazed spider, I focus just on the tunnel ahead. I sing the tune back to him as I go and in this way I follow his route – the comms tunnel, then a stormwater drain, then up into the walking tunnel at Mill Wall.

And to my surprise, the network of tunnels we've moved through, that spun round me without name in an untethered melody, all shift and settle into place. It's as if I'm blindfolded and then the blindfold is taken off.

Lucien nods. 'Now,' he says, 'sing me the way from there back to here . . .' and he whistles the melody of the Limehouse Caisson.

Before I lose my nerve, I'm off. I take a more complicated route than intended. I get myself lost and tuneless for a while before finding at last a way out, a tiny rivulet of melody that pulls me through. By slow degrees and without anything you could call an elegant tune, I arrive at the contours of the caisson. And it's like I'm there in body. I can almost see the fastrunning greengrey of the Thames, feel the grit of shells and mud and rock through my thin plimsolls.

But if I blink, I'm back in the candlelit space of the narrowboat, with the low chug of its motor and the sway and slap of the water passing.

Lucien watches me and smiles. 'Not bad. Not bad at all.'

We have travelled four nights when it happens.

It is early evening and the smell of pepper fills my nostrils for Chimes as usual. We stand on the deck of the narrowboat. A light rain has started and it drills holes into the water around us. No movements anywhere except the steady, light rhythm of rain on water.

In spite of what I now know about the Carillon, Lucien continues to conduct solfege, Matins and Vespers both. When I ask him why, he pauses as he does when he's looking at a thing from every angle and thinking how to explain. In the end he says not much at all.

'If you have an enemy, you seek to know as much about them as possible, don't you?'

I nod lento.

Then he thinks a bit more. 'Why does Chimes deaden us, our memories? Infrasound, the vibrations in the air. But something else as well. When you don't grasp something or remember something, I think your mind at last says, "OK," and part of it accepts this. In the end your mind gets to welcome that deadening. That's what I believe anyway. Half of our memoryloss is by choice.

'Vespers is difficult. The most highly trained musical minds compose it. And who are they talking to? A handful of other musicians and scholars. Those who can understand how a certain

174

phrase is a witty play on one from Buxtehude or Brahms. Or that a rhythm is a graceful nod to a Vespers chorale from a month back. Nobody else is meant to understand this. Not really. And what is the cost of all that lack of understanding?'

I look at him, shake my head. I don't know.

'The further we can follow in solfege, the better, that's all.'

Callum stands on deck with us, though he does not follow our solfege. Jemima disappears below and I wonder again how the music strikes her. Do the vibrations speak to her body in a different way?

Chimes comes.

It starts piano. Brings the long, slow progression of the melody simple. Muted, plain. Today it's two lines of tune, intertwining. The first is stately and simple. The second lighter, presto. They interweave: half-competition, half-friendship. But something jars, a buzz in my ears. It comes and goes, a tune in the bass progression, something familiar.

The first theme is almost at an end when I realise what the falling minor seventh cadence reminds me of. The bass is tracing an inversion of our comeallye.

By the time I realise, it is too late to turn to Lucien, too late to move at all as at once the chords come thick and heavy and full of thunder.

Our pact tune, split open into arpeggios and scales. Robbed of life and movement, but clear as ours. Chimes slows and examines the tune and it becomes impossibly rich, encrusted with harmony and ornament, and it stretches as if it would last forever and break open the sky.

After, I am kneeling on the deck of a narrowboat, perilously close to the water, my forehead touching a plantpot and one hand gripping tight to the brass track that runs the edge of the deck. The rain is falling fast.

I rise up slow. The shock stays with me. Deep in the bone. Our comeallye flooding the sky. The message clear inside it. Two pactrunners, escapees. Warning. Reward. It makes a joke of the meandering rumour tunes of the narrowboaters.

We go back to the bunkroom in the hold. I stand there shivering, still hearing our comeallye and reeling from the strange violation of hearing it aloft in the sky like that.

'Who will remember it tomorrow, though?' I say. 'Who even knows our tune? Most people listening won't understand.' But I know I am speaking just to say something. The Order don't care who understands. The real message woven into the melody is one we hardly needed reminding of. It is the Carillon's vast strength as it fills the whole wide air with our pactsong, the private tune we hum between ourselves in secret in the under. Two pactrunners are no match for the power of the Order.

'You're soaked,' Lucien says. He rummages in the drawer beneath his bunk, throws me a clean shirt that must be Callum's.

'Here.'

I pull off my T-shirt without thinking. The candle flickers. The light is low.

'What's that?' says Lucien. 'On your arm.' He points to the place on my forearm where I scored the memory with my knife.

'Nothing,' I say. I pull the shirt on and the shirtsleeves down.

'That's not nothing.' His voice is dangerous, piano. He grabs the sleeve and pulls it back up. His eyes go thin. 'How in hell did that happen?'

I can't think of what to answer.

'It's a memory,' I say, because in the end it seems I have no choice but to tell the truth.

Lucien's indrawn breath is fierce.

'Fucking stupid,' he says. 'Clare may need to do it and I'll say nothing further about that. But *you*? I thought you were smarter.'

I have never seen him so angry. He swears under his breath again and turns away.

I want him to understand that I did it not only for myself. I did it for Clare. A sign of solidarity, wasn't it? An apology for what I somehow knew was coming – our leaving, our betrayal. But it will only seem like an excuse, so I say nothing. Lucien gets up subito and stalks out of the cabin.

The cut on my arm is painful, but it stings less than Lucien's anger.

He is gone for a long while. When he finally returns to the cabin, I'm sitting on my bunk. I am playing the recorder tacet, melody without breath.

Lucien says nothing. He rolls my sleeve up again rough and takes a tube from his pocket. He squeezes a white paste on his fingers and rubs it into my arm. The white stuff burns the skin around the cut. Lucien rips a strip from the bottom of my old wet T-shirt and binds it twice round my arm, tighter than is really necessary.

'Do me a favour, Simon,' he says with a cold voice. 'Next time you get some idea in your head, some noble plan for saving memory, don't act on it.'

We are sitting side by side, but the space between us is immense. I don't know how to talk to him.

'Can you see much in this light?' I finally ask.

He turns his face so that he is looking right at me. He is still angry, but there is something else there too. He has been surprised by his anger as much as I have.

'Some,' he says. 'Not as much as you.' His voice is dark. His eyes meet mine, then move away.

'Lucien,' I say.

I do not know what I am doing, but before I can question it, I put my hand on the side of his face, though I know it by heart and don't need to recognise it by touch.

I touch his brow with my fingers. I move them down over the fine skin at his temples, the plane of his cheeks, the sharpcut lips. I study his face as if I were blind too. My heart is going so hard he

177

must be able to hear it. It must deafen him. And I am shaking like I've been pulled from the river with the cold still on my skin. We sit there like that for a long time.

Then the folly of what I am doing, the gravity of the overstep, hits me subito. I draw back like I've been stung. 'I'm sorry,' I say. 'I am really sorry.'

Lucien shakes his head from side to side. He hasn't moved away from me. He sits there.

'That's not a good idea, Simon,' he says. Says it slow. 'It's too dangerous. It can't happen. You do not want it.'

I find myself shaking my head also. A slow mirror of him. I don't know what I am refuting exactly. If I'm saying yes or no to what he said. No, it cannot happen. Yes, it cannot happen. No, I do want it. Yes, I do want it.

'All that time,' I say, 'I followed you. You had my memories safeguarded. You knew where I was from and what had happened to me and you knew who I was. You knew . . .' I stop.

Then the shame rises up and it burns. He knew this, the other thing, the secret of my regard for him. Of course he knew. How much longer than me? I think of my heart's keen leap in his company, my eyes on him always, my fear on the race when I held him, and I cannot believe how bloody ignorant I have been. The embarrassment flares up inside and I know I have to leave.

He shakes his head. He has not turned away. He has not moved.

'You shouldn't think so,' he says. His voice is rough, and catches. 'You are not so easy to know as you might think. Not so easy to know at all.'

His hand goes to the back of my head then. His smell of river-mud, sky, smoke, as he leans forward and kisses me.

My whole body in my heart and mouth. His hands in my hair. The long lean of his body hard by. The candle flickers.

After a while he pushes me back. He is breathing hard. His grip on my shoulders is so tight I can't move my arms. I can't help the huge foolish grin on my face either. The only thing I can think to say is his name.

His grip gets tighter. What is he scared of? It's simple, I want to tell him. His name then mine. Question and answer. 'Lucien,' I tell him, and kiss him.

'Simon,' he says at last.

His face is so serious, yet I am grinning away and my whole body feels light. I lift his fingers from their grip.

We take his bunk, though it's much too narrow for both of us. My bare back to his bare chest. All night the edge of the bunk cuts into my hip and I lie awake listening to his breath, breathing in the same air as him. I feel my happiness turn and wheel overhead.

Into the Belly of the Whale

We travel and the countryside changes. It becomes greener, lusher; the river gets narrower. On the fifth night the moon is full, and there are tall buildings, twisted and bent, in the distance. We go past two small islands in the river. To our port side runs the wide, ugly scar of a concrete road with many tracks. Above it, tall, dead lamps like those still left in parts of London.

Lucien comes to sit next to me, where I'm craning my head out of the porthole. He's holding the paper map that Netty gave me.

'Callum says we're here.' He points to a place near where Netty has marked with an X. 'The village is called Reading.'

We stop just before a large lock. Rushing water speeds past in the dark, and the wind pushes between the broken buildings on either side of us.

We hood up. I sing Lucien the tune that Netty gave me and he sings it back.

The village is grey and ugly. We walk through a huge concrete tunnel lined in yellow-painted mettle. The tune takes us along a wide sunken road with half-broken walls high above it. It feels bare and exposed in the moonlight. After walking through the wide, quiet streets and rubble for ten minutes, the tune takes us down a narrow, straight street of houses. Those houses that are still standing are small and redbrick and all the same – jammed together with windows along the front like staring eyes.

There's no glass left, of course, but about half have the windows boarded on the inside. Those are the lived-in ones, I guess.

Lucien counts off the beats from the corner and we reach the middle of the street before the tune runs out. The house looks the same as all the others. There's a garden in front with overgrown hedges. Lucien pushes the gate open and it swings with a mettle note, C sharp. The grass out front is covered in moonlight. There's an old concrete fountain sitting in the middle filled with burnt paper, flakes of ash sprinkled around it. At its base is an old leather shoe half eaten by foxes.

The moon makes strange shadows with the shapes of the scrunched-up paper in the dish of the fountain. We both look at the door. All is silent. Lucien turns to me.

'I'll wait for you here in the garden.'

'You're not coming?' For the first time I notice the cold slip around my shoulders and ribs like a wet garment.

'No.'

'Why not?'

'Look at my eyes. She'll see I'm from the Order. It's best if you go alone.'

'What am I meant to do?' I don't like the weak sound of my voice. I have been going along this road because it's Lucien's road. I know I have anger kindled down below, for what happened to my parents, for the things we have all lost, but it is out of reach. I feel like I'm listening to a song around me and I have no idea what part to take.

Lucien looks at me and his eyes are lunar also, casting out into the night. His hair is silver. I straighten my back. I am ashamed of my uncertainty.

'None of us knows what we are meant for,' he says. 'Even if a person keeps their memories intact, don't suppose the way forward is always clear. But we know a thing that needs to happen. So we must get help.'

Behind my eyes, I see black shapes, as if against a white sky, coming together in patterns like water does. Turning, wheeling, dispersing . . .

If only, I think, the way forward and the given meaning were lit clear. If I had a name or a meaning that was one single note.

181

'Take this,' says Lucien, and reaches inside his T-shirt. He takes his mother's ring from the pouch, flicks the catch and removes the guildmedal. Then he puts the medal back into the leather pocket and puts its cord over my head. I feel the Lady's mild pulse.

He walks away until he's standing under a half-dead oak tree in the corner of the garden. For a beat it looks as if the branches are growing from his head, crowning him. Then I turn, crunch up the gravel path, take a breath, knock.

Silence. I put my ear to the door. It was once green, but now its paint is curled and peeling off in flakes.

Far off inside the house, there's a bang like something falling off a shelf. I wait and there is silence again. I might have imagined it.

Behind me in the garden, I can feel Lucien watching, blind as the moonlight makes him, but still watching. I reach out, grasp the door handle and turn.

The door opens partway and my eyes adjust slowly. My heart is beating tight with fear. The hallway is dark, but there's a window at the end that gives onto a back garden and lets in a thin corridor of moonlight.

Once in, I see why the door did not open fully. The corridor is packed. Above me, the walls are lined with boxes of every colour and size. Stacked to twice my height on haphazard shelves made from thin wood and bricks, from rope and cardboard, from para cartons, from instrument cases. Crammed into the shelves, like a crazy person's market stall, are strange objects.

Silver forks and knives sit next to strings of bright coloured para beads. Piles of sheet music leaf out of rough piles onto children's toys. There is old electrickery, paraboards with keys of code printed on them, antique clothing. There are ancient shoes, board games. I see a boat anchor, a dead pot plant, small mettle men holding weapons and crouched in still poses, mould-covered pillows, dolls with staring eyes. And hundreds of instruments, from the cheapest to the most valuable. One side of the hall is straddled by an old upright klavier, half of its keys gone like gappy front teeth and the top lifted off like an emptied skull so that more objects can nestle into the strings. There are clarionets, viols, tambors and, down in the corner glowing softly, a transverse flute made out of pure palladium.

I feel dizzy, like my knees are going to bend. Before they do, I sit down, close my eyes for a beat. I think of the stripped-clean spaces of our storehouse, my quarters with hammock stowed. My memory bag and candles the only objects on otherwise bare shelves. And then there is a shift in light. I jump up. Standing in front of the window to the back garden is an old woman.

I had thought that Netty was old, but I had never seen age. Not like this. The woman's face is all wrinkles, like all the years and all the living of several people have been pressed into one body, one face. Her hair is as white and straight as the horsehair that viol makers buy from the tanners. She wears a cloak. I do not have time to be afraid.

I open my mouth, but before any words can come, the air around me is split by a scream. A shriek that has at its core the caw-caw of some strange animal – harsh and wild and black and frenzied. The sound is coming from her open mouth and it is rushing toward me so that I hold my hands up over my ears and face, and as her cry comes shrill and swift, she comes with it down the hall faster than is possible, with her cloak sweeping and flapping behind her like wings.

Before I can move, she is on me. Her two hands bent like claws round my throat. Nails in my skin and I cannot breathe. I am choking, drowning. In my nose is the smell of unwashed hair and rosin, as if her hair has been used to bow a viol's strings after all.

Then suddenly I am released.

In the clawed hands, she has the leather pouch. She is hunched over it and I see a flash and feel the Lady's small vital pulse of silence. She has removed the guildmedal. The next thing I see is the old woman's head go back and her eyes twitch and roll. Her head goes back and something goes out of her. Or perhaps something goes into her. I cannot tell which.

I back away towards the far window. The glass cold on my back, some distance between us. The woman stands, still as still, the pouch in her clawed hands, the cloak settled over her.

After what feels like a long while, she emerges, blinking. Down her face, bright in the moonlight, are the wet tracks where tears have run, their simple lines gone crazed across the tricky wrinkles of her skin. Her head cocks to one side, and her eyes look out at me beady and wet and twinkled. Her face cracks and is remade into a smile. She opens her mouth and I tense for another screech, but what comes out, cracked and broken, is a tune.

'*Sing a song of sixpence*' – her voice is like gravel – '*a pocket full of rye.*'

I stand there baffled, with my heart banging and my arms held up against my chest as if I'm bracing against something.

'*Four and twenty blackbirds baked in a pie.*'

Her voice is full of mirth, as if she has told a wonderful joke. I look around. Junk. A house full of junk and a crazy old woman. We were fools not to listen to Netty. To hope that we would find some answer or help here, some mystery that would equip two pactrunners to bring an end to the Order.

'*When the pie was opened, the birds began to sing,*' the old woman croons, and it seems as if she intends the song to reassure me. Her cracked voice falls from song into chant. '*When the pie was opened,*' she says louder now, insistent, motioning with her head toward me. I look around to see if I can leave without pushing past her, as I don't want to get close to those fingernails again. My throat stings where she grasped me. To my left is a kitchen. Like the hallway, it is crammed with junk, the only clear space the narrow bench and sink. An old gas oven sits next to the bench, its innards removed, a fire kindled inside it, a kettle atop and a cast-iron tureen directly on the coals. There is no other way out.

'The pie, lover, the pie! All the darling birdies. Must let them

184

out. Time to let them sing. You hungry, my love? Whistle up a cuppa, will you? Brown Betty's behind you.'

I twist round fast. There is nothing behind me but a tall ladder of shelves stacked with eggcups, toast racks, candleholders, plates. She comes up behind me, a dark shape in her cloak, and reaches down a large brown teapot covered in a wool cosy. Then she kneels in front of the stove, gathers her hands in folds of the cloak.

'Tea, tea, tea,' she says under her breath. 'Tea for two and tea for memory. Leaves are in the lolly box, lovely.'

On the shelf, there's a tall red mettle tin with a picture on it. For a moment I am sure I have seen it before. The woman removes the green iron tureen from inside the cookstove. Then she takes the kettle hanging over the stove's mouth. She puts the teapot and the tureen on a small table and gestures to the mettle tin again. In a dream, I reach and take it from the shelf. Bright red, beaten mettle. A strange old man in a black suit hacks into his cloth-covered fist. Where have I seen it? From a cupboard below she removes two plates, two forks and two cups, and puts them on the table.

Then she turns and grabs me. She holds my arms down and brings her face right up into mine.

'Let's have a good look at you, my dearling.' Her eyes close to mine, her lips creased in a grin. 'My dearling, my darling, my lily-livered starling.'

She smiles and then she whistles a tune into my face. The tune is our comeallye. I start back.

'Scared, are you? Surprised, are you? Why should you be? Bells tolled to tell me you were coming. No knowing of mine. Memory's my toll, not telling weather.' She shakes her head. 'Cloudy, though, very cloudy I'd say your outlook was. Don't need much to telltale that.'

I pull my arms out of her grip.

'Do you know a woman named Netty? She told me to find you.' Her word mess is getting into my ears. I shake my head.

'Netty. Netty?' She pauses as if to ponder. 'No . . . Don't know no Netty. Not a Netty in the pretty lot of them. Not a one in the net, you know. And you should knot a net to keep it. Keep it from slipping out, dear.' She looks at me as if she has said something final, conclusive.

Then she continues, 'No Netty. But he hasn't a worry, not *he*. A bird in the net's worth two in the bush. Or in the moon,' she says brightly, flinging a hand toward the window as if to release something clasped inside.

Then she turns back. 'Tea, that's the thing. That's the stuff to patch it.' And she breaks into song again.

> *'The fishers of Galilee,*
> *they never had enough tea.*
> *With a net and a line*
> *and a stitch in good time,*
> *there'd be more than enough for all three.'*

She looks at me as if expecting a response.

'Yes?' she asks.

'I . . .'

'Your fellow, your pretty one, waiting under the tree out there. Tea for him?'

'No,' I say.

No, I think. Let Lucien rest for a bit. Let him think we are moving ahead.

'Right, then.' She pours tea and opens the tureen and dishes what is in it onto the plates. 'Drink up. Eat up,' she says. 'Remembering is hungry work, you know.'

I hesitate, smell the pie, thinking of her rhyme about blackbirds. But under the crust is a gravy with mushrooms and potato. The sauce steams and the smell is savoury. I feel my mouth fill with water. I can't remember the last time I ate.

She watches me for a while; then she eats too. We drink tea without milk from the big teapot. After we have eaten, she gets up. She holds a hand out to me.

'Now we've broken bread, you can't go back, my dear. Only way out is through the belly of the whale.' Her palm held out, wrinkled. Her nails long and clawed. I take her hand and let her lead me. I follow her through the kitchen to the cluttered hall.

The room we enter is a maze. Boxes form corridors that stretch above my head. Cloths hang down and filter the moonlight that is falling from somewhere, a window high above us. Twists and turns of boxes and finally into a clearing. In the middle of the room, there is a space of cleared floor and on it a woven rug of many colours. A solid bookcase leans against the back wall behind. Ahead is a skeleton leaning slack against a mettle stand, his legs bent in a strangely casual way, from the hip. The skeleton wears a woman's straw bonnet with faded red grosgrain ribbons and tuberoses made of starched silk. Above him, propped against a machine like a tiny klavier with codeletters instead of keys, is a boar's head, the mouth open and eyes glazed in surprise. Next to that is an immense stoppered jar filled with glass beads of all sizes. I wonder how it survived Allbreaking.

'Sit, sit,' Mary says. 'Or kneel. Knee to heel. Kneel to pray. Pray to heal. Have you ever seen anything so lovely?' She gestures at the mess all around us. 'No! Never!' she answers for me. 'Don't be afraid.'

I watch her move lightly around the room, darting, alighting, swooping from place to place. She ducks down corridors, returns, flits off again. As she goes, she touches objects. At first I think it is at random, a sort of crazed dance, but then I see there is intention in it. She moves across and reaches an arm to grope up to a piece of fabric that hangs down from the ceiling. Then back to a patchwork-covered cardboard box that sits next to me on the floor. She pirouettes over to the skeleton, bows at the waist, then reaches up to tip his flowery bonnet. Subito a picture flashes up of something I saw once; it must have been in Essex. An old memory, at our crosshouse hall. Exhibition Chimes and an organist brought in from the Citadel to play along on our hall organ. A small man in his white robes darting light like that, like a butterfly, changing the stops, tapping the bass out with his feet, the same look of rapt, joyful attention on his face.

As she goes, her eyes flit and shift, open and close. Expressions enter and then leave. Joy, wonder, humour, affection, love, pride, contentment and a constant stream of patter . . .

'Oh, the beautiful boy, yes, eyes only for him, a mouth like a knife and hair like sunset, ah, my darling. Come, unbutton here. Loosen your collar a bit, that's it. Yes, of course I remember. Hopscotch and the daisies out. A fine time we had. Five under your feet and it's springtime. And in the swim we were. In the Isis. You carried me home the whole way, soaked to the skin, never stopping for a breath . . .'

She stops, turns like a spinning top until she's standing still at last in front of me on the rug. She closes her eyes and her face glows with happiness and I can imagine her young.

'Such love, my dear. Such capacity for love! The beauty of the world! The paragon of animals! But I forget – you can't see it yet, can you? Not standing there like that, or sitting. Patience on a memorial.'

I shake my head. I look around the room and all I can see is junk, debris. Rubbish. Then her face changes again. She looks tired, even older, if it were possible.

'Oh, but I am glad you are here at last, ducky. I admit it's getting too much for an old bird like Mary. The pretty ones. I love the pretty ones, but it's the bad ones, the sad ones, the heavy ones. Too heavy for an old back. They need young shoulders. But we can't pick and choose to suit ourselves.' She walks slow, as if she is being forced, and I almost see her back bending, hunching further. She stands in front of a pile of old paintings in frames. On the top sits a small white leather shoe, a slipper.

Her hand swoops and she clasps it, and as she does, her face crumples. Tears fold out of her eyes. Her mouth opens in a wide broken arc.

'The pretty one,' she calls. 'Oh, but I loved her even though I didn't know I would. There were curls there.' She strokes her temple, the old white hair at the side of her head. 'Curls, and they smelt of sunshine.' The tears are running steady down her face. She holds the shoe under her breast. 'Curls and a birthmark on her little left leg. And when you tickled her, she laughed and laughed. As if she was made for laughing.'

She stops abruptly, puts the shoe down carefully in its place. She closes her eyes and breathes in silence. When she opens them, they are clear again.

'And what would she be in music, do you think, my dear? A baby with curls like sunshine? A flute, a piccolo perhaps? If they cared for such a pursuit, that is? No. Chimes could not capture that. Where's the basso profundo for a dead baby, darling? What's the discant for the mess of loss?'

The mess of loss, I think. Chaos. Disorder. Junk. And it brings home what I had known but somehow managed to ignore. Before I can think further, I am on my knees and retching. So many memories, so many lives. So much pain, so much forgetting. I want to vomit, but I cannot. I retch until my throat is raw and my head is throbbing.

When I open my eyes again, Mary is kneeling next to me on the mat. She wipes my mouth with a corner of the cloak.

'Who in the guild sent you?' she asks. 'I thought they were all gone. I'd almost given up hope that they'd find the next keeper.'

And I understand what the whole performance has been. She thinks that I've come to replace her. She wants me to stay here with her, with all of the memories. I shake her off.

'No,' I say. 'That's not what I'm here for. Not to keep the memories. I need your help.'

'Are you sure about that, my dear?' Her voice wheedles and curls. 'You've got the gift, don't you? Who else is going to take these when I'm gone? They've left me alone here for too long.' Then she pulls in close to me again and I hear her voice in my ear.

189

'They're all here now, you know. All the memories have found their way back to me. The whole story is here in my keeping. They're all mine, and they can be yours.'

She pulls back as if studying me, and she strokes my forearm.

I shake my head. 'No,' I say again. No to the thought of dwelling here in the twilight of all of these forgotten lives, living off the borrowed honey of their pain and joy like a strange insect. I pause and a picture comes. Not like an insect. Like a hunched bird waiting on a treebranch for flesh. Carrion. Carillon.

'I'm not a memory keeper,' I say again. And then, because she appears to be waiting for more, and because there seems little harm in it, I tell her.

'We are travelling to the Citadel. We are going to destroy the Carillon.'

Whatever I expected her response to be, it was not laughter. Mary flaps away from me and hoots, her lips tucked over her teeth and tightened like a beak.

She gasps, breathless. 'Hoo, hoo, hooo,' she cries, and wipes her eyes, folds her cloak around her. 'But I *am* pleased to make your acquaintance. How gracious of you to call in on your *journey* to the Citadel.

'So you're off to overthrow the Order? Ah, my dear, how many pairs of plucked dicky birds have I seen on that errand? And I suppose you're just going to fly over the wall, are you? Easy as a pie full of blackbirds.'

I shrug, feeling the anger rise.

'The one I'm travelling with, he has a gift for hearing, and he remembers without aid, without objectmemory,' I say. 'He was born in the Citadel, though he broke away and got to London. His sister is there still and waiting. She will help us to get inside.'

She stops laughing subito. She blinks, and she hums something to herself. She is peering at me. 'And you?' she says. 'What do *you* do, my fettered kestrel?'

I stop for a minute because how do I explain my place? I'm here because of my mother's gift, and because Lucien caught me by chance with the hook of some memories. Mary interrupts my thought.

'He has hearing, your moon-eye out there, you say? A good singing voice? And you'll follow that voice to kingdom come? You've given him your word along with your heart, and you'll keep it, come what may? And you go, the two of you, to meet another. A girl, you say. Not of the city?'

Her head twists, swivels, on her neck, up to the corner then back to me. Eyes slitted as if she's willing something gone. 'I hear the chime,' she says to me, or to the invisible thing in the air.

I stand still. How to answer that?

'I hear it. Oh, I hear it,' she says, trying to silence the thing. 'Don't think I don't hear it,' she mutters.

I wait, confused. She hums again; then she sighs, as if I have forced her to explain a thing against her will.

'Just a silly ditty. A fairytale for fools. Hope is made of feathers, I told them. And we all know what happened to feathered things.'

'What are you talking about?' I ask.

'What they sang in the guild when it all fell down. Grasping at pieces. Trying to put it together again. *One to sing and one to tend the plot*, it went. *One forgetting and the one forgot. One who hears and one who keeps the word. Two will come and join a third.*'

The sound of it makes me laugh, though I don't know why. Tend the plot. Whatever it means in her mind, it makes me think of our fields marked for planting, the bulbs with their secret of colour held close.

'Tell me, lad,' says Mary, and she looks at me sidelong. 'How long have you been able to see others' memories? When did you know you had the gift?'

'I can't,' I say. 'I can see my own, not those of others.'

Then something breaks between us, the thread of her attention perhaps. She stares at me as if I have slapped her. 'What are you doing here, then?' she cries. 'You shouldn't be here at all. You're not the one in the forecast, are you?'

I feel hot and then cold. 'I never said I was. I don't even know what that means. I told you what I knew and I told you what we were going to do. I don't need any more riddles,' I spit.

She stares at me, like I'm a creature she's never encountered before, and she mutters, shakes her head. Then after a while she smooths her hands over her face, pushing deep into her eyes as she does. As if an ache will heal an ache, I think.

'Ah well. I'm sorry for that. But you've been a diversion, my dear. A bit of amusement.' She looks up, a beaked half-smile. 'How about you bring in your pretty friend, then? A long time since I've had company.'

I feel her focus slipping away. And something comes to me. The broken plate, the flash when I touched it. It seems a small and uncertain thing, but there is nothing to lose.

'Maybe I can see others' memories,' I tell her. 'At least, I saw one. A flash when I held it, and memory in her eyes, not mine.'

'Really?' She comes close again and studies me again. 'Really? You're not teasing Mary?' She looks around her. 'Well, then. Let's see what you can do.'

I wonder at my stupidity. What possible point will this exercise have except to extend the time I spend in this cluttered room? She retrieves a nondescript mettle bowl with a deep lip and brings it back to me.

'Here, my lovely. Touch it. Don't be afraid. There's nothing to be afraid of.'

I shake my head. 'No, I can't do that.'

Mary chuckles. The sound is unpleasant. 'What do you think is going to happen, little fool? That the Order will break in here and take you? Why do you think the law is there anyway? To stop people like me and people like you. Those who can see, and those who might be able to stitch memories back together.'

'It's not that. It's my stomach . . . I can't.' Just thinking about touching another's memory makes my throat close and my gut clench.

'Sick? It's not in your stomach but in your mind, my darling. They've gone deep, haven't they? Chimes almost had you. Thank Moon-eye there for pulling you out. Love goes deeper than hearing, does it not, dearling?'

I pull away in surprise. I look down at myself, pat my clothes. What memory has she touched without my knowing? How did she see what I feel for Lucien?

Her eyes are canny and shrewd and I realise that the nonsense bluster is like the cloak – something to put on or take off.

'Nothing there gave you away.' She taps her own face between hooded eyes. 'It's all right there. Bright and clear.' She pauses. 'For his sake, then.'

She takes my hand in her dry wrinkled one and places it on the mettle bowl. I wait, unsure what to do. I close my eyes. After a long, tacet pause I open them again. I am sitting in the cluttered room filled with moonlight. The old woman crouches wrapped in her cloak next to me.

'Well?' she asks. Her voice is eager. 'What did you see?'

I look at her, the wrinkles, the clawlike hands, and fear fills me. I am not the person in the forecast. I am not the person Lucien thinks me. I am not meant to be here. I wonder if I could make something up, broider a tale to tell her.

'I didn't see anything.'

'Didn't hear anything either?'

'No.'

Disappointment crosses her face and disappears.

'But it takes a while. You have to be patient. You've only done it once before, you say?'

'Yes, but it was only a moment. Maybe I imagined it.'

'Another one, an easy one.' She sweeps off again through stacks of memories. I watch her move back and forth between two piles, looking. She locates a mettle urn and holds it up to her eyes and shakes it. Then she empties its contents – old jewellery, coins, chess pieces – and uses a broken wooden peg to pick through. Finally she plucks out something and brings it back to me. I see from the look on her face that wheels are turning in her mind again.

She opens her palm and on it I see a roughmade bracelet. It is gold with a chip of red stone. For some reason it sets up a strange ringing inside me.

'Here you go, darling. Better to start small.' She nudges me. 'London is waking. Daylight is breaking,' she sings. 'Ding dong the bells are going to chime. Quick smart now.'

I look at the bracelet and I know I have seen it before. Is that how it starts? I take it obediently, fight the rise of sickness in my throat. I squeeze my fingers tight around it and I push myself into it, into the story of it, the past of it. A small gold bracelet. A tiny dark red stone lit in its band.

A long while passes and I open my hand. I have pressed the bracelet into my hand so hard that it marks red then blue in the flesh of my palms. My fingers are numb. I have failed. But as I release it, I know where I have seen it before. The answer is simple and impossible. My mother had one just like it. A chip of red stone in a light gold setting.

'It's my mother's,' I say flatly. 'How did it get here?'

She leans in. Her breath smells of strong tea. 'Did you see? Did you see? Did you see?'

'No. I didn't *see*. I remembered it,' I say. 'Isn't that enough? My mother used to wear it on Sundays. My father gave it to her. How in hell did it get here?'

'Then you were right the first time,' she says, and her face closes. 'You are not the one after all. Not for the forecast and not to keep my memories.'

I feel angry. I am tired of questions, of being tested. I am sick of the very idea of ransacking memory, which is private and silent and should remain so.

'It is my mother's bracelet,' I say into Mary's face. I stand up. 'I'm keeping it.'

'But you must give it back. It's not meant for you. I should have never let you touch it. Her husband gave it to me. They were happy. Red was her favourite colour. Red tulips. Red amaryllis.'

'It's not yours to remember,' I say, and I push her away.

'He wanted her memory to stay alive, and so it will, with me. Go back to London. Be happy with your blind friend while you can. Shut your eyes at Chimes. Keep your memories close.' She claws the bracelet from me and clasps it to her lips.

'Take this instead.' From under her cloak she takes the leather pouch she snatched from me at the door. 'Take it back with you. I am the last keeper and the guild is gone. Dead. Buried. Long, long ago.'

She pushes it into my hand and I feel the animal texture of the leather, the silent reproach of the Lady.

And as I hold it, something shifts.

A familiar feeling comes into me. Water rising. Darkness rising. Rushing in my ears and a swoop as air and earth change sides. Through the haze I see her staring at me. I feel myself fall and there is nothing I can do to fight. I go down . . .

I emerge and I am standing in front of a small stone crosshouse next to a wooden hall. It is familiar. It takes me a beat to see why – it's our village crosshouse in Essex. Where we went every morning for Onestory and every evening for Vespers. But it is different. The wooden wall is unpainted and raw-looking. I can smell pine and the sap bleeds in places from the wood. I search for a way to understand this. It comes to me. The hall is new. It has not yet been weathered by wind or sun. It has just been built. I am inside a memory that is not my own. That occurred before I was born perhaps.

I look around and I am surrounded by people I do not know. The ground in front of the hall is churned-up bare mud, not the grass I remember. The raised beds that my parents donated bulbs for each year are not there.

People are massed around and pushing against each other. There is a low droning sound of voices. It doesn't rise or fall, but plays a constant thrum, like water at a slow boil. It is a mix of two notes – fear and excitement.

The crowd moves like an animal, forward and back, testing its muscles. They are farmers, tradespeople, ordinary villagers. Their faces are both blank and keen, and I feel their special fear start to move in me. I push forward with the crowd, and when it pushes back, I resist and move through between those in front of me. I move in the smell of mud and sweat and woolfat and rosin. I push through the crowd until I'm breasting the front line. Ahead of the crowd stand a line of men in brown cloaks, a dam against the tide of villagers who are straining to see. The men are members of the Order. Their transverse flutes are slung across their backs with fine cord.

In the middle, between the members who stand solid and tall and calm like trees, there is a clearing of mud with three mounds of mudded dirt in the centre.

But they are not mud after all. One of the mounds turns against its earth trammels and I see that it is a human head buried up to the shoulders. In the clearing and in the middle of the circle of the Order, there are three people buried in earth, only their faces above. The faces are streaked in mud, the eyes and nose thumbed clear of it like the indentations in a child's pinch pot, ready for kilning. On each head is a wreath of leaves, splashed with silver paint.

But none of this is the true horror. The true horror is that their mouths are silenced. Each is stopped with a dead creature. The still-living eyes of these buried heads strain as they fight to breathe against the obstruction.

The creatures are black, tawny, wild-looking. My head casts around for some word that will fix them. So black they are almost blue. Not rodent. Not cat. Not lizard. A snakelike head, a small beaded eye, a hooked beak. Blood at the corner of the beak. The words come to me unbidden. Bird. Raven.

And then I understand. The buried are Ravensguild.

I come to. Emerging out of the memory is like rising out of sleep, out of water, out of mud. There is a rushing as if of a great weight pushing down on me. Then a popping sound deep in my ears and the pressure shifts and I am blinking and back in the moonlight.

Mary stands in front of me. A look of hunger, almost jealousy, on her face. Her mouth is open and loose with emotion and I can see her gappy teeth.

'Well,' she says, eager. 'Tell me. Tell me what you saw.'

'I saw the dead of Ravensguild,' I say.

She nods avidly. 'How did you know? How did you know they were Ravensguild?'

'Because they had been buried up to their necks and crowned with leaves,' I say. 'Because they had been gagged with dead ravens.' I imagine feathers, the taste of dust and mites and earth. I feel the bile sting the back of my throat and I force it down.

Then she says, 'Fetch him, your dear one out there. There is much to do. Much to do.'

Taking the Memories

Outside, the garden is empty. Moonlight raked across the over-grown lawn, under the oak only a pile of dry leaves. A bubble of fear rises in me, but I press it down. I want to call his name, but I let out a soft whistle instead.

Then I see him. He is lying down behind the oak, like a statue. His head pillowed on his arm and his eyes closed. He is sleeping. I have never, to the full extent of my memory, seen Lucien asleep. I stand and watch him awhile. His face is calm and beautiful. The thought that I should wish to protect him seems somehow as backwards as blasphony. But I can't help it.

Lucien hears me watching and opens his eyes.

'Well?' he says. His voice is as clear and imperious as ever. My thought seems foolish, as I had known it would.

I say, 'Come on.'

'What?' Awake presto, standing. 'What has happened? You saw her? What did you learn?'

'She wants to meet you,' I say.

Inside, Mary makes more tea and examines Lucien.

'Your friend here,' she says to him after a while, gesturing with her thumb to me. 'What is his name?'

The reversed echo of downsounding makes me twitch.

Lucien looks oddly bashful.

'Simon,' he says. He stares straight at Mary, though unseeing, as if I were not there and he must hold her gaze.

'His name is Simon.'

My heart stops and starts, as though I've never heard him say my name before. His voice gives it a silvered edge.

'And do you know what skill Simon has?' Mary asks.

'No,' says Lucien. Then if my eyes tell me right, he blushes. 'That is to say, Simon has many skills, but . . .' Annoyance springs to his voice. He is not used to being the one who answers questions. 'What do you mean exactly?'

Mary smiles and she winks at me as if she has caught Lucien out in some sort of game.

'Simon can see memory. Like I can. *See* it! Not just his own, mind. Minds of others. That's a rare thing, a fair thing, a precious thing. There were fewer of us in the guild, and then fewer still. Leaves on the tree after the winds came in . . . and I was all that was left. Last and lonely.

'But now there's Simon. Simple Simon. Simonides. And he will be the last after all. Not Mary.'

She says that thoughtfully, as if remarking on the weather. Then she comes to stand between us. 'And now you two want to travel to the Citadel.'

Lucien is pale again, controlled.

'Yes. To destroy the Carillon.'

Mary's lips open in a strange smile, and she starts to sing again in her rough voice.

> *'Simple Simon went to look*
> *If he could pluck the thistle;*
> *He pricked his fingers very much,*
> *Which made poor Simon whistle.*

'You need more than a whistle to destroy the Carillon, my darling. Chimes are strong as mettle can make them. A dangerous nettle indeed. How do you plan to pluck her?'

Her smile is full of relish.

Lucien turns to me. The plan is a sketch in the air, thin as the broidered river of his mother's map. Go to Oxford. Get a message to Sonja. Enter the Citadel with her help. And get inside the Carillon. Beyond that we have not talked.

The thought returns. I've been stuck in a dark room that I thought was the whole world. But now I see that, even if the doors in that room open, the difficult part is knowing which to choose. How does any of us know, after what has been taken away? And I see Clare again, on the strand, cutting her own path of story. I see the mirrorsmooth reflection of mudflats, a flatness unbroken. And I see that we cannot destroy the Carillon without returning some part of what has been taken from us.

'We need memories,' I say. 'We need memories that tell the truth of the Order, and what they did in the time after Allbreaking.' Lucien is looking at me. 'We need to put them together so that they form a line that starts in one place and moves to another place.'

They're both looking. It is Mary who breaks the silence. 'Yes, and what then, my darling?' she asks, coy and with cocked head.

'Then it will smash the circle that is Onestory. We will return what's been stolen by the Order and by Chimes – time past and time hereafter.'

'And say I help you, my dear. What then? If you are successful, well and good – no need for Mary in that sweet hereafter. But what if you fail, as in all likelihood you will? What happens to Mary then? I'll be here, still here. Still keeping the memories. That's no good for me, I'm afraid. I'll help you, but I'll need something of yours in exchange.'

Neither Lucien nor I say anything.

'I need to know that if you fail, you will return to me to take over your duties.'

I look at Lucien. There is no picture in my mind of a time in which we succeed, and none of one where we fail either. Would either of us survive it? Mary's is a blind bargain, but I don't see a way out of it.

'Yes,' I say, turning away from Lucien. 'If we fail, I'll come back.'

'Good, good,' says Mary. 'That is honourable. And if we listen to the forecast, you're a man who keeps his word.' She winks conspiratorially at Lucien. 'He'll not let you down this one, smitten as he is.'

I flush against my will, but Lucien acts as though he is deaf as well as blind.

'But, my dear,' says Mary, turning back to me, 'you won't think ill of the old bird if I insist on something to secure the deal? It's not that I don't trust you. Just that youth has its own code. If you give your word to him and your word to me, in a pinch which of them will you follow? I can't let love get in the way of what's rightfully mine.'

'What do you want?' I ask.

'You need memories. Memories in my keeping, to forge this story of yours. The important ones.'

I nod, impatient.

'Then you must give me some of your own in exchange,' she says, and eyes my memory bag.

I look at her. Doubt fills me. Can I keep them alive? I know I have no choice. I nod once, without looking at Lucien.

Mary examines me, like she is tasting the quality of my agreement. Checking its balance of fear and folly.

'Good,' she says. 'Come with me.'

And so we begin. Lucien enters the room with us, carrying my memory bag. He and I sit in the clearing between the shelves.

Mary looks at us both and then seems to disappear somewhere inside herself. Her eyes cloud and she stands apart. She looks like a moony, as if at any moment she might begin to make the starburst hand movements of their kind.

She is travelling, moving through the map of the memories just as Lucien navigates the map of the under. I imagine the constellations of memory pulsing out at her like nuggets of Pale.

Then her eyes sharpen and she suddenly moves forward with

purpose. She ducks round the shelf to our right and after a few minutes returns. Her eyes twinkle with triumph. She is holding an old book, or what remains of it. The leather and gilt-embossed cover is charred, the edges scalloped, as if eaten by some large black worm.

'Hot potato,' Mary calls, and throws the book across the room to me. It flutters in the wind of its arc and I see words in formation. Code, like birds flying.

I catch the book. It is very old and has been burnt. Flakes of ash still cling, delicate as feathers, to the edges of the thin paper inside. I turn blank pages until I see code.

THE

TRAGE

OF

HAML

Prince of Denm

William Shakesp

it says.

I feel a rush of hot air hard on my face, so hot that it tightens my skin and my eyebrows stir. I go down . . .

I am standing in a small public square. Behind me is a low fence with black spiked railings. In front, consuming all of the surrounding air, is a huge bonfire. The smoke is fragrant. To my left and right are tall, filigreed buildings made of pale honeyed stone. The building behind the fire stands on a small, neat apron of green grass, now scorched black. The building itself is circular and self-contained, somehow confident. It makes me think of a beehive. Or a walnut. A clever casing to protect a small, hollow universe.

King of infinite space, *says a voice in my head. The voice of the memory's owner? Where am I? Not London. Nowhere I have been before, as far as I remember.*

But the feeling inside the memory, that's familiar. Because it's one I know well. Helplessness. I look down and almost expect to see arms or legs bound. But I am standing free. Black robes hang around me. I watch.

The neat circular building is being gutted. Men and women in brown cloaks emerge from its many doors. They stream from other buildings to the left and right. They carry books. Books stacked so high on platformed arms that they can barely see the path ahead. Books laid on cloaks and pulled behind like threshers pulling hay.

One by one the cloaked figures enter the neat rectangle of the public square, bounded by the black rails I lean against. And one by one they throw their burden into the flames.

The flames leap. Sparks wriggle through the air like bright insects. The fire towers hungry in the night. And through the smoke and flames and the tread of feet, and the whump as books take their flight into fire, I hear chanting. I recognise the tune. It is Onestory.

> 'Out of dischord's ashes, harmony will rise.
> Order of the Carillon.
> Music of the skies.'

The voices are so beautiful. They weave in and out in complex harmony. Each cloaked man and woman sings, and their faces are lit. I feel myself rising up, pulling away.

The voices float up with me, never broken, circling and perfect.

I emerge with my face in my hands as if I am shielding myself from heat.

Lucien is next to me, his hand on my shoulder.

'What did you see?' he asks.

I shake my head, still half inside. 'They were burning code,' I say. 'Members of the Order. At least, I think it was the Order.'

But there was something wrong with the picture. The jangling of a note out of place. The circular building so confident in the meat of its own secret. It had windows. And all of its windows were made of glass. Unbroken glass.

'It doesn't make sense,' I say.

'What doesn't?'

'None of the windows were broken.'

'Where were you?'

'Standing in a square watching a bonfire. There was a round building with a mettle roof.' I think how to describe it. 'Like the middle dome of Paul's crosshouse in London, but just sitting by itself.'

'And the windows were glass?'

'Yes.'

'There is a building like that in Oxford,' says Lucien thoughtfully. 'But it's not in a square – it's built into the East Wall as a gatehouse. And it has para windows like everywhere else.'

'There were tall buildings around it,' I say. 'Tall and thin, made out of the same golden stone.'

Lucien breathes in. 'I think it was Oxford,' he says. 'I think you saw Oxford before Allbreaking.'

'But the Order were there,' I say slowly. 'They were wearing travelling cloaks. Brown like now. They were singing Onestory.'

I look at Lucien and see understanding reach him the same second it hits me. It fills his eyes like a wave. Huge and dark.

The Order didn't rise up out of the ashes of dischord at all. They were there, waiting. They knew what was coming. They had already started burning code.

And then the next wave swoops in, carrying the full weight of its sickness. Allbreaking was not the end of a long conflict. It was just a necessary step. A harsh chord before their resolution of new harmony. Allbreaking was brought about by the Order.

Mary is behind us.

'Chop, chop, lovelies. No time for talk. I've given you the first one, an important one at that. Now you must keep your side of the bargain.' She points with a wrinkled finger at my memory bag, which is sitting on the floor beside me.

I nod my head lento. Waves and ripples crashing around. My own memories are distant. How will I choose what to give her? How can I trust myself to choose?

'Here,' she says, impatient. 'Give it to me. Lucky dip.'

I pass the bag reluctantly. She wraps her hand in a fold of her cloak and reaches in.

She pulls out a big old burberry. Dip of mud at its hem as if it has been dragged through a puddle. *The arrival in London*, I hear in my head, *what was it like?*

'The arrival was mud,' I whisper.

'Don't worry,' Lucien says. 'You won't forget. Don't worry.'

I feel light, a bit empty. Mary wraps the burberry inside itself and places it on a shelf. For a moment I see the carter sitting heavy on the strut of his cart, his neck jerking with chimesickness as he breaks his journey to help a half-drowned farmboy. The coat was my only shelter from Chimes that first night in London.

I force myself to look away and I flex my fingers.

'What next?' I ask her.

Mary moves from the corridors and back into the clearing. Forward and backward, stitching memory as she goes. And time after time I go down . . .

In memory, I give my name to a strange man guarding a door, sing a few notes of melody and walk into a candlelit kitchen. A group of men and women sit in a ragged circle of mismatched chairs and they shuffle back to make a place.

The circle is one of chanting. First it carries names round and round. Eyes flick back and forth as it goes. Listening, watching, nerved with mistrust. After a while stories come. A young man to my left speaks of how he came to get the name he's called by, a long, winding tale of mistakes and lost chances. Then an old woman takes over and all she says is the list of her family as far back as she can remember till it's a litany and a marvel and the others in the group slowly clap in rhythm as she chants. Then the next in the circle is me. And I tell of how I came to meet my wife at a winter dance in the neighbouring village, but that she died, subito, not much after. My hands shake as I tell it. How long ago now?

Afterward we share other things. Why some winters wheat rots and not others. How best to help a baby sleep. What to do when your daughter falls from a tree and breaks her leg.

The people in the circle nod. Each story and each piece of knowing is repeated back until the memories are spread like cloth that you could take up and fold into smaller squares. And I go down . . .

In memory I am pacing across a narrow kitchen. What's the word for the feeling that sits heavy in my chest? Clinging as a baby. Arms of it round me so I can't put it down. It takes all the space I have in my lungs and mind. Takes all the time I have left.

My husband holds our boy in his arms and they watch from the kitchen table as I break the butterknife trying to lever up the floorboards. Use the broken blunt hilt of it to get behind the loose bricks of our chimney. Empty the broderie box for the silver scissors and slit the linings of our wintercoats up to their armpits. Memories. All the memories. I pull them from where they're hid and pile them in the middle of the kitchen. I see myself and what it must look like. As if I've taken leave of my senses. But I cannot stop because if I stop, I will never leave.

Is it wrong that I pray for forgetting after all? I don't want to keep the picture of my husband watching me go and my baby with his face turned. When I lift the bag of memories, it is very heavy. What use are words in the end?

I kiss the two of them goodbye without ever looking once at their eyes and start walking and I go down . . .

In memory I leave home. I say goodbye to children, to lovers, to parents and friends. I sing journeys backward and forward. I enter new towns and villages, and I carry memories in knapsacks, in bags made of roughcloth and of stickwrap. I travel by cart and by foot and on horseback. In new villages, I convince wary strangers that I can keep their memories safe. I blend into the crowd and keep my eyes blank and forgetful as browncloaked men pass.

Lento, as I come in and out of memory, I see a web spread out across the country. The web is Ravensguild.

I go down . . .

In memory I am in the head of a young weatherman. Under a tree that spreads its branches wide like a tent. Lightning carves the sky and catches the rain in its path so that it could be either rising or falling. Falling or flying back upwards to whence it came.

Something is near and I cannot run. The runes are waiting to be scattered. Weather waiting to be told.

Broken code from a paraboard. Bits of lead from crosshouse windows. Fingers of leaf and other fragments.

Keening forward and back like the clapper of a bell. Forecast comes out of me whole and it whispers, 'One to sing and one to tend the plot.' Though what that means who can say? I say to myself as I go down . . .

In memory I hold a small mettle bell. I am talking to a friend, a tall woman who is standing close and smells like smoke. Another memory keeper, and the object is a tool that I am using to illustrate my point.

The bell is small and its hood curves down like a tulip, as if it wants to hold its sound close rather than let it go free. It's threaded on a wool ribbon broidered with leaves and flowers, felted up in age. Brightly coloured like something a child would own.

I am explaining something. I gesture up at the sky. I am talking about Chimes. 'They come down from the sky,' is what I am saying. 'And they take something with them. The birds are leaving. When was the last time you saw a starling?'

I extend my hand with the bell held dangling from its ribbon.

'This is what they do,' I say. And I shake it. There is no sound. I turn the bell over on my hand for my companion, whoever it is, to see.

'Chimes makes of us silent instruments,' I say. I shake the bell. Tacet. It has no clapper.

Each time I come up out of memory I feel pressure pushing down on me. It builds up between my eyes and then rises like bubbles. Each time I come up, Mary swoops across. She stands over me as I hold my memory bag open, and she waits to take one of mine.

After the burberry, I pull out a dog collar. It's the memory of our first dog, who used to run in circles when she saw me and pee in the corner out of excitement, and who died when I was still young.

Then my recorder. Which is actually several memories, though I don't bother to protest. Each part – beak, body, flue – has its own associations. As I hand it over, I see the day I chose it. The ceremony held in our village crosshouse. All the children paired with their instruments. Klaviers for the clever; trompets for those with brass; a beaked recorder for a farmboy with no prospects. I see my mother teaching me the fingerstops in the kitchen along with solfege. Then playing duets with my father. And, finally, I see my audition for the pact in the storehouse on Dog Isle.

Mary takes the paralighter my father gave me that is the memory of our first trip to London together for trade. I remember the pleasure of its sound and the spark as I sat across from him in the cart and flicked its burred wheel again and again. My irritation when he told me off for wasting petrol.

And other memories large and small, important and incidental. None of these scare me, though. I can live without them, I think. I feel lighter, a bit weaker, but still myself.

At last I fetch out a piece of wood with a sketch on it. Two figures in pencil, the outlines drawn over and over until the impression they give is of blur and movement.

'You can't take this,' I say. 'It's my parents. It's the memory of my mother dying of chimesickness. That's important and I need it.'

Lucien's hand moves to my shoulder again. Things are leaving me. I am floating. A feeling of tugging in my arms and legs.

'It's just one memory,' Mary says. 'One family. One boy. One mother. One father.' She waves my protest away. 'How many memories like it do you think there are here? What makes yours more important?'

I am too tired to fight. She takes my parents' picture and places it among the others.

After that, things seem to both slow and speed.

In the memories Mary gives me, the Order closes in on Ravensguild.

Village crosshouses chime local curfews. One by one the evening meetings of memory keepers and villagers are broken and dispersed. In memory I sit and watch with other memory keepers as the door to my home thuds and splinters and finally cracks. A browncloaked arm comes through, clasps the door handle, turns.

In memory I stand straight as a tall, browncloaked man with a broken nose stops me and orders me to strip with a sneer. 'Where are the memories, witch? Where are you hiding them?' he asks.

In memory I see a fellow keeper pushed out of his village and barricaded in a wooden hut in the fields outside it. I hear his cries and chants as I walk past each day. His words lose meaning as he loses memory. What could I smuggle into that place? I wonder. What would help him? But I do nothing. Chimes takes it all, until he's free to go. Memorylost, starry-eyed, thin as a stick and covered in rags.

And I go back and forward along what I guess is time like a ribbon stretched. Once into a pale and clear-skied time of silence where I watch people walking streets emblazoned and lit in streams of code. Letters everywhere. People carrying small, flat boards backlit and breeding code, and code on vehicles that move without fire or horse. Code in the very sky itself that is revealed as flat and depthless as a blank page.

I see people at Allbreaking as I have always imagined it. Glass stirring in an instant so it breaks white and clean as ice. People striving to shield their bodies from the deep phase of chords that take root in cavities of chest and lung. The bridges rocked as if by giant hands.

I recognise the massive redbrick ruin near Pancras on the edge of its vast collapse. People young and old pour out of its cracked glass doors and into a broad stone courtyard. They cover their ears and go down into their last hunches. And the huge mettle statue that is hunched there still watches them, measuring, always measuring, as he seems to be, the silent ringing of an invisible string into pure and perfect fifths.

I see as if watching from a far-off window a field in London, Lincoln's Inn or Coram's, as brownrobed members of the Order move on it. It is night and they walk among the memorylost and they stoop to each and gag them. From the distance their movements are gentle. Bind them and blind them with cloth, tie their hands behind their backs, corral them and herd them like animals from the square – going where? – the blank figures walking.

Everywhere I see flame, as memories are burnt in their thousands. And everywhere, through the ones that remain, the Carillon tolls and it takes on a tone I had never before heard. I understand as if for the first time. Chimes are tolling out death. Human death and the death of stories.

I emerge finally from the tide. Tired like after a long run in the under. But weak too, as if from hunger or missing blood or air.

I catch Lucien up on the memories I have been given, and he places them carefully in the stickwrap bag from Mary. They look so jumbled and meaningless in there. A small mettle bell without a clapper. A handful of lead and some para squares lettered with code. A burnt book. A bundle of twigs bound in red string. A picture of a child painted on cloth. Flotsam and jetsam.

'Last one,' says Mary. 'Are you ready, my dear? You look all in.'

I take a deep breath and pull my shoulders down. The story I will need to tell is all there in that bag, but I feel uncertain whether I can untangle it, what I can make out of it.

'The last one is here.' She points to her closed left hand, fingers shut in tight keeping. 'But I need my last one in exchange.'

Without waiting, she picks up my memory bag.

From it, she brings forth a candle. It is my memory of the night in the narrowboat. Our bunks next to each other. His hand, that strange moment when the distance between us was crossed. The hardest journey of all of them. The feel of his hair against my hands. His face in the tawny light. The taste of his mouth.

'No!' I say, forte. 'I need that one. I have to keep it.' I am so tired that I feel my knees bending.

'What is it?' asks Lucien.

'A love token?' says Mary, her beaklike mouth pursed. 'I understand, my dear, but we have an agreement.'

'The candle,' I tell Lucien, because there is little point being embarrassed now, if I will forget it anyway. 'From the narrowboat.'

Lucien takes my hand. His is dry and cool. He squeezes my fingers hard and he brings his head close to mine. His breath against my ear.

'I won't let you forget.'

But I am filled with dread. What if he is not able to stop it? I look up at Mary.

There is no choice. Even if there were a choice, there is barely enough of me left to make it.

'Take it,' I say. 'You've got it all now.'

She inclines her head, places my last memory on the shelf and moves toward me. She extends her hand and waits until mine is open before pressing the object into it and closing my fingers one by one.

'The last one,' she says, and smiles at me.

I breathe in and wait for the memory to take me, but nothing happens. I clench my hand tighter, close my eyes. But there is no movement.

I open my eyes.

'This isn't a memory,' I say. 'I kept my side of the bargain. Where's yours?'

She is looking at me again with the wry, amused look on her face.

'It's more important than even a memory, lovely. It's a little piece of acquired wisdom from one memory keeper to another.'

I open my fingers. On my palm is a clot of thread. Wool, cotton, silk, different colours all knotted together tight and hopeless.

'What the hell is this?'

'It's a question,' she says. 'The question is, even if you have all of these memories, this grand and noble history of ours, how will it help? What is to make it anything but another version of events, another Onestory?'

I stare at the knot of threads on my hand. I feel raw and empty and blank. Some part of me refuses to think, refuses to engage in her puzzle.

She comes in close. 'A clue, my dear. Where is the Order's weakness? What is it they are afraid of?'

The tangled heap of threads is an irritation, a stupidity. It gives me a headache just thinking of untangling them, and then what would I do with it?

And like that, like a candle being lit, or a chord being struck, I understand the answer to her puzzle. I stare at her.

Mary nods to encourage me.

'Yes?'

'Mess,' I say. Both Lucien and Mary have their eyes turned to me. They seem to sway in the lanternlight, but it's just me.

'They can't stand mess,' I say again. 'Human mess. They can't abide the things that don't fit into a perfect harmony, a tidy chord. They wanted to perfect us. Their music doesn't have a place for mistakes and errors, for people who love the ones they're not meant to love, for babies with noses that run and those who are deaf and alone. In the end it can't fit in things like grief and loss and stickiness and dirt.'

I think of the members of the Order I have seen with their shaved heads and their spare, nearly skeletal, frames. Their paleness not Lucien's living pale, but of cloisters and practice rooms without sun.

'And bodies. They are afraid of bodies. Because bodies betray us. They grow and change and they love and they leak and they get tired and sick and old and they shake and die.

'They are afraid of these things,' I say, 'because they are afraid of dischord.'

The Map

We are sitting in the narrowboat, having returned through the dark streets of Reading. The sky was getting pink as we walked back the way we came, under the concrete overpass and the craned necks of the tall, broken lamps.

I paced behind Lucien, out of habit, as if we were in the under. He carried the stickwrap bag with the memories Mary gave us. I heard it crackle as he ran.

I sit on the bed now and it's as if some part of me has been cut off. I keep going to touch my memory bag, to check it, then stopping myself as I remember it's no longer there. The repetition starts to get irritating. I realise that I am afraid. It is a dull fear, boring and familiar, and it makes everything go flat around me. Like things are stuck to cardboard and I could hit out and knock them over. Only Lucien's presence is real and solid. But I don't want to look at him because then he might see I'm flimsy too. Paper and cardboard. There's nothing inside me and I don't want him to know this.

Lucien moves and the stickwrap bag rustles; the new memories jostle. They are full of sickness and pain, and I shouldn't touch them anyway.

'Simon, are you all right?' Lucien is leaning back propped on his elbows on the bed.

I don't want to speak because I don't trust my voice. I nod. Then I just say what I'm thinking.

'I have no idea what to do,' I say. My voice is flat like the room is flat.

'Just what you said,' he says. 'You will put them together so that they make a line that someone can move along. Like you did with your own memories.'

For a moment I am amazed that he thinks it has been, and could be, so simple. 'I didn't do that alone,' I say. 'I needed you in order to do it.'

Lucien studies me. 'It's strange that you see everyone so much clearer than you see yourself,' he says soft. 'You don't know your own gift, Simon.'

I don't look up at him as I don't know what is on my face.

'Most people I've met, inside the Order and out, never ask themselves what their own thoughts mean. Never seek to put them together like that. It's always just one and one and one, and no one ever gets beyond that, in my experience. But you, you puzzle on one thing and you seek to link it to the next thing. You ask where it came from, and why it came. And you seek to hold both things in your hand and move on to the next, to three.'

I am not sure I understand what he is saying.

'Do you trust me?'

I nod.

'Then trust that you can do this,' he says.

'If I make a story that puts the memories together, what then? How do we share it?'

'You tend the plot. I sing,' he says. 'Isn't that how the forecast goes? I will put the story to music, and we will play it using the Carillon.'

The full risk of this, said out so plain, shakes me. It seems small to raise the other thing.

'I'm not sure I can keep them.'

'You mean your own memories?'

'Yes.'

'You're not going to forget now, Simon,' he says. 'Think of all the work you've done. We've done. Your memory is much stronger now. You're not really scared of that, are you?'

But something, whether my breathing or my silence, must let him know I don't believe him. He sits back up.

'OK, here's what we will do. You're not going to forget anything. Not your own memories, the ones that make you who you are. Not these new memories, which are our task and our test at the moment. There are things that go deeper than Chimes, correct? Bodymemory for one. We're going to use that.'

And then he sings our comeallye and orients it to the line of the river and the Limehouse Caisson.

In my mind I am standing in the amphitheatre. I hear the ferns, the outlines of the tunnelmouths.

Lucien sings a tune and I follow it through the under. I see the tunnels, the turns he takes, the shifts, the corners. Then he stops.

'Where did I get to?' he asks.

'The entrance to Mill Wall Tunnel.'

'Good. Now sing it back to me.'

I do. As I sing, I see myself running.

'Good. Now, you are going to hide your memories in mind's ear.'

I look at him to see if he is joking, but his face is serious, intent.

'What do you mean?'

'I mean, for each of your memories, you'll find a turn or a landmark on this run, and then you'll put it down. If you want them back, you simply need to retrace your steps on this run.'

And so we start. Back at the amphitheatre. Each turn I stop and I search my memory, and I consult Lucien to check them, and I choose one and I see myself putting it down in the under.

The burberry I place down in the muddy water of the sluice gate by the first cadence of the first tunnel. The riverstone I place next, where the next tunnel meets the river inlet. I bury the woodblock at the start of the comms tunnel that breaks off from the river inlet and leads south.

At each turn, each shift in the melody that tells of a split in the tunnel or a change in direction, I place a memory. A roughcloth strip, a bar of chocolate, a dog collar, a paralighter. Until the tune is the tunnels and the tunnels are littered with the story that is my life so far.

'Now we both have the tune,' says Lucien.

I sit there, wondering if it will work, wondering how solid a foothold my memories can make in the spiderweb of the tunnels. But Lucien's voice is confident and it makes me feel somewhat better.

'You can run whatever direction you need through it. Do it presto, lento, da capo al fine, whatever. The memories should stay in place. I can downsound it with you, anyway, if you want.'

'Thank you,' I tell him, and get up. I don't know what to say. The space between us has become charged with a silence that seems to be growing.

'There's one missing,' I say.

'Which?' says Lucien, but he doesn't look at me. He lies back again, staring at the ceiling and rubbing the spot between his eyes as if he has a headache.

'The last one I made. The night before we arrived in Reading.'

Lucien doesn't reply. The silence is thick and it's like sightreading a difficult tune in front of a cold audience.

'What happened in the memory?' asks Lucien.

My mouth is dry. What to say to that? Either he's forgotten it or it meant nothing to him. Whatever the case, the message is clear. He is not going to help me.

'Don't worry,' I say, with a hot flush of blood in my face. I stand up. 'I can remember it by myself.' I pull my jacket back on.

'Simon,' says Lucien. I can't read his voice at all. But he's trying to return to the way things were. Before. And I don't want to return.

I need air. 'I'm going on deck,' I say.

'Don't,' says Lucien, sitting up.

I turn to him. 'Why? What's the bloody point in staying here?'

'That memory is harder than the others to tell you about. To ask you about. Can you understand that?' His voice is strained.

I look at him. I don't know where this is leading.

He takes a breath.

'There's no single memory of it for me,' he says. 'There's no single memory for the way it makes me feel. I promised that I would help you remember it, but I don't know if I can. Do you understand?'

His voice has a demonic clarity that makes my chest feel bruised and open. Like I've run too far, too fast. Like there's something inside me that shouldn't be there, a nameless element. Subito I know that it doesn't matter what he says, whether he feels what I do. Because I'd do anything for him. The knowledge gives me freedom somehow. And a kind of elation. His voice is as clear as a knife and I let it cut through me with its silver light.

He is still facing straight ahead, staring at the wall above my bunk like it's something he wants to break in half. I have to know.

'Do you *want* me to forget it?'

Lucien turns to me and I can't read his expression either.

'It's the thought that you might be able to forget it I can't stand,' he says. 'For me, it's in everything. Everything I hear. The map of the under, the shape of the river. This journey, the sound of it, it's you. And that sound is better than any other in my life. Do you understand? I can't keep it separate. If I could, then maybe I could downsound it for you. But if I did that, I think I might end up hating you. Do you really need schooling in knowing that?'

The current of what he has said rises through my body, up to the top of my head.

'I don't need you to remember it,' I say. I walk over to where he sits. I put my palm against his chest to hear the sound of his heart. Rhythms turn and tumble against my hand, mapping a run entirely his own. Violent and painfully clear.

He looks up at me standing above him and he starts to say something else.

I silence him in the best way that I can think of.

Oxford

Barnabas's Crosshouse

'Louse Lock,' calls Callum from the deck. Then there is a window of light in the black above us and his head appears. 'This is as far as we go, lads.'

I sit up. How have we come into the city without my hearing? I listen for the noises of boatpeople, tradesongs, prentisses. I listen in vain for the hungry whistles and furtive tunes of early evening. The air is still. The rushing of the lock, the sound of insects. Then at last I hear a faint, dignified tradesong. It runs right through to its end before another begins. Nothing like the clash of life and colour and song I know. I miss London in a sharp burst.

In the dark, the four of us stand on deck for a brief while. Then I reach out to Jemima and hug her. She gives me a quick smirk and signs something in solfege, the only part of which I catch is to do with luck. Lucien shakes hands with Callum and then Jemima, and we jump presto from the boat to the towpath.

The riverwater is deep green. We cross a moss-covered stone bridge that looks like it will collapse into the water at any time. Then we're on the banks and scrambling up scrub and over rails and into a small concreted park at the arse end of an ordinary enough street. This is strange. I thought all of Oxford would be the Citadel, but we walk now along a street with houses just like anywhere. The same staring redbrick terraces as the one where we found Mary in Reading.

One thing is different – I can already feel the low, thronging call of solid palladium. Down the narrow grey road, the Carillon's silver arms are reaching toward us. I feel as if I am walking without touching the ground.

The two-floor houses are quiet above us. No one on the streets. But the day is lightening and I see curtains begin to twitch behind para windows. I have my head down when I nearly bump into a smartly dressed man walking out of his gate carrying an embossed leather valise and a clarionet case. He curses politely under his breath, sidesteps me and continues on his way over the broken concrete.

'We need somewhere to shelter,' says Lucien. He pauses for a bit. 'I know a crosshouse where we can wait. Come on.'

Not much further and subito Lucien pulls me into the doorway of a large white building. The wooden door gives and he pushes us inside. There's the smell of old beer. I can just see out past the green wood of the door.

Lucien is breathing fast.

'What is it?' I whisper to him.

'Ssh,' he says, and places his hand gently over my mouth. We flatten to the paint.

And then I hear voices. Voices chanting, coming nearer. And footsteps in a clear and clever rhythm. It is impossible to judge how many they are because the pattern is so neat and the footfalls so precise. It never wavers.

Straight ahead are blank redbrick houses. To our left, not far off at all, I see a wooden tower that must be the crosshouse we were heading toward.

The voices approach steadily, and as they come, they become clearer. They are moving in some kind of game. It reminds me for an instant of our own practice in the crosshouse.

One voice begins a tune. A few beats and a second voice enters. The same tune, exact. A strict canon. The two voices intertwine and I marvel at the skill. Then a third voice enters. The same tune a major third below. Then another voice reverses the melody and sings backward against the dense tide of counterpoint. The notes pull and press against each other, but the miracle of it is that the voices are still in harmony, still calmly moving in perfect accord.

They are so clear and they echo off the grey streets and float upward in the still morning air.

Then a sixth voice enters. It takes me a while to understand that the sixth voice sings the first tune as if a mirror were held up to it – each note reversed across the stave. I stand still in disbelief. The tune weaves in and around without speeding or slowing. The voices make a magical game of it, throwing the notes like golden balls lightly in the air, juggling them, tossing them from hand to hand. It is one thing to listen to the immaculate canons of Chimes, quite another to hear such music sung in the streets.

Then they come into view. Walking down the street. Three boys and three girls. They walk side by side: boy–girl, boy–girl, boy–girl. They are all tall and wear plain white gowns. Over these a white tabard broidered with gold threads. Their heads incline slightly each to each. Across their backs they carry small transverse flutes in palladium.

They move at a steady pace. I breathe in deep of the stale beery air and hold my breath. The group passes. I hear them turn east and head back toward the Lady's pull. We wait, hardly breathing, inside the doorway. After a while I see the door of one of the redbrick houses open and a woman comes out, woven shopping baskets held in each hand. Lucien relaxes his hold on my arm and we move away from each other.

'Who was that?' I ask.

'Novices. Probably just about to be ordained. An excursion outside the walls.'

I stand still, dazzled by those golden balls juggled so briefly.

'Come on,' Lucien says after a moment. 'I'll show you where we wait.'

Lucien checks inside the entrance for memorylost; then he leads into the dark. The space is quiet and clean. It rings with the odd echo of stone floor and high arches. I hear mice scuttle. The beams are half broken, but the roof is sound.

It's a small, simple crosshouse with aisles at north and south divided by stone arches. The blank walls above the arches are painted rough, like something has been covered up. A few figures in gold robes emerge in a shadowy line and make their still journey toward something long gone. Lucien leans against one of the brick-bottomed columns. There are piles of broken chairs. That will serve well for kindling later, I think. And I slump down. The light is fading. I am tired, but I sit on the floor and I take out the memories one by one.

All of the last slow days and nights in the narrowboat I have worked with them. I began by placing them out in front of me and looking without touch, trying to feel the weight of them in my mind that way. I thought about where they were from, how they might talk to each other. I tried to empty my mind of the other things that it was full of. The pale of Lucien's bare back in candlelight. His clean, hard forearm cushioning his cheek in sleep. Faces that come up out of the murk of my mind. My father's. Abel afraid, the scar showing white along his jaw. Groups of people moving like sheep across a green.

Tried to clear past all of that. Empty enough to go down. And I have gone down into the memories again and again. I think about what Lucien said, that it is a gift, that hunger to find how one thing links to the next thing. To wish to find an answer to the questions 'How did this happen?' and 'Why?'

But this is not enough. I want something more than that. I want to show an all of us. And I want the story to hold and keep our separate strangeness and the broken pieces of all the human things that do not fit.

So far the story tells about the world before Allbreaking. It tries to conjure the density and slipperiness of written words. It talks of a world in which ideas are in formation and can be released and yet return at will each night. It shows the Order burning books and destroying words long before Allbreaking. It shows how Allbreaking started, and the bonfires of burning pages. It tells the bodies and faces of the people killed in the blasting chords, brought down in the buildings, drowned as the bridges collapse. It tells that the weapon was a Carillon built by the Order.

It shows the broken memories and the burnt memories and the memories scattered, and it shows those without memory, wandering lost and helpless, worse than blind. It shows members of the Order binding their arms and eyes with great gentleness before taking them to be killed.

It tells the legend of the ravens and the growth of the guild and its clever network, and of dead birds stuffed in buried mouths. It tells about the last keeper, Mary, in her memory palace of hoarded precious junk and nonsense.

It has all of the memories in it, the ones I exchanged for my own. It has babies born and people dying and missed. It has mess and dischord and pain, and it has falling in love. It has my father slumped beside my mother's bed, holding tight to what he is already forgetting. It has Clare stockstill with terror in the crosshouse by the embankment, carrying nothing of her past except cuts and bruises and the blade of a broken plate.

This is the story I am working on. But it isn't yet complete as I don't yet have the right way to begin. I sit on the crosshouse floor and look at the objects. I see the different ways they could be put together and the way the story changes each time. The objects fall into their groupings and they talk to each other in different fashions depending on where they're put and at first it makes me panic. I put the memories together again and again in their different patterns and try to understand which is the correct way. Then at last I see that there isn't one. I see that if I am lucky and I do it right, the story will not ever come together in one final meaning. Because there is not yet any end.

When I surface, Lucien is watching me. I walk over lento and take a seat, and he pulls me rough toward him. I tip back my head so it meets the hard bone of his shoulder. I feel torn between the clear, strong pull of his body and the weight of the memories that sit in their temporary arrangement on the crosshouse floor.

'You are working hard,' he says.

I nod. It's true. It is pulling something out of me. Going down, and surfacing. 'What happens tomorrow?' I ask.

'Tomorrow we will try to get word to my mother.'

I have been pondering the question for a while, but it still feels awkward. I think what to say.

'It would be useful if we knew more about why she got the ring out. You know, I could touch it – the ring I mean. Look at the memory.'

Lucien sits up straight. 'Yes. I should have thought of it.'

'I don't know if it will work. If a person doesn't need to make memory, it might not hold in the same way.'

'But you can try,' he says.

'Yes.'

I must look as sick as I feel, because Lucien elbows me. Then he takes my hand, places the leather pouch in my palm, folds my fingers over it. 'Go on,' he says. 'I've seen yours. I've heard yours.'

I take the pouch and open it. I feel the silver of the Lady slide down my fingers and through my joints. And with it I feel my arms go heavy, and slow and sure the deep rushing of water in my ears. Adagio, cantabile. I go down . . .

I am walking through a room. Maybe the most beautiful room I have ever been in. Pale plastered walls, high eaved ceilings. Light enters and shines into my eyes as I walk, so for some seconds I cannot see.

Someone is there behind me. I can hear their quiet threat. The threat is not just in their presence but in their hearing. What are they listening for? Hesitation? Fear? My feet tread a skilful bluff. Clear and measured and irreproachable.

There is a bed and it is covered in a white coverlet.

I look at the bed; then I allow myself to look at the person who is lying there.

'Mother,' I say. For it is her. Hold my eyes steady. Do not blink. There are small broidered figures along the edges of the bedspread. Some are playing instruments, and some are dancing. A small cellist with golden curls. They are caught in motion, as if time has stopped for an instant but will soon resume.

My mother's hair has been combed back from her head and lies on the white linen of her pillow as if floating in water. It has been twisted in fine strands. On the strands are threaded coloured glass beads. The beads form an intricate pattern, a map, a series of constellations. I stare at them and at first what I am looking at makes no sense.

But then I see. Or rather, I hear. The hair is a stave. The beads are musical notes. The melody is writ upon her, and the melody is her death.

I am kneeling. Something moves in me, an emotion I thought was beaten. 'Don't leave me,' I say. What I want to say is, 'Don't leave me like he did.'

'I'm sorry, Sonja,' she says. Her eyes are calm and remote.

Then a cold touch at the back of my neck, my hand on hers. And a tune that comes from her lips and leans into the arms of silence.

I'm too deep. Deep in the black water that is pushing down heavy on me. I cannot see which way to go up or down.

I kick up toward the light, but it is wrong and the pressure deepens. A rushing comes and it is not the rushing of movement but of blood in my ears.

A hand shaking me. Too fast. Too soon. And I can't stop the ascent. I feel the bones in my skull move and my vision blur and then I'm out and the hand shaking me is Lucien's.

He's leaning right over me, his hands clamped round my head. 'Simon,' he is shouting. 'Simon.'

I can't answer for a few seconds. Lucien's voice is drowned out in the sudden thumping in my ears as the pressure ebbs. I feel his hands leave my face and go to my throat to test my pulse. I lie there, let the world find its right sides again.

'What happened?' he says. I hardly know his voice. 'You keeled over. I couldn't hear your pulse.' He touches my forehead, then my chin as if reassuring himself I'm there. 'And you're bleeding,' he says. 'Where's it coming from?'

I reach up and my nose is wet.

'It's the pressure. I have to dive down to get there. When I come back, it feels like something bubbling.'

'You scared me.'

'I'm sorry.'

Then the memory comes back. I will have to tell him.

'Lucien,' I say.

He sits back on his heels, his hands streaked with my blood. His whole body has gone still. As if he can tell by the sound of my voice.

There's nothing else in the crosshouse but the silence.

'It's not your mother's memory,' I say. 'And it's not yours either. It's Sonja's.'

Lucien stares blank. 'But it's my mother's ring,' he says. 'She never took it off.'

I think through the pictures of the memory lento. I want to tell him exact. 'I was walking down a white corridor. It was, I think, inside the Citadel. Then I was with your mother in a room at her bedside.' I pause. I don't know how to say it. 'Your mother's hair . . .' I start.

Lucien pushes himself to standing. He does it presto like if he moves fast enough, he can push away from what is coming. But when he speaks, his voice is calm.

'Her hair was combed out and twisted, and it was threaded

with glass beads,' he says. 'Her hair was like a stave, and the beads formed a melody that sounded along it.'

I nod.

'I always hated that ritual,' he says, and his calm scares me. 'How can you take a person's life and make a single melody from it? Everything they've ever said or done. All they were to other people. As if a tune can sum that up.' He spits on the ground. 'The magister musicae composes all of them, you know. And then he sings them into death. People he probably barely even recognises. People he wouldn't have deigned to speak with. Whose names he never even knew.

'I hate it. A neat glass tune for a life and how grateful we are all meant to be. But it's just lies.'

He stops. His shoulders are shaking. His voice is cold, as if I am a student and he has been given the task of stripping away my illusions. '*Grief is not a note to be sustained after death*,' he says. 'The threnody becomes the melody simple of the funeral mass. I must have been in London when they played my mother's, then. I didn't even get to hear it.'

I sit next to him. He looks up like he is surprised. His eyes are dry and staring. I take his hand.

'I'm sorry,' I say. Then, 'Don't.'

'Was it easier?' he asks. 'Knowing you would forget them?'

I don't answer that. Just sit with him while he cries.

Sonja

The next morning is cold and sharp. I wake on hard ground in the corner. From where I lie there's a clear view of the wooden cross at the end of the room. The wooden man on it stretched somewhere between life and death. The look on his face like the rigor of chimesickness. Lucien's arm lies over my shoulder and my chest. I lie as still as I can so as not to disturb him.

It's a while before Matins. The window at the end with the chips of coloured glass still in it shows no light shining through. I would gladly lie still with Lucien's arm over me until next Allbreaking, but I can tell by his breath that he is already awake. He sits, stretches.

I watch him. He stands and shakes the stiffness out of his legs, and then he walks from one side of the crosshouse to the other, turns and returns to stand just behind me, out of the line of my sight.

'I dreamt that I could see,' he says. 'I was due to go on stage to play the Carillon for the induction ceremony. I was all ready and I sat down. And it was as if my fingers were sick. The muscles acted against me. They didn't believe anymore what I was doing. I could hear the music, but it meant nothing. There was no time in it, and no time for it. No future and no past . . . I can't explain it. I knew it wasn't part of any world outside of the concert chamber. There were red velvet drapes drawn, beautiful heavy velvet. They were there to keep out light. And they were keeping out time, and death also.

'I was so desperate to leave the stage. I couldn't even remember what I was meant to play. But I didn't have anywhere else I could go, and I didn't know what to do, so I sat down and played the piece through. I could see the audience's faces, and they were horrible. There was nothing inside them. No pleasure or disappointment or anything. And it was like I was crumbling on stage, cracks forming in my fingers and through my head, and I knew I would break at any moment.

'I tried to tell them. It seemed they should understand – they could see it in front of them. But I couldn't stop playing. My fingers wouldn't let me. The playing was ugly and clumsy, but I couldn't stop. I wanted to shout out that they needed to let me stop, but I couldn't. And they just kept staring, waiting for me to finish.

'I must have finished at last, because at some point the hall, the magisters, the students, all of them rose up in one single movement to applaud. I saw their dead eyes and their hands clapping and it was just the same empty sound and it meant nothing. So there I was dying, and they clapped. And I realised that not a single person among them, including my father, cared who I was, cared if I lived or died.' He takes a breath. 'That is the life of the Order. I've been deaf to it as well as blind. We go on as before,' he says. 'There's nothing else we can do.'

'We need to get a message to Sonja,' I say.

Lucien is silent for a while.

'There used to be a viol maker across the east side of the market place,' he says. 'He was the best in the city. He and his prentiss used to enter the Citadel every eightnoch to sell bowhair and strings to the Orkestrum and do repairs. I am sure he is still alive.'

'We gave the last of our tokens to Callum,' I say. 'We've nothing to trade for a favour.'

'Then you will have to rely on your good looks and native charm,' says Lucien.

After Matins I leave Lucien, whose eyes will betray him, and I head east toward the pull of the Lady. The streets are filled with people. I watch the ones carrying shopping baskets and follow their path until I reach an open market in a large cobbled square.

Buyers walk calmly, and talk is muted. All the flinty chaffer and dash of bargaining is missing. No roughcloth on the cloth vendor's cart, just linen in pale creams and whites. Gold and silver broderie thread on large wooden reels. The traders' eyes slide over me, too full of their own dignity for spiel or swagger.

Off the market street and down the wide avenue to its east. All of the shops are large and well kept, and they're hung with the guildsigns of instruments. Highboy. Trompet. Clarionet. Flute. The thick, clear para windows are polished bright and behind them strange and inventive displays. I stop at a casement backed in rich blue velvet. Dozens of trompets hang inside, tied by invisible thread and spinning tacet, sending out sparks and rays of golden light across the street.

Basson. Klavier. Slip horn. Cello. I stop in front of a red door. Viol.

A low chime from the doorbell and I'm inside. Candles bright against the dark of the windows and the smell of rosin rich and piney in the air. Scent of glue and varnish and the warmth of wood. Viols hang on the walls, their scrolls resting between specially turned pegs. The bows lie in a field of green velvet inside a low case. They are wonderfully beautiful, inlaid with ivory and coloured stones. I can see through to the adjoining workshop. A bench covered in leather. Two heads, one grey and one blond, inclined over a curved piece of wood, the belly of a viol.

The viol maker takes his time in looking up. When he sees me, he hands the woodplane to his prentiss and says something under his breath.

Then he walks into the showroom slowly, rubbing his hands on a cloth.

'What can I do for you, young man? A new string, perhaps? A block of redpine rosin? Or does something else catch your eye?'

There is humour in his words, but he moves with caution, a wary eye on the precious goods around me.

The prentiss watches from the workshop. He has taken in my ragged clothes and grimy face and is waiting to be entertained. I will not disappoint.

I stand taller, look for the right words. A stammer, I think. Proud and poor. Nervous as hell.

'You . . . you go into the Citadel often, I think, sir?'

'What business is it of yours?' he says.

'I need to speak to someone . . . to get a message to them.'

'And I need three hundred tokens and a new coat. What of it?'

'Her name is Sonja,' I say. I think of what Lucien has told me. 'She's tall. She talks as if she is somewhere far off and much better, but her eyes look like she's trying not to laugh. Her hair is blonde. Paler than his.' I gesture to the prentiss through the open door. 'She's high born, a member of the Orkestrum. I need to get a message to her.' I think of Lucien. The strain in my voice is real at least.

A small smile comes to the viol maker's mouth.

I push my hands through my hair. 'You will know her if you see her,' I say. 'She is beautiful. Tall. Her father is high up in the Order. She plays the cello.'

'And does this beautiful, tall cellist know you exist?' the viol maker asks. He walks to the case of bows and picks one up, tests the balance. 'Why would she accept a message from a boy so clearly beneath her in status?'

My face returns to the truth of my own doubt.

'She spoke to me once,' I say, drawing myself up again. My voice is tight, trying for dignity. 'In the market place. I bumped into her and she dropped her bag and the scores went everywhere. She was very angry at first, but I helped her gather the music. We talked.'

Strangely enough, as I say it, I see it. The tall girl bending in anger and the white pages of music flying from her grasp. The awkward bulk of the cello case resting sidelong on the cobbles.

'Look, it probably meant nothing to her, but I need to speak to her one more time. Please.'

If I'm not mistaken, there is a softening in his face.

'And if I were to see this Sonja, what then?'

'Would you tell her that Lucien is waiting for her?' I sing the message, the name, the location of the crosshouse.

'Lucien,' he says thoughtfully. 'An odd name for a rough lad. I'd forget about love and get yourself prentissed if I were you. You're too old to be out of work.' He nods at my chest, bare of guildsign. 'Knock at the bakery, three doors down. They had a call out for prentisses yesternoch.'

'Will you tell her?'

'Not that you have a hope in hell, but if I see her, I'll sing your ditty. I was young once, however little I remember of it. Now, get yourself down to the bakery and say I sent you.'

I nod my thanks.

'And keep your memories close,' he says.

It is late evening, after Vespers. Lucien tells me of vast libraries with corridor upon corridor of leather-bound scores. He speaks of chamber concerts given by the magisters in gilded and lamplit rooms. He talks about the Orkestrum, where the students move from room to room with the tolls of the Carillon, and from lecture to rehearsal to lesson. Days spent deep in music, living and breathing it until it shapes your dreams.

'Meditation is a form of hearing,' Lucien is saying. 'A heightened form. You clear your head of all thoughts. When the music comes, you try to see it shining between your eyes. Like threads stretched taut and the notes as coloured beads threaded on. When you get very good, it's as if you can see inside the music, through it. You bring the music alive, bring it into being. As if you're the one composing.'

234

I watch him speak. His eyes are fixed on the candle. The shadows are on the planes of his face.

'I can see you, you know, Simon,' says Lucien.

'What do you mean?'

'I wasn't sure if you knew this. I mean not with my eyes but with my ears. I can hear your face. What you look like. I can hear your breath too.'

Subito he turns to the door. There is nothing there.

After several beats I hear it also. Low footsteps around the side of the crosshouse. Lucien stands, motions me into the north wing, which is shadowed by the stone arches.

In the dark, the door creaks open and there is the faint whisper of robes on stone.

A girl stands just inside the door holding a lantern.

My description to the viol maker was accurate. She is tall, almost as tall as Lucien. Her hair is blonde and her nose a sharp line. She holds her head with her jaw tilted up. She is dressed all in white, her robes as austere as those of the novices we saw. Her hair is cropped but not short enough to remove the curls that stand around her head. Her expression is empty, no expression at all. Not calm, not cold, not angry, not afraid. It reminds me of nothing so much as the dead room we found at the heart of the weapon.

'Who is he?' she says, looking direct at Lucien. And I realise she means me. She has not looked my way.

Her voice is blank too, but under is an old emotion, something soured, painful.

A quick exhalation of breath from Lucien.

'Come out, Simon,' he says to me.

'You've been away too long, brother. I suppose in the city you're the only one with any hearing. Deafness isn't tolerated long here.'

I walk back down the arched corridor until I stand behind Lucien, in the shadows. Sonja sets the lantern on a nearby pew without taking her eyes off her brother. She looks around the room like a soloist who had hoped for a bigger audience. Her movements are precise, as if her physical body is just a hindrance she has mastered.

'It poses an interesting question, doesn't it?' she says.

I can read Lucien's impatience clear from where I stand. But there is no sharp answer. I am surprised to see him incline his head in a half-bow. And then I see that he is scared of her. Not of her anger, but of what has caused it. He is afraid of the hurt he's given her by leaving. The damage there not far from the surface still, not quite hidden. It lends her a strange power.

'What question?' says Lucien.

'Why am I even here speaking to you, when you're dead? You *are* dead, aren't you? Dead, all these many years of – what was it? Riverfever? It was too risky for me to see your body. They are so afraid of contagion in the Citadel.' She laughs. 'Poor Lucien.'

Lucien regards her steadily. 'But you are here. You got the ring out to me.'

'Yes,' she says, as if reminded of a past whim. 'My mother's ring.'

'*Our* mother's ring,' he says.

'I saw her before she died at least. Though it was you she was thinking of.'

Her laugh isn't for humour, I realise then, but for giving herself pain.

'Tell me what happened,' says Lucien.

Sonja shrugs. 'She died,' she says. The words staccato in the cold crosshouse.

'I know that much,' says Lucien. 'Tell me what happened.'

'It was about a year after your mysterious death. They all assumed that she was mourning you, that that killed her. The magisters attributed such crass sentimentality to her low upbringing no doubt. They were wrong, though, as it turned out. Whatever she died of, it wasn't sentiment.' She pauses. 'What else is there to tell? She gave me the ring when she was dying. It was her way of telling me you were still alive and that she'd lied all that time. She meant it for you.'

'How do you know?'

Sonja sighs. 'Because she sang it,' she says. When Lucien says nothing, she continues. Like someone used to waiting for the other to catch up. 'Do you remember the game we used to play?'

'The singing game? In the Purcell Room?'

'Yes. Do you remember the tune?'

'Of course,' says Lucien. 'It wasn't really fair, that game, you know. I could hear you without the melody. But you refused to change the rules. I sang *Ray Me* to signal you. Then you had to answer *Ray Me Doh*.'

Sonja ignores this. 'When Mother died, she gave me the ring and she sang your name. Not in the official melody, but in that tune. *Ray Me Doh*.'

Lucien wrinkles his brow and subito I'm watching a whole world I do not know. The vast territory of secrets that has passed between them. A picture floats up of them walking in lockstep like the idling novices, their heads inclined. I feel for a moment apart, alone.

'I didn't know she had heard us.'

'Neither did I. It took me a while to understand what she meant. Of course, it was obvious. She was telling me that you were still hiding, that if I listened hard enough, I would find you.'

'And the magisters? How did they learn I was alive?'

For the first time since she started speaking, Sonja's voice falters.

'After I knew what she had meant, I studied the ring again. I found the hidden catch, and what was there in the space behind the stone.'

'The guildmedal?'

'No,' says Sonja. 'Not a guildmedal. It was a key.'

Lucien doesn't show any surprise, just stands there waiting.

'The small key to the broderie box in Mother's room. I looked inside. Hidden at the bottom was a soundproofed bag. Inside the bag was a transverse flute. A novice's flute. Made of palladium.' Sonja looks hard at Lucien. 'So I knew that I was right. You weren't dead. If you were, they would have buried the flute with you.

'But I made a mistake,' she continues. 'I didn't lock the door.' Her face changes. 'They are never very far behind. Always listening. Two attendants were following me and they heard it too. They must have understood the flute's meaning as clear as I did. There was nothing I could do about it.'

'How did you get the ring out to me?'

'As it happened, only one of the attendants alerted the magisters. The other came to my quarters that evening after Vespers.'

'Martha.'

Sonja nods. 'She didn't say anything else that was useful, only that you had gone to London. It was she who insisted on putting the coin inside the ring for you. She said that you would understand. She seems to have forgotten a lot, but then she was never very disciplined.'

Lucien is looking at her. I see he is processing what she has told him. 'Thank you,' he says at last.

'Don't thank me,' she says, sharp. 'I didn't do it to save you. I did it to bring you back. You need to stand before the magisters and learn what it is you have done.'

Lucien's voice doesn't shift in register. 'Do you think the magisters want to hear why I left? What do you think they'll do if they find me?'

'I'm not in a position to speak on their behalf.'

Her voice is closed and tight, and it contains something I recognise. Something I know from experience: it is harder to be the one left behind.

I walk into the circle of light that binds brother and sister.

'Lucien told me of you,' I say. 'He told me of your skill. He said that you were always smarter than him. So you must have seen yourself what is wrong with the Order. What the Carillon does.' I say it presto and straight as if I'm speaking to Clare. It's a mistake.

'What did you say his name was?' Sonja asks Lucien, not breaking her gaze to look at me.

'Simon.'

'Well, Simon,' Sonja says, turning at last and fixing me with dark eyes, 'don't talk about what you don't understand.'

Anger rushes into me. Like water into a vessel pushed under the surface. It floods my head and stomach and arms so fast it scares me. She might be Lucien's sister, but her face in its cool blankness is that of every member of the Order, their privilege and cruelty.

'I understand enough,' I say. 'I understand what it's like to watch someone die of chimesickness, when they're trying to hold your hand, but their muscles won't even let them keep that last grip. And what it's like to forget who you are and where you came from and the people you love. Every part of the place you live in is soundproofed to protect you. You have no idea about damage or pain.'

'Chimesickness? A sickness given by the Carillon's music? That's not true. That's a rumour started in the cities out of envy and ignorance.'

'Believe what the hell you want,' I say. 'I saw my mother die from it.'

'If they knew, they would not allow it,' she says. She is speaking to herself. She taps the fingers of her right hand, bow hand, on the wood of the chair's back. 'It can't be true.'

'It's true,' says Lucien. His voice is somehow apologetic, which makes me angry. Why should she be protected? 'I have heard it. And I've felt it myself. It attacks you in the joints. You can't do anything to stop it.'

Sonja looks up abruptly.

Lucien continues. 'Onestory teaches that the weapon was built out of dischord and turned dischord on itself. That the Order and

239

Chimes saved us from the chaos after Allbreaking. But that isn't true. The Order built the weapon to clear the way. To clear it for the Carillon, and for their harmonies. In London, under the river, parts of the old weapon remain.'

'The weapon from Allbreaking?' Sonja is pale and I think of myself in that dead room, my confusion. I almost feel sorry for her.

'Yes.'

'But how do you know the Order made it?' Some emotion is fighting in her face.

'Because the weapon is soundproofed in the same way as the Citadel. The Order omits an important fact from Onestory. The weapon was a Carillon.'

'That is impossible.' Sonja looks as though she is about to cry. She turns to face the cross-stretched man. Her hands tense and release on the wood. 'They don't lie,' she says.

'They lied from the beginning,' says Lucien. 'They think it's for the greater good, but it is still a lie and the Order is built on it. Outside the Citadel, they can't keep memory. Chimes brings sickness, and then it kills.'

Sonja's thoughts have moved back inside, too deep for me to see, and she stands straight and unmoving. Somehow that stillness is a dark thing to watch and I feel that I should turn away. When you have kept your memories with you forever, I think, it might be harder to have their meaning destroyed. I turn away from her to the far wall of the crosshouse and I see a picture in my mind. A silver structure, an unsound platform held high in the air. The scaffold holding it sways, but it stays up as though by sheer force of will.

The silence lasts for a long while. Her voice has changed when she speaks again.

'Father once showed me an object he had picked up in one of the cities as a souvenir. He said that citizens kept them to ward off memoryloss. He said that it was just superstition. That in the cities they had forgotten what was important, and they didn't care for learning or contemplation.' Her voice higher, strained. 'He said they were ambitious, hungry for money. There was no discipline. No discipline, just ragged striving. He said that if people conducted solfege at Matins and Vespers, they would learn from the Carillon just as we did.'

Lucien and I wait. She speaks lento.

'And I knew that he wasn't telling the truth. Does that surprise you? I knew and I decided not to care. It was my decision.'

She tilts her head back and I see the tears she is fighting and will master. The fine blade of discrimination turned inward, cutting herself with it. And I see how her self-control is its own punishment. Close as she can come to remorse. She knows it also. I see Lucien in her then, his pride.

'Why are you here?' she asks at last, though I can see she already knows the answer.

'We are here to broadcast what we know,' says Lucien. 'And then to destroy the Carillon.'

'How do you plan to do it?' she says. 'Is it even possible?'

I walk away then, toward the chancel and from there toward the door to look out at the yard. I hear Lucien's voice telling her. He tells her how we will put the memories in a line that shows the Order's rise to power. How the story will be sounded out in music by the Carillon itself. Because how else can we give back the story of what has been stolen? I hear his voice speaking the story low to her, and the smoke of the story seems to spread and spread through the half-light of the crosshouse and wend through the pillars toward me. Burnt books, burnt words. Memories that move in flame through the night sky. If we borrowed the Order's lesson of fire, would that do it? Wood struts around the Pale pipes and bells? A tall scaffold. I listen to the foxes calling to each other outside.

At last Lucien has finished speaking. Sonja steps away from the chair like someone who has forgotten how to walk. I go forward and let myself look at her. I figure I have earned the chance to judge what she has decided for us. In her eyes, when I see them, there is something new. Whatever Lucien told her, there's a hunger in her now like she has smelt the smoke as well and wants to follow it to the flame. Maybe something in her wants to burn too.

Lucien looks across at me. 'Will you help us?' he asks.

She pauses; her hands clench and unclench. And at last she nods.

'Yes.'

Past the Wall

Sonja leaves us only with the instruction to wait. She will find some way to get us inside.

And so we wait. We sing the composition. Lucien downsounds my memories. I share stale bread with the foxes, and I try not to think about what is waiting for us behind that golden wall.

Past Vespers I'm sitting watching the foxes in the crosshouse yard when a large, stout shape looms over me framed in the sun's last rays. The shape moves and there's a flash of sun on clean white cloth. 'Do you know how to scrub dishes?' it says.

I shield my eyes and blink.

It's a solid, strong-armed woman with dark hair. She's wearing the robes of the Order. On her, they don't look austere or graceful. Just aggressively, impossibly *clean*.

She stands in front of me for a few seconds, then, as if concluding my answer is not worth her time, walks past me toward the door of the crosshouse.

'Hey,' I yell. 'Where do you think you're going?'

She stands in the door, turning her head this way and that on a well-fleshed neck, looking for something else altogether. Someone else. She blinks in the dark of the crosshouse. She looks back to me.

'Where is he?' she asks. 'Where are you hiding my boy?'

I come up behind her at the doorway, and as I do, I witness the wholly unexpected vision of Lucien walking slowly across the flagged floor of the crosshouse and into the woman's arms.

Martha spreads a cloth on the dusty floor between the pews and the cross. On it she puts a meat pie, two cheeses, half a dozen small wrinkled apples, a bottle of currant wine and some strange cakes that are seemingly made from nuts and eggs and air.

Lucien and I eat as if we have been starved for weeks, which, when you think of it, is not far from truth. All the while Martha barely lets Lucien out of her grip.

I am transfixed by this strange sight. She squeezes him, ruffles his hair, pinches the muscles of his arms like she's planning to bid on him at market. I keep waiting for Lucien to snarl as she prods and pokes. To assert his rightful dignity. But the snarl doesn't come. I try to keep my laugh stifled, but he hears it in my throat. He looks at me and rolls his eyes, shrugs.

Martha's questions come in a steady rattle, as constant as her pinches. Where was her boy, and how has he been? She thought he was dead and never had word. And did he get the ring? And did he remember her when he was in the city? And what did he do all that time?

But the questions are odd, I notice after a while. Like some of the ruins in London. There are houses and buildings you would swear have been untouched by Allbreaking. But when you walk and see them side-on, it's their front preserved only, perfect stone with open-eyed windows and nothing behind. And it makes me understand how much stronger my own memory has become.

Martha asks about the man who took Lucien to London. She remembers the colour of his horse, what he wore. But when Lucien asks about his mother and her death, about Sonja and how they got the ring out of the Citadel, Martha's answers are vague. At one point she talks of someone called Frieda, how worried she has been about Frieda's illness. Lucien blinks, and subito I realise that Martha is speaking of Lucien's mother as if she were alive. Her eyes cloud then and she returns to stable ground, to the matter of the boy in front of her, how tall he has grown, how handsome. She recommences her squeezing. What hair he has. And so tall.

When we have eaten and finally sit in silence, she turns to me at last.

244

'You didn't answer my question, lad,' she says.

'What question was that?'

'Can you scrub pots?'

'Yes, of course.'

'What's your name, then?'

'Simon,' I say.

'And you're a friend of Lucien's, from the city?'

I am dazed with food. I smile at her. It is a strange question really. A question from a world where people have time and leisure and space between themselves, space to sort and choose. I didn't choose Lucien, I think. Lucien was there always. His voice speaking out of the darkness.

'Yes,' I say.

'Good. He'll need one where he's going.'

'Why do I need to know how to scrub pots?' I ask.

'You both will,' she says. 'Or pluck chickens. Or peel carrots, or what have you.' She pulls a flat bundle of pressed material from her bag and unfolds it. Two linen tunics, gathered and trimmed close at the sleeves. Dark breeches. She tucks one of the tunics under her chin and smooths it down over the steep bluff of her chest, ironing out the creases. I take the other and hold it up, look at the guildsign. Kitchenhand. Potboy.

'There was a call out for kitchen prentisses yesternoch,' says Martha. 'Two needed. I've taken it upon myself to recruit them.' She reaches into a pocket and takes out a pair of bone-handled scissors, soap, a razor. She puts them down between us and gestures at me. 'Cut his hair and shave yourselves, both of you. I'll be back tomorrow before Matins.'

The water in the font is freezing. You have to laugh or you'd scream instead. Lucien dunks my whole head under and scrubs my hair hard with the solid bar of soap that Martha left. 'No one will believe you're a well-brought-up serving lad with such a ridiculous amount of hair,' he says. And he's quick but

245

not as quick as me. I catch him at the chancel and show no mercy.

When we're washed and shaved as clean as cold water can get us, he cuts my hair. The crosshouse is quiet, the only sound is clumps of my hair falling on the dirty floor. He turns my skull with precise, hard fingers as he cuts. Then he wipes the scissors on his robe and blows out the candle.

At half-toll before Matins we're waiting for Martha, dressed in the tunics and breeks. Lucien is too tall for his and his wrists show a couple of inches below the gathered sleeve ends.

When she arrives, Martha tuts and mutters about what to do with Lucien's eyes. Paraspecs are only worn by the Order here. Finally she rips a band from the edge of her own petticoat, folds it twice and ties it tight over his eyes. He looks like a moony.

'If anyone asks, you lost your sight to fever when you were five,' she says.

We follow her through the just-waking city. Through the streets of houses and in towards the thronging silence of the Carillon.

The few people out at this hour pay little attention to us. Traders sluice the frontages of shops with buckets of water, their eyes kept low. As we enter the Lady's silence, I begin to hear movement in the streets, a high murmuring passed from voice to voice.

We walk through the market place, past the instrument makers, down a narrow, gently curving street. We follow the curve. And then subito, like in a dream where the thing you fear is in the room with you all along, the tower rises above us at the end of the street.

The face of honey-coloured stone seems to stretch forever against the clouds. Heavy at the base and narrowed toward the top. At first glance it is blank and unified, a solid mass. But step-wise closer I see the sheer weight of it is built up from stone upon stone of different sizes. Stones broad and thick, flat and flagged, some like cobbles, some small as teeth. The honey-coloured stones of Oxford's Allbreaking. They're pieced together so clean and perfect that you can hardly see the gaps. The look of it fills me with dread. Power lives in it. Power and a cleverness I can't understand.

We follow the broad foot of the wall, walking in its shadow until we round its curve and there are no streets beside us. We have entered a wide open square in which the wall stands clear and tall and proud. At its centre is the circular building of the scholar's memory from before Allbreaking. The place where the Order started burning code. The wall cuts through the circular building, grows round it, making of it a gatehouse and the entrance to the Citadel.

We follow Martha, who walks without falter through the press of people that stand in the square. Throated murmuring of speech all around me, but I can't make out words. When I trip on a loose cobble, Martha catches me sharp by my elbow, walks me forward.

As we reach the gatehouse, the murmuring heightens and I realise that people are craning their necks, looking up to the ramparts above. Then I feel a steady throb of Pale coming forward, nearing the wall from the other side. The pulse of silence comes forward; then it breaks into three separate points. Then the trio of silence is climbing. The crowd murmurs and subito, above, the early sun catches on white robes and pale silver.

Three members of the Order stand on the ramparts. They are magisters, members of the elect. I recognise them, the white robes, the tall proudness. But they are different, different from any I saw in London. They stand on the ramparts with their blind eyes uncovered instead of behind dark paraspecs. And their transverse flutes are not of silver as the ones they carry in London, but are made of pure palladium.

The crowd's murmur forms a low continuo. The magisters play the announcement in unison. It carries far off into the city. Two pactrunners. Escapees. Traitors. Traced from London and a narrowboat they travelled on seized. Warning. Vigilance. Reward. Among the people standing below, the announcement is whispered, whistled, passed from voice to voice and breath to breath.

We stand in front of the rounded gatehouse. My heart is going presto as I think of Jemima and Callum and I do not look at Lucien.

Martha steps forward toward the closed doors; then she takes a short wooden baton, like the stick of a tambor that hangs there by a linen cord, and knocks a complex rhythm on the door's mettle ring.

After a slow beat a small door within the door swings open and a man's face looks out. He is wearing white robes and over them a garment of fine woven mettle. His expression is that of a martyr to unbearable boredom. He takes in Martha, her clothes, Lucien and me standing behind her. Then he opens his mouth. I expect a speech, but his question emerges in melody. His voice is pompous and reedy and mannered, and he sings a long interrogative phrase in which I catch only glimpses of meaning. Martha waits and then sings back. Answering phrases, clipped and stout and impatient.

The man nods with the same lazy worldweariness and then gestures at us. He asks in words, as if for our benefit, 'And these two? What are they doing?'

Martha bows her head. 'Kitchen prentisses for the Orkestrum, sir. Hired yesternoch and due to start training today.'

The guard narrows his eyes. 'They look old for prentisses,' he says.

Martha nods. 'You're right, sir. Yet they won't ever be more than prentisses, either of them. This one's slow, poor lad' – she gestures at me – 'and that one's been blinded since he was small. But they're steady workers, or so I was told. And they come at a good rate.' She winks.

The guard turns to speak to a person behind him. Then he looks straight at Lucien and me, ignoring Martha. He studies our faces.

'We're looking for two young men from London,' he says. 'Traitors to the Order. Word is, they've arrived in Oxford. You wouldn't know anything about that, would you?'

We are both silent.

He looks at Lucien. 'You,' he says.

Lucien keeps his head low.

'I'm speaking to you,' the guard says. 'Where were you working before this?'

In the pause that follows I wonder whether there would be any point in running. Then Lucien speaks in a voice that isn't his, a voice with low-lying muddy vowels.

'In the kitchen of the Child,' he says. 'I've scrubbed pots there since last year's festival Chimes.'

The guard pauses. 'And who's the landlord there?'

There's another pause, but this time Martha interrupts.

'Every man and his dog knows Annie Kerwood, sir. I have a better question for you. Who's going to explain where the magisters' supper is if I don't get these two to the kitchen?'

The guard flicks his eyes over us again, but he feels he's done his duty and the boredom has returned to his face.

'Get them in, then.' And he waves us through.

Martha sings and signs a few notes of respectful obeisance. They are cut short by the quarterdoor swinging back into its place. Then there is a creak as the vast wooden gates open a fraction, as if for an entrance only reluctantly allowed. Martha shoulders the door and we walk in past her.

Out of the shadow of the wall we walk.

And we are inside.

The Citadel

Where we are is a place of open space. Greenness. Grace. Before us are curving paths laid out between carefully pruned low hedges. Along each edge of a wide green square lie covered corridors in the same honeyed stone as the wall. The heights and proportions of the stone construction seem to follow an invisible grammar. Through the corridors, and through the patterns of light and shadow the arches cast, figures stroll in white, carrying their instruments in silence or playing them. Conversing in melodies tossed from voice to voice. Speaking together in solfege with hands that move more rapidly than I can read. They are tall, and their movements are graceful.

We proceed down the corridor and I snatch sideways glances at Lucien's face, trying to read his expression. I try to see the buildings through his eyes, what it must be to return to their elegant proportions, the harmony of their colour and design. It twists strange in me. I wanted to hate this place for its cruelty and power, but I find the beauty working its way inside me. I want to walk straighter, as if my own rhythm has been altered in some subtle way by the austerity and calm.

Might Lucien realise his mistake in leaving this world? Would he not regret the disorder and dischord of London? And in me, what must he see? Somebody confused, rough, improbably shorn. I reach up to touch my head and its strange stubble.

I try to keep my eyes down. We follow Martha to the end of the many-arched corridor and through a set of windowed double doors. Then down a long, echoed marble hall and three flights of stone steps and into a long, cold corridor.

The floor is polished from many feet, and the echo tells me we are below ground. The corridor stretches ahead, and as we walk along it, I begin to hear noises. Water boiling. Feet shuffling. A curt voice calling out rapidfire orders. The ringing sound of someone chopping firewood.

A few steps from the corridor's end, there is a narrow wooden door, and a stairwell that presumably leads back up into the light. Martha pushes us toward the stair and up the first few steps.

'All of the kitchen staff live extramural,' she says, somewhat out of breath. 'They leave before Vespers.' She turns to me. 'Did you see that door down there?' she asks.

I nod yes.

'That's the coldstore,' she says. 'When the other staff leave, hang back. Hide in there. It may be a few days, but Sonja will come for you.' She hands me a mettle key. Then she pushes us before her, back down the few steps and through the open arched doorway.

The kitchen is dark and my first impression is of unformed shapes buzzing sharp and purposeful. Rich meat smells. Sharp bursts of laughter. And the heat of several fires. A thickset man in an oilspattered apron walks up to us. He speaks an order to Lucien, and when Lucien does not move, he pushes him forward with a rally of impatient blows, towards the end of the room, where there are sinks piled with dirty dishes.

A small woman walks up and speaks to Martha. When she has had her words, she grabs me by the shoulder, as if convinced I am blind also, and propels me forward with a sharp push towards another sink and an enormous pile of potatoes.

It is a stretched and sleepy afternoon in spite of the grip of fear beneath. The repetitive task and the noise and the sun coming in through the low grates and I find myself several times almost falling in sleep. I look for Lucien, but he has been shifted from washing dishes to some other chore and I cannot see him anywhere.

Each time I pause in my task, I see the small woman's eyes on me, measuring. The day is broken only by the tolls of the Carillon.

At one point in the long afternoon a magister enters. The silver of the Lady spills into the kitchen and at first I don't understand it. I feel rather than hear the shrinking back of the kitchen staff against the walls. The faces people wear while working, the unguarded resting expressions of humour, irritation, boredom, each goes inward and closes, and a conscious hush comes from each so that their silence is somehow joined.

The magister treads out onto the silence like it's a cloth beneath his feet. A small man, but the glow of white from his robes seems somehow immense in the unlit room. I cannot tell if this is a routine visit or not. Their eyes and faces do not offer any clue. When the magister speaks, his voice is fine and steady in pitch. Not forte or piano, but a carefully graded middle tone that does not strain.

'There will be ten more of us for supper,' he says. He looks to the thin woman who spoke to Mary when she brought us in. 'Please open the additional bottles beforehand. And we will need an extra server, I think. Somebody presentable.' That light tone, even, calm sends a shiver down my back. His milky eyes move lento across the kitchen, over my face. Then he walks a few steps forward and points to a boy beside me. 'He will do.'

The mountain of potatoes never shrinks. It's a toll before Vespers when a bright little melody flutes through the kitchen. It is clear what it means. All around me people step back from their tasks and stretch bodily. Subito the workers who have blended into their chores and the shared rhythm of the kitchen take their own shapes and movements. I watch a tall, thin girl pile kindling and coal in the mouth of the largest oven. Two boys push a wheeled trolley laden with meat back out into the corridor. The man who shoved Lucien counts knives back into a safe in the wall. I feel Lucien then. He is standing a few yards away, hanging polished copper pots of all sizes on a huge pendant iron rack above the central fire. I wait.

In pairs, the workers remove aprons and take their turns at the sink to wash their grimed hands. They leave by the sole corridor, talking, humming, laughing. I imagine them going out through that vast blank gate and back into their streets and homes, and it makes me feel stronger. The kitchen is half empty when I nudge one of the peeled potatoes at the bottom of the vast stack and the whole pyramid collapses. Potatoes bounce and roll like marbles over the scrubbed tiles and I swear convincingly.

Lucien and I on hands and knees. It's empty enough in the kitchen now that nobody thinks to remark on how a blind prentiss can put his hands so unerringly on the scattered potatoes.

It's after and we are standing in the freezing dark of the coldstore. Whole pigs hang from mettle hooks beside us. The candle's shadows bloat and swell the lines of their flesh. I examine my blisters by touch. Walk round to see if there is anything we can use for blankets. Lucien, slid into a crouch against the wall, removes his blindfold with a grimace of relief and watches me. When Vespers comes, it is both strangely the same and entirely other. How to explain? The sounds come down from such dread proximity above our heads. Almost as if they are in the same room. I feel them in my body, but the resonance slides off from me. Like I am covered over in a sheet of clear para, it cannot touch. I follow Lucien's solfege right through and my body never seizes.

What makes me wake is Lucien's arms tensed tight round my chest. I hear that he is awake and listening. I hear the slow sound of mettle on mettle. A key in the lock and the handle turning.

Lucien's grip tells me to keep still. We're in the corner of the coldstore. Between us and the door there are several ranks of shelves piled with dry goods. We lie in the dark. There is the hungry hiss of a match and a glow of light catches and blooms. A bare few footsteps and our small dark corridor is filled with candlelight. Lucien swears, shields his eyes and sits up.

Martha stands there. She is out of breath, and her face has changed. It is fixed, and her eyes move in it like things trapped.

'Where's my sister?' asks Lucien.

'Not safe for her to come,' says Martha. 'Now that the magisters know you're in the city, they are watching her. We can't wait either. We need to move.'

The cold presses in on us and I have the same feeling I had in the dead room. Like something dark and heavy is sitting on my chest.

'What do we do now, then?' I ask.

'You come with me,' Martha says.

'Where?' asks Lucien.

'Somewhere she thinks you'll be safe for a while. Safer than here.' Then she sings a tune in her stout voice. It's short and it plunges and winds. I see Lucien following it, dredging through memory, piecing the directions together. He waits and looks up at Martha.

'She's serious?'

Martha nods.

'The novice cells?'

'That's what she told me.'

'I hope to hell she's right,' says Lucien. 'We could not get any closer to the Carillon.'

Martha gestures for us to take off our shoes.

'Never quieter, boys. Never quieter in your lives,' she says. 'You don't touch the ground. You float.'

We follow her down the same stone corridor we came in on. But instead of continuing back to the garden, Martha turns left and down another two flights of stairs. Then through a series of corridors and down further flights, getting lower and lower until

254

we enter a long, straight hall. It's being used for storage – there are shelves filled with scores lining the walls.

We are deep. Though the walls are sealed in plaster and painted white, I can feel the cold breath of earth coming through them. At the end of the hall is a heavy double door. Martha removes a key and unlocks it. She opens it wide and we walk inside.

I hear space unfold in front of me.

I hear Lucien's lungs open as if a part of him has come home. For a moment I'm back in London, standing in our amphitheatre at Five Rover, waiting for the map to settle. What we hear is tunnels.

In the mouth to the under, I wait for my ears to sharpen as I always do. The room we are standing in is not large, and it opens into a simple network at first, just one tunnel leading each way, left and right. Then I listen out further and I learn that this family of tunnels is as far from the crazed tangle of our territory, with its wormed maze, its spiderweb of ways, as it's possible to hear.

I can't hear the full extent of them, but the opening phrases are as careful and precise as a partsong. They are concentric, coiling like the shell of a snail, and cut through with a grid of straight tunnels. Lucien turns to Martha and quietly sings the winding tune she gave us in the coldstore. She listens with care and then she nods to confirm that he has remembered right. We enter.

We tread light and presto. Martha goes first with the candle, then Lucien, then me. The tunnels are rounded and easy to move in. They are taller than our heads and wider than an armspan, and they have little echo. They are lined in flat white tiles. Our tunnels were built, I guess, to carry other things. Water. Words. Carriages. Sewage. These appear to have only one purpose, to take people from place to place beneath the Citadel.

We follow the tune as it winds, walking tacet. And I get the strange feeling that somehow we are not moving at all. There are no landmarks down here, nothing to offer cadence or modulation. The corridor never changes, just follows the same slow, patient curve. At regular intervals we pass the open mouth of another tunnel in the grid. Keep treading, never quieter. I think of Martha's instructions and imagine that, after all, I could be floating. I have forgotten which way is up and which down.

Subito, between Martha and me, Lucien stops.

A few paces ahead, Martha halts and looks back at where Lucien is frozen. My throat closes. A dead sound chimes inside me. Then I hear what Lucien has heard.

In the under in London, it is the sound that signals the end of a run, a pleasing glow of luck and reward. Here it means something else.

Far ahead in a tunnel perhaps two from ours in the concentric spiral, there is a pulse of silence. Its whispered hush comes to us through mettle and tile and stone. Martha has not heard yet, but she can read the fear in our eyes. No one moves. I barely breathe. Far ahead in its tunnel, the line of Pale is moving. It moves smoothly at a walking pace. Northeast.

At first the panic drumming in my ears makes me mishear, but after a few breaths I understand. The Pale is moving away from us. As if it will help him on his way, I try to imagine the magister's steady tread, the glowing flute slung askance his white robes. It is moving, far ahead, in the same direction we are going. Then it turns down one of the bisecting tunnels, farther off. I watch Lucien's eyes. They are fixed, as if even their movement might reveal our presence.

The constellation of silence traces its journey and we wait. It moves away from us. Steady but sure the silence fades. I feel the blood begin to move more calmly through me and I let my muscles ease a bit. I breathe.

And then I freeze.

In the candlelight, Lucien's eyes have widened and flared. I train my ears again. The pulse of silence flickers on the edge of my hearing. It is still. Still with the magister's listening. I look at Lucien and he at me. In the moment that passes, far off in that northeast corridor, the silence makes a small movement back towards us. Almost grudging, like someone pulled back to a task they would rather avoid. The Pale turns and begins its tread back.

Lucien's jaw is rigid. The bones of his face are raw and stripped. Some awful recognition has bloomed in his eyes. Lento, lento he reaches into his tunic and pulls a leather cord from round his neck. What it draws up is a leather pouch. Muddy from where it was buried in the paratubs on the balcony of the storehouse on Dog Isle. Inside it is the silence of his mother's ring, and inside that the smaller silence of the guildmedal. A tiny droplet of quiet signalling out to the keen ears of whoever is now walking steady towards us, at the pace of someone who has no earthly need to hurry.

Lucien's anger as clear as speaking. To have come so far. To have come so far and to have made such a mistake. All I can think is that if we are going to be taken, I don't want the last sight of Lucien to be in this tunnel, underground, far from sun and air.

Then subito Martha is standing between us. She grips Lucien's hand open and sees the pouch, the stitched tune. She cannot hear the Lady's homing pulse, but she knows what it contains. In the tunnel's slowed time, Martha pulls the pouch from Lucien's hand. She doesn't look at him or at me, but walks past us and back down the corridor.

The last sight I have before I push Lucien forward into a run is that of Martha standing solid at the next tunnelmouth, waiting for the coming wave of silence to swallow her.

Out of the tunnel Lucien and I push and fall, and Sonja is there in the corridor at ground level. She is crouched pale against the wall and leaps to her feet as we shoulder the wooden door. She grabs me and pushes me ahead and I'm almost stumbling as I go.

Three doors and we enter the last and we're inside, locked in soundproofed quiet.

I'm shaking. I see my hands through a blur as if they're apart from me. I try to clench to stop it. I rest them on my knees, but that's useless as the tremor is in my legs too. It seems to be in my whole body.

Lucien sits a foot away with his head bowed. He has wrapped his arms around himself. His hands are tight to his upper arms and they're kneading, punishing the flesh. I get up and go to him, try to pull his hands clear, but he pushes me away, doesn't look up.

Sonja is silent.

'Martha?' she asks. I nod.

'What happened?' And I tell her.

Lucien looks up then. His eyes are wild and strange in a way I can't remember seeing them. 'It was my fault,' he says. 'I made it happen. I cannot believe I was so fucking stupid.' He pronounces every syllable mercilessly clear. 'I carried that thing the whole way from London. I brought it with me into the Citadel.'

Sonja stands up and walks to him, sits down. She puts her hand on his shoulder.

'What will they do to her?' I ask. I can't rid myself of the picture of Lucien's eyes in the tunnel as he realised his mistake. The anger at himself.

Lucien doesn't answer, but Sonja looks up at me steadily. The first time I think she has done so.

'Nothing,' she says. 'I mean, they'll question her, of course. See what she knows. But, remember, the magisters didn't know the ring was my mother's. They won't be able to connect it to Lucien.'

'And the guildmedal?' I ask.

Sonja is silent for a beat. 'Martha will buy us time. She's lived on her wits for a long while. She'll think of some explanation.'

'They won't harm her?'

Her look takes on a hint of disdain again. 'Of course not,' she says. 'The Order practises mercy.'

When I have gathered myself enough to look around, I see that we are in a small room. At the far end is a window. The floor is woven matting, and the walls are soundproofed. But not with the ornate white tiles I have seen elsewhere. Here the tiling is dark brown wood and there are cracks in parts of it, though the silence is intact. There's a washbasin at one wall and a recess to the right for a narrow single bed. On the left-hand side, there's an internal door covered in the same soundproofed material.

True to its name, it is a cell. A room meant for nothing but to hold a person and an instrument. A place for seclusion and meditation. For stripping away everything but music.

Lucien has looked up again. He's listening intent to the room. Then he rises and goes over to a precise spot on the right-hand side. He feels with his hands and then he laughs. There's not much humour in it, but it's a laugh and I'm thankful.

'Look. Here!' he says to me, and I go to him.

Carved into the wood where he points are a cluster of notes.

'It's my name. It's the cell where I domiciled as a novice.' He looks over at Sonja and she nods, almost shy.

'That's what made me think of it,' she says. 'I realised that you would have left by the tunnels. And the same tunnels will take us to the campanile, to the instrument's tower.'

I go to look out of the window. We're just barely above the ground level and the clear, thick para looks out over a long slope of grass not much above eye level. The block we are in forms one side of an eight-sided, watching shape. The lawn rises gently. In the middle is a cobbled square. And in the centre, the hub around which everything gathers, is the structure that houses the Carillon.

I turn away. Lucien is sitting again.

'How did you get in here?' he asks. 'Why isn't it in use?'

'This row was decommissioned after your death. It was too old, they said, and the new block was nearing completion. But I really think that they were scared of the infection.' She smiles. 'It was a waste, as the practice console in this room is in perfect condition. I had a key made after your death,' she says. 'It wasn't hard to do.'

'Why did you need the key?'

Sonja stands straight beside the soundproofed wall. She is talking only to Lucien now.

'Do you know, I used to feel so sorry for you. Because however clear you could hear it, you'd never see the gardens. The way they plant them so the textures and colours of the flowers and trees all speak together. Nobody else would probably ever admit that to you. "Blind of eye is true of ear" and mothers pray for children with milky eyes, after all. But I was always glad that I could see.' She pauses, leans back a little.

'They ignored me. Not just the magisters in the Orkestrum, but Mother and Father when we were growing up. I didn't blame you for it. It wasn't your fault, and you were special, of course. Destined for great things.' She pauses, the hesitation of somebody not accustomed to sharing thought. 'As long as there was you and me, I didn't care much about them.

'After you died, they continued to ignore me. It suited me by then, though. They ignored me, so I ignored them. The less attention anyone paid me, the more time I had.'

'For what?'

A slight halt from Sonja. She is letting him in on something very private.

'For practice.'

'What do you mean? Why practise here, away from everything? Why not in the Orkestrum?'

She looks hard at him and I see a glint of pride. She does not answer his question straight away.

'I wasn't born with your gift. But I knew that I wanted it. And I had something you never had, brother.'

'What?' says Lucien.

'Perseverance. I know how to work. I'm not afraid of my lack of gift. I wasn't called to be a novice. When I got over that, it struck me. What was there to stop me teaching myself what they would learn?' She straightens her shoulders.

260

Lucien nods. 'You mean you followed their training? Meditation? Composition?'

'Yes. And the instruments. I taught myself the viol and the bass. Then brass. I learnt the trompet and the slip horn. I wake two hours before the Orkestrum for meditation. It's hard.'

She closes her eyes. She is thinking how useless words are to explain what the endeavour makes her feel. But it's plainly visible. She is lit from within. A dread certainty and humility shines along her cheekbones. Along with a fear that something, someone will take it from her.

Lucien nods again, not smiling, not saying anything.

She stands and walks to the door in the opposite wall, opens it and goes through and lights a lantern. Lucien and I follow behind. It is another soundproofed chamber twice as large as the outer room. On the left and right sides of the wall, hung by turned wooden pegs, are instruments. A heavy maple cello. A lute. A bass viol leaning roundbellied in the corner. The military lines of brass trompet and slip horn shine up high above the strings. There is a transverse flute of silver. A clarionet neat in black and gold.

Taking up the whole front wall is a huge klavier. At least, it looks to me at first like a klavier. But instead of a single keyboard, it has seven, one on top of each other, ranked in terraces. On either side of these are neat rows of wooden pegs with rounded handles that jut out of the instrument's flat sides. Beneath the piano stool are pedals, dozens of them, and then another keyboard at foot level, made of slim, long levers of light and dark wood.

Sonja walks toward it. She takes a cloth from a pocket and polishes the keyboards. She does it with pride and deference. I know that she is watching Lucien, waiting for his reaction. Her movements have changed again. The precision has lost its sharpness and returned as grace. It's too bright for Lucien to see, I realise, and I am unsure how much detail he is able to hear.

Sonja solves this problem by sitting at the stool. She reaches to the side of the instrument and makes a series of adjustments to the mechanism there. Then she places her hands on the central keyboard. The instrument is so large it seems to swallow her.

A second's pause and then a muted miracle of voices springs up. Her hands play clustered chords and her feet too, moving deft over the lower pedals like a dancer. It is a simple Bach prelude. Halfway through, she changes the stops and the plain voices are joined and sustained by throaty woodwinds. The simple melody doubles and twists like a wonderful heavy rope of gold.

At the end she sits back, her hands still alive and alert on the keyboard. She doesn't look away, but every part of her is listening for Lucien's response.

If only she could see him, it would feed whatever she is hungry for. Lucien's face is wide in wonder.

He walks forward to stand beside her. 'May I?' he asks. Sonja nods. He places his hand carefully on the upper keyboards, runs his fingertips over the drawerknobs to left and right.

Sonja takes Lucien's hands and places them in the correct configuration on the central keyboard. With efficient movements she lowers the stool for him. He sits and his attitude is one of reserve, almost constraint. His head is bent and he listens close to what Sonja is telling him.

In undertaking to learn, to teach herself the skill reserved only for the Order's elect, Sonja has done something I would have never thought possible: she has surprised her brother. There is nothing much for me to do but sit and watch and be silent. The room has filled with a buzz of excitement and concentration that rises off the pair of them and threads through the honeycomb of the wall's carving.

Sonja is blinking fast. She has dragged a chair in to sit next to Lucien at the stool. He plays an experimental scale. She flexes her fingers back, elbows him out of the way, demonstrates something. Lucien nods twice, replaces his hands on the instrument, repeats a phrase. 'Like this?'

Sonja has turned the bellows off now, so the instrument does not sound, but it is clear that for the two of them, there is no impediment to the music. In their heads, it is as clear as a bell and echoing into the soundproofed chamber.

'Yes, that's it,' says Sonja.

Then, 'No, the fingering's wrong. If you do it like that, you won't be able to keep it sustained. Here, swap the thumb under.'

Then, 'Here.' And another demonstration. After a while they are playing music. I hear the complicated runs as they swap places back and forth.

'Use the pedal to play the cantus firmus here. It's louder than the manuals. No. You need to use the other stop for it. That's right.'

I sit in the chair and I doze off and on. They work together through all the minor hours of the night.

I come awake at some point and Sonja is curled up like a cat on the rush matting with her cloak over her and Lucien is thundering silently away. His elbows are out like wings and I can tell he's playing the Bach prelude. He moves from the top keyboards to the bottom in fluid movements. Again and again. Then he breaks and plays repeated phrases, selecting different stops. His feet tread light on the pedals.

I sit and wonder for a while. In the two or so hours since I was awake, he has gone from awkwardness to near-mastery.

Before Matins tolls Sonja leaves, as she must, to return to the Orkestrum. Anything else would arouse suspicion, and they will be listening closely to her movements, she says. Keep to the room, stay away from the windows. If anyone comes to the door, do not answer.

Lucien is practising what we have written so far. Putting the music into the Carillon's voices, changing the story into imaginable and unimaginable sound.

I hear him singing repeated phrases, the tamping sound of the keys moving, presto and then lento. Every now and again he comes out to me to check a story, a phrase, a detail. I play it on Sonja's recorder. Then he disappears and it transmutes into that soft, deadened sound, the keys hitting muted strings.

I count the tolls, and time creeps on. I lean against the tiled walls of the practice room and I wait.

At None Sonja knocks a trick rhythm to signal us and then opens the door. She is carrying a plate of bread and a bowl of thin vegetable soup with herbs. She places it on the floor where I'm sitting. Her face is white and strained.

'I'm sorry it's not much,' she says. 'I said I had a headache and needed to return to chambers. I couldn't take more without making them suspicious.'

'What is happening in there?' I ask, gesturing toward the Orkestrum.

Her words are clipped. 'It is hard to know. Things continue as normal. There is no word of Martha. But they have started searching the students' quarters. We do not have much time.' Then she breaks off. 'Where is Lucien?' she asks.

I point to the practice room. 'He has not left there all day.'

Sonja goes into the inner room briefly, then comes out. She is tacet for a while after, and when she speaks it is as if we are continuing an argument.

'You know that it is very dangerous for anybody without the correct training to enter the sacrum musicae,' she says. 'Let alone to be in the tonic chamber, to play the instrument.'

I suppose that I did know that. If Chimes can damage human ears and minds as far away as London, it follows that to be within the Carillon would be much worse. I have tried not to think about it.

'But Lucien is not untrained,' I say. 'He was selected as a novice. He started the training process. And what about his gift? He was marked to play the instrument from birth.'

264

Sonja looks at me. She speaks piano.

'You really have no idea, do you? Of what is required. Of the kind of sacrifice involved. To play the instrument, the priests give up everything. Not just family or time or a so-called ordinary life. They give everything to the Order and to the Carillon. Their hearts, their bodies. Their minds.

'When Lucien left the Citadel, that's when his real training would have begun. He would have started with four hours of meditation a day. Broken up into blocks at first. Then the rest devoted solely to practice and study. The novices must master all instruments. A mastery that outshines that of the finest soloists you can hear in the cities. They study until they know rudiments and counterpoint inside and out. They fast and they meditate and they work. And after five years they're allowed to *enter* the sacrum musicae. Not to play, not to even touch the instrument. They are allowed to *enter* the first of the seven chambers.'

She stands straighter. 'At any time in the Order, there are only three or four priests who are able to enter the tonic chamber. Always at least three, never more than four. And that includes the magister musicae, the one who composes the Chimes you hear every day in the city. Being in there while the Carillon is sounding would break a citizen's eardrums.

'You have no comprehension of this world. None at all. The sacrifice they make is immense. It is beautiful.'

She is so unhappy. She stands in her fine robes and my mind flashes up a picture of the first time I saw Lucien, covered in thamesmud, his roughcloth clothing, his shoulders broadboned and lean and his hair full of light.

'The sacrifice might be beautiful,' I say, and I try to keep my voice somewhat gentle. 'But that's because it is chosen. Because it is made freely. We don't have that choice. Our memories are taken from us by Chimes without choice or will.'

The look she gives me is one of pure hate. Her neck lengthens and she tilts her head back in a familiar imperious manner.

'Do you think I don't know that? Why do you think I'm helping you, though it could cost my life? Certainly it'll cost me everything I've ever worked for.'

'I'm sorry,' I say.

'I don't think you understand enough to be sorry,' she says. 'To you this is all evil, all built on loss and suffering.' She fixes me with dark, fierce eyes.

'But the Order is not evil.' She pauses. 'Not at heart. The ideals it holds are good. Beauty. Truth. Knowledge. And they are generous. At heart they are generous. Why do you think Chimes is told for all, if not to share this knowledge? The magisters want what is best for the people. It is not their fault that people are not always able to choose the best thing for themselves.'

Like something made of clockwork, her familiar speech slows and she runs out of words. As if trying something for the first time, swallowing a new substance, she takes a deep breath. I see with a shock that there are tears in her eyes.

When she speaks, her voice has changed.

'I wish she had got me out too. He was always the chosen one. Me, she was happy to leave to rot.'

I shake my head.

'I've seen your memory,' I say. 'Your mother's death. She gave you the ring because she knew that you would do the right thing. Your task was harder. And you had no one to help you. You had to see past what was there in front of you all along.'

Sonja is crying. It comes hard to her. She jerks away so I can't see her face. After a while she wipes her eyes with impatience and a kind of scorn and turns to me, her face white and set.

'What is he to you?' she asks. But before I can answer she continues. 'I have seen how you look at him, so perhaps you can understand. I missed him. I missed him very much.'

She turns, then, back to the window at the end of the room. She stands still and then she crosses the room toward the window like someone pulled.

I stand up. Something in her stillness is new and wrong. A look in her face like she's been hit across it. Her mouth moving and her eyes wide and too bright. I begin to walk towards her, but she is moving already, away from the window and pushing past me. She reaches the basin at the side of the wall and she vomits into it.

I do not want to cross the room to see what is waiting beyond that window, but I do it. I do it lento. I reach the para and look out, out across the grass and toward the tower of the Carillon. In the public square that stands between us and the tower, a wooden post has been erected. Two men in brown robes are working diligently, fastening something to the post. They are efficient. No movement wasted. At last they stand back to view their work, to ensure that it is done well, that it sounds a message clear for all to hear.

Lashed to the post is Martha. Rope crosses her body in a cruel pattern. Her head slumps down as if she were asleep, though she is not asleep and won't ever sleep again. The rope crossed under her breast forms a stave and arrayed across it is a message in rough wooden beads. I do not need to read it to understand. Here is a traitor to the Order. There are dark streaks all over the once-clean robes from the blood that has run from her ears.

Leavetaking

When Lucien turns at last from the window, he looks at his hands.

Then he looks up at his sister. Their faces mirror each other. Pale and broken. What is not spoken is clear in the room. Sonja says it at last.

'Tomorrow before Matins,' she says, 'I will come. The door to the instrument has two guards only at that time. I know the key tune. We will have the benefit of surprise. Whatever they are afraid of, whatever they think you are here for, they will not believe it is this.'

I look at her. 'Why?' I ask.

'Because it is beyond their imagining. I did not believe it myself. I am not sure I do even now.'

If she does not return, says Sonja, we should not risk an attempt to enter the Carillon. Lucien will need her to enter. If she doesn't return, she says, we should try our best to escape with our lives. She sings us the most direct route through the tunnels to the least-guarded section of the wall.

Lucien returns to the practice console and every moment that passes I expect the knock at the door to come. I think of Martha and what killed her. I think of what Sonja warned, about the danger of entering the instrument. If a citizen's eardrums could be destroyed by entering the tonic chamber, what will happen to somebody who attempts to play the Carillon untrained? The clammy feeling in my heart grows. *What is he to you?* asks Sonja. *I love him*, I say silently to myself.

And because my mind moves slow, it is only then I realise that since our entry to the Citadel, since we came into the arms of the

Carillon's silver shadow, we have not spoken of destruction. We have planned how we will play the story on the instrument. We have made the choice to broadcast what we know. But we have made no plan for how to destroy it.

I hear the echo of Mary's rune in my head. *Simple Simon went to look / If he could pluck the thistle.* I think of the Carillon destroyed in fire and know that it was a false imagining, never possible. *He pricked his fingers very much*, I think. The plan we have had all along is only this. We have never expected to leave.

After Vespers Sonja returns. We wait in the cell together, listening to the silent symphony that Lucien musters in the inner room. We wait and I feel the tension build, lento but sure. We do not speak. Sonja's face is tight with its old control and I think again of the picture I saw in my mind in the crosshouse. A high silver platform held up by an impossible invisible force.

The door in the wall opens. Lucien walks out.

'I'm ready,' he says.

We follow Lucien in, taking the chairs with us. Where before it was Sonja's room, now it is somehow, undeniably, his. He commands the space as we enter. I can see that Sonja has noticed this. She is quiet and doesn't meet my eyes.

My heart is beating presto and my scalp prickles. But Lucien is calm. He gestures to us to sit down; then he sits himself. He checks the stops on the console, turns the bellows on, arranges his feet at the pedals. He raises and drops his shoulders once, twice. Then he places his hands on the top keyboard and begins to play.

What is it, the difference between ordinary people and those with genius? Not just ordinary people either. Intelligent people, sensitive ones, exceptionally talented ones. Even people like Sonja who give everything and then more, who work harder than seems possible on the thing they love.

I have slept next to Lucien. He eats the same stuff as me,

breathes the same air. He sweats, shits, bleeds, all the things that ordinary people do. But yet there's something inside him that can make this music.

His hands pull music out of the air. They carve it up; they split the chords. They render what I wrote – what we wrote together – true and beautiful. Notes of dischord, notes that don't fit neatly into their key or the expected line of a melody, but nonetheless true, and because of this beautiful. Listening to him play is the first time I understand what his hands are really for.

I sit and listen and I know that whatever comes at Matins, whatever the day holds, I am lucky that I can hear this thing that we have made. And I am lucky that when he finishes, he will step across the room and come back to me.

Then I turn to Sonja and I understand something else. I am lucky to feel the gladness of his gift. Because Sonja's face is frozen and under the mask of control something hangs broken.

That difference, that indefinable difference between talent and genius. It is as fine as a hair, invisible to the eye and even, most of the time, to the ear. But in her face when she looks at her brother, I see that it may as well be a huge, uncrossable chasm.

Sonja sits straighter in her chair. She looks at Lucien. 'Play it through again,' she says.

The Carillon

In the Citadel, the violet hour of morning comes with peace and beauty.

Lucien and I sit side by side on the bed where we have lain through the night, not sleeping, not moving. Sonja paces the matting floor, muttering as if rendering an invisible account.

Then she stops.

'We need to go,' she says. Her face is tight, and her eyes hardly shift. Her hands pull at the folds of her robes. 'The priests will be gathering for meditation in the hall.'

Lucien and I stand. He puts the white and gold tabard that Sonja has given him over his head and smooths it down. I look at him. He has become part of the Order.

'What is your name?' I ask him.

'My name is Lucien,' he says. He takes my arm and pulls me in close. 'My name is Lucien. I live in the storehouse on Dog Isle, in the city of London. I am a member of Five Rover pact.' He holds me chest to chest, arm to arm. Our foreheads meet. I breathe his breath and try not to let my fear pass to him. I grip his shoulders hard.

Sonja looks away. I take Lucien's head, kiss him once, whisper luck in the raven's tune. 'Let Muninn fly home as he will,' I say. 'You must come back to me.'

Then they stand together at the door, tall, pale, dressed in their white. I see them framed for a second and I feel memory form then, all the other moments rushing in to collide, to bring the past into the instant of the present and make it ignite in the golden light. Brother, sister. Two faces, gentle and hard at once. Then they are gone.

The room is quiet. I feel nothing, just low fear that has become like breath to me. And emptiness. It's like when you fall and hit the ground, or when someone lands a clean punch right in your stomach. The second after the air has been forced out, you feel nothing. It's only on the first inhalation that the pain begins.

I wait with my empty lungs for time to start again, for breath to start again, dreading the pain and wanting it to come, and yet not knowing what it will look like when it finally does.

I wait for the dead sound of the fourth toll that signals Matins. I try to imagine where Lucien is, whether they have entered the inner chambers. I try to believe that his gift will protect him from the Carillon's assault. I am sure time has passed, but it is impossible that Chimes would be late.

Then I hear a sharp knock at the door. A knock then a voice, cool and hard.

'Simon? Simon Wythern? Open up. Open up or we will break this door.'

I reach to my ankle. Bodymemory feels for the knife that should be strapped there. But it has gone.

There is no moment of surprise. I walk and look out of the window, across the curved distance of the grass. Through it, people are moving in their ordinary days without any knowledge of any of this. I stand there halfway across the room and wait for them to break the door.

When they come, they are many. The poliss enter the room as if to fill it and the thought comes that I must fight, because the longer it takes to remove me, the more chance Lucien will have. Even as I think it, I see it is probably not true. But somehow I have been waiting for my pain and it is a relief when it comes even in this form. Through the legs of the poliss while I can still see clear, there is a whiterobed man who looks down with great disdain. 'One pactrunner, far from home,' is what I hear him say. 'As she told us.'

When the poliss at last pull me from the room and the pain is singing high through everything, the words still come and go in my mind. As I'm dragged down the corridor of the decommissioned cells and into the sunlight's pale violence. As they pull me across the public grass and round the cobbled square at its centre with the magister walking free and graceful ahead. All the way past Martha, slumped at the wooden pole, and the presence of her body and the crossed stave and the mockery of a threnody strung along it, I hear the words. *As she told us.*

Perhaps they've deafened me with their blows, I think, and the last thing I heard is what will stay. But who is *she*? I think. And they pull me towards the pale stone of the tower, and the arms of the Lady reach out as if to offer up their consolation.

Then I am pushed through doors of pale wood and into a massive hall.

I'm on my stomach, but against my will I look up.

The hall is fluted, elegant, like the body of one of the giant shells that are washed up on the strand sometimes. Yet it is human. My mind struggles to understand the time that has been given to it, whole lifetimes between the laying of its first stones and its completion.

Columns stretch up as if they have grown out of the floor like immense trees. They are carved in hard white stone that somehow looks soft to touch. Three, four floors of fluted columns stretching up to a ceiling that seems to breathe and move like the many mouths of a giant creature. All white. I recognise the intricate lace stone carving on the walls as soundproofing. The mouths at the ceiling are open to swallow music. Light fills the hall through high windows, and the smell of incense is strong.

It was not Sonja who gave us away, I think. She was ready to release all of this, to give it up.

But what did we have to offer her in return, next to this beauty? the voice in my head says. No answers, no order. Nothing but mess, questions, fear.

273

In the middle of the hall, around a table of pale wood, sit the magisters, some in travelling cloaks, most in the white robes of the elect.

'Bring him in,' says the one in the centre, the one whose beard is the same white as his robes. I manage to get half to my knees. Because I want to see him. Something in me needs to see him. When I look, it is blurred. My left eye feels broken, and the pain in my head comes forte. I shut the broken eye and it is clearer. I can look then at the man of power who is sitting in front of me. The one responsible for so much death.

He is tall as they all are, and old. Very old. So old that you can see how his power has grown up slow around him. The weight of it in the room like looking at stilled time, the rings on a cut tree. The features in that face are long and sharp, eyes deep set in their sockets. Yet the horror of the face is not the age, but its wonderful smoothness and flexibility. Each line in the fine-grained flesh is exact, somehow articulate. Speaking. It seems to express a living and elegant discrimination. A face that has tasted of things if only so it can choose to renounce them.

Then a door opens in the east wing, the place where, in a cross-house, the chapel would be.

I see two poliss walk across the floor. Pushed ahead of them with his hands tied is Lucien. A trail of blood from a deep cut on his temple follows the line of his face. I hear a noise leave my mouth. Behind the poliss, a tall man with a hunched back. Next to him stands Sonja.

Lucien is pushed toward the front of the table, directly opposite the magister musicae. Two blind faces stare at each other across the plane of wood. The hall is silent.

'Who is this boy?' asks the magister.

The hunched man leaves Sonja and walks forward to stand at the table.

'This is my son, Lucien, your honour. I should say, he used to be

274

my son. As you know, I believed he died of riverfever at the age of fifteen, before his ordination. I learn now that my wife smuggled him out of the Citadel and he has been living in London since. He tried to use my daughter, Sonja, his sister, to gain access to the instrument. He has brought shame on our family and on the Orkestrum. It would have been better if he had died as we thought.'

Lucien draws himself up slightly. He starts to say something.

'You will not speak,' says the magister musicae. 'You have not been ordained and so have no right to utterance here in this hall.' He turns back to Lucien's father.

'Your wife was Frieda, I think. She was from outside the walls?'

'Yes, Your Honour. But she had embraced our ways. I had no indication that she was not loyal to the Order.'

'Your ignorance is hardly an excuse and does little to recommend you.'

'I am sorry, Your Honour.'

The magister musicae turns to face Lucien directly.

'Due to your actions today, the Carillon is late. For the first time since Allbreaking, Matins will take place after sunrise. It is the only distinction you appear to have achieved in your short life. And a pointless one, as it will make no difference either in the Citadel or to the people in the cities. Chimes is always coming and always here.

'I remember you. A gifted boy. You still bear the mark of your birth, I hear. Your talent was fine. You had the skill to rise high, to gain the immortality that only music can bestow.' He stops speaking, closes his eyes. 'I cannot tell you how many times I have seen the same error. They mistake the individual hungers and desires, the wants and needs of the solo player, as a source of meaning. Think they can live for themselves and for the pleasure of others. Yet there is no truth in that; there is no way forward. Where did the cult of personality take our predecessors? Into a mired, frantic world without foothold of truth or understanding.

'You may look at our decisions here, but you are not adequate to understand them. You will never grasp the principle of hierarchy, the sacrifice of the individual for the greater good. We have opened the people to the possibility of a higher, an enduring, beauty. We have shown them that perfection is within their reach.

'Some might say it has been punishment enough for you to leave the Citadel, to witness and partake of the corruption of city life, to lose your education, your skill, your chance to pursue the high and only ideals. But to my mind it is not enough.'

He points to a young man in white robes who sits down the length of the table from him.

'Magister Joachim is our youngest magister. Look at him closely. He is what you could have become.'

The young man inclines his head slightly, as if embarrassed to be singled out.

'Magister Joachim, when you enter the inner chambers, this boy will accompany you. He has been away for so long that he has forgotten the transformative power of music. Before you reach the sacrum musicae, you will leave him in the fifth of the inner chambers, the dominant. You will seal the door. He will listen to your concert from within the instrument.'

'No.' Sonja breaks out of her father's hands, half falls forward. There is silence from the table. 'No. Please,' she says.

The old man looks up, fixes his blind gaze on her.

'You did not ask leave to speak here.'

'Your Honour, I am sorry. He is my brother. I know that he has betrayed the Order, but if you make him listen from the dominant chamber, it will deafen him. He has no training. He will die.'

I stare at her. She must have known all along that our quest was without hope.

'I am sorry, discipula. We practise mercy as a rule here. There is no benefit to be gained from cruelty. It is ugly, and it aids no one. But your brother abandoned the Order. This is a betrayal from within and must be recognised as such. *Grief is not a note to be sustained beyond death.* Perhaps you might choose to see this not as a punishment but as a reclamation, an atonement. The instrument will open to him for a last time. Perhaps in its embrace he will learn what was lost.'

I see Sonja open her mouth and close it again.

I move forward.

'It was not him. It was my idea,' I shout. 'He had no memory of this place. I made him come. Take me instead.'

The magister musicae does not address me. I am beneath his notice.

Lucien turns and he looks at me and holds my gaze. His face is calm and open. He holds his bound hands out from him, and in the narrow air that he can command, he conducts the solfege for my name and then the solfege for forgiveness. I hear it in my head in his voice. I hear it in my head as the single chord inside me that cannot be understood or broken into its different parts. I hear it as love.

The poliss take him. They leave the hall. The young magister goes too, and Sonja's father pushes her to follow also. 'To your quarters,' he says.

I go to my knees then, and my last glimpse of Lucien is the straight pitch of his neck bending as one of the poliss cups his head to push him under the low door that leads towards the Carillon.

I stand in the hall. The stone is cold and empty of life; the ornament is toothed with cruelty; the golden light is cheap.

I feel a hand at my back pushing me forward. I stumble, clumsy. Lucien has gone from me. My body feels made of wood.

'What to do with the pactrunner?' says a voice.

I force myself to speak.

'Take me as well. Let me die with him.'

'You would profane the instrument. That punishment is only for one who was born here.'

The magister musicae is speaking, but I cannot see him. In

277

front of my eyes are bright moving lights. They are inside my eyelids, moving with them.

I see shapes on the fringes of the brightness, but nothing is clear, a dull throbbing in my brain.

'As I said, we practise mercy in the Order, as a rule.' His voice is fastidious, cold. 'Take him back to London and leave him. He will soon forget what has happened here.'

Hands on my shoulders again. The voice comes again.

'But no,' it says. 'Leave him for now. It may near to deafen him, but what other time would a layperson be privileged to hear the instrument at such close quarters? Such an opportunity will only come once in a lifetime. Who are we to prevent it?'

The hands are removed and I am allowed to slump down.

Pain climbs into a corner of my skull and sets up a rhythm of throbbing. I close my eyes, but the lights cluster and play, following their tracking behind their lids.

I pull my hands taut against the rope as hard as I can, not because I think I can free myself, but because I need to feel something, anything, or I will go mad. *Lucien,* says the deep throb in my skull. *Lucien.*

In the hall around me is silence. A new silence, that of their cruel, hallowed ritual. I pull my hands taut. I bring my head to the cold tile.

Silence opens. The smell of pepper fills the air. A dry cough in the upper reaches of the vaulted ceiling. A dead chord breaks the air.

It is Chimes.

Head in the water is peace. I go down, down, down into a place of cool darkness. But in the darkness there is a different voice. It is singing. I think for a while it is my mother's voice, and then it becomes Lucien's voice, and then I understand that it is neither of these.

The voice is the voice of Chimes, the melody simple. It is not song at all, but the clearest and sweetest of the bells sounding wordlessly. The words are those that come into my head with the tune as somehow, at last, I hear it.

> 'In the quiet days of power,
> seven ravens in the tower.
> When you clip the raven's wing,
> then the bird begins to sing.
> When you break the raven's beak,
> then the bird begins to speak.
> When the Chimes fill up the sky,
> then the ravens start to fly.
> Gwillum, Huginn, Cedric, Thor,
> Odin, Hardy, nevermore.
> Never ravens in the tree
> till Muninn can fly home to me.'

The tune comes once, twice. It is raw and simple. It has the open fourths and fifths of a folk tune. There is no harmony or embellishment, just the tune sounding simple and sweet.

Sounding down from the instrument and to me. What my ears tell me is impossible. My mind freezes with it. It cannot be true. Lucien is within the terrible embrace of the instrument, and he is playing.

Around me, in the hall, people are running. I do not follow their movement. I keep my head down.

The guildsong comes to an end. Its end is a crashing chord and the chord is pain. It is jagged and crooked. It is broken and splintered and uneven, and it's sustained for so long at such a pitch that I think my ears are going to burst.

The chord is death and sorrow and torture. Like millions of people all screaming at once. Just when I think I can't stand any more, the harshness fades and crumbles. It doesn't resolve. That is the wrong word. It doesn't move into harmony, but it breaks, and as it breaks, it shows the possibility of change. It walks forward. It carries the pain into the next chord, but it softens there and there is sweetness again.

Those two chords are like gatekeepers. And then the story starts.

It starts with water. A river flowing. It flows from the source down to the sea. Its source is a field, trees all around, flat, undulating green grass. And under a tree a spring. The spring is the origin of the river, and the river is memory.

It was the only way I knew how to tell it. The water is born up where the river starts, and it is fresh and new. It springs up, and there is birdsong. Lucien has put this in with the highest stops of the instrument. I have no idea how close they might be to life, but I somehow recognise them straight away. The sound bubbles up through the air. It's free, clear and free, flying around up there.

It is so strange listening to Chimes use music that isn't ordered and dense, perfectly neat and rich in counterpoint and all the voices sounding at once that I forget for a while, listening to the simple running melody and its new, true meaning.

Then I remember that Lucien is in there somewhere, playing. The notes run clear and smooth, and somehow I have to believe that it's going to be all right. He is going to survive.

After the origins of memory, Lucien plays the world before Allbreaking and then the birth of Ravensguild.

Different voices talking. Folksongs. Forecasts. There's no grand structure. No sonata form, no canon. Just the individual stories coming and going, different currents. Which is not to say there is no harmony or repetition. The same things circle round in their own ways. Babies are born. People are married and die. Songs for planting and songs for harvest, patterns for journeys forward and back. I let myself look up a little from where I've been crouched forward, my head on the floor.

The magisters are still around the table. They are staring all of them at the magister musicae, who is listening with his arms outstretched as if holding captive the attention of a vast orkestra. Then he points to the Carillon's chambers. He bellows, a bullish, strange sound, 'Stop the instrument!'

Three of the magisters jump out of their seats and run to the door.

I dip my head again. 'Hurry, Lucien,' I whisper to the floor.

I hear the shift in the tune in my head before he plays it. Part of me wants it to stop there. Maybe we all want time to stop, or to be coming the same always. But I know it can't. Under the green melodies that we carved out and practised together, I can hear the dark rumbling of what happens next.

Fire starts and it burns books, maps, stories, documents. It burns old electricks. It burns memoryboards and paraboards. It burns music, old scores from before Allbreaking.

And it burns memories too. In the music, I hear the flames leap up, hungry. Crashing, devouring, turning code to dust and ashes.

Lucien plays the lives cut short, fragments of story riddled with the black wormholes of sated flame. He plays the memorylost herded, the minds wiped clean, the frenzied dance of chimesick-ness. He plays the dead of Ravensguild. He plays mouths stuffed with dead birds.

The music gets louder and louder. Some of the magisters still sitting at the table are bending their heads and covering their ears, their mouths open in sounds I cannot hear. Their despair not at the music's volume, but the blasphony of it, the mess. The music gets louder and louder, but the playing is triumph. I hear every note as we wrote it and it makes me think of what Lucien said about meditation. How you can hear the forward and backward of a note as if you were bringing it into being. And I hope. I hope that some miracle means his skill is strong enough.

In the music, something else is coming in. I hear it once and at first think I am mistaken. It is something not part of the melody or harmony we made. Something not part of the Carillon's voice at all. It is a sound like you hear on the race sometimes in a high wind, when the boats that are still docked there strain against the wood and rope and rubber of their berth. A kind of resentful creaking. The sound of something yearning to pull apart.

The frenzied melody continues. Death and breaking. I know the fragmented violence of the rhythms so well that I am holding my breath.

And then wrong notes come.

Not just the ones we have written, the known dischords, but other notes, notes not intended. Notes stumbled. Two into one. One into two. The wrong chord. Notes missing. The devil in music held long and awkward and loud. The augmented fourth shrieks like pain through the hall and I see several magisters shrieking too, as if they're vibrating in sympathy with the instrument.

The rending sound comes again as the pitch gets higher and higher, louder and louder.

Through the din I can see the magister musicae gesturing wildly in solfege, his arms moving like a crazed windmill. And something calm comes into my head. A still spot. A voice. It says, *The Carillon can't withstand this.*

I stand up. I hold my hands over my ears. I think of Lucien in the tonic chamber and there are tears running down my cheeks.

Then silence. In the silence, creaking and a sound I can't describe. A slow sound of something falling. An arc of silver planing through the air, and then a crash. I feel the whole hall shake from the ground upward. The noise pushes me down.

Then the instrument resumes like a fallen horse stumbling back up to its knees. What I hear then is awful in its volume and harshness.

A chord, then another, then another. Cruel, pitiful, violent. The Carillon is playing a mockery of Chimes. Chimes through a black mirror of dischord and heaviness. It pushes and pushes through the rending, as silver crashes all around and as the pipes and bells of the instrument pull apart from each other. Until there is nothing left, only silence, only despair.

I think, How could you leave me like this, Lucien?

The story we wrote had a different end. The cruel mirror of Chimes was meant to end in a different song, a new one that Lucien wrote to mean hope and hereafter. But there is no one to play it anymore.

I get up slowly. The arches still stand upright, but along the left side of the hall, they stretch up into air like hands held in supplication. The roof is broken. Slicing through the immense hole is the silver lip of an immense bell, deformed and broken by the weight of its fall. Huge splinters of wood have come with it, piles of rubble and stone and white tiling. Dust rises up through the air.

Silence. Creaking, and the intermittent crashes of debris still falling. Wind plays through the hall from the broken walls and ceiling.

'Lucien,' I yell forte. My lungs are useless. I get up and run down the hall and toward the damage. I run toward where I saw Lucien disappear into the stair that rises to the tower. Though I know that there is little chance anyone in the chambers could have made it out alive.

The opening of the stairway is covered with rubble. I find a thick piece of wood and use it to wedge and lever the heavy concrete blocks aside. Then I push the door open. Fallen debris has broken through the inner wall of the stairwell, so the steps are held by one side only, splayed like the struts of a fan. Through the broken ribs to my right I see the silver pipes that formed the instrument's core. I keep one hand on the outer wall and climb the stairs, pushing over the rubble. Up some way I go and there is an opening to my left, from off the stairwell. One of the chambers of the instrument. I crawl into the carved narrow room. Its outer wall has been shorn clean off and it has collapsed inwards, catching and trapping Magister Joachim where he was trying to escape. From his waist down he is covered in rubble. One of his arms is broken, and his face is turned to me in profile. It is covered in white dust like flour and for a moment I think of my mother making bread. His eyes look surprised. Blank. Blood in a line from his mouth. I try to pull his cloak over him, but it's caught on rubble, so I gently thumb his eyelids closed instead.

Then I return to the stairs. As I get higher, they become more unstable; they creak with pain as I crawl. At last it is impossible to climb any higher. Dust clouds around me like smoke. My eyes are running with it, and my lungs are full. Then I look up. Hanging above is a skewed platform with no visible means of support. It must be attached somehow to those of the silver pipes that are still upright. And I know that it must be the floor of the tonic chamber.

I force myself along the creaking tongue of the step on which I'm standing. I stand at its edge and it gives with a sickening downward flex. Then I jump. I jump upwards and into the fretting that holds the instrument's remaining pipes. The core of the destroyed Carillon. Its backbone. I use it as a ladder, and I climb upward. Up into dust and blindness.

At last I am level with the dust-covered floorboards that form the base of the tonic chamber. I am reluctant to add to it my weight, so I stand with my arm hooked through the fretwork of the instrument. I squint through dust and at last I see the thing that I don't want to see. The impossible thing.

At the far end of the small chamber, tented by fallen arms of tiling, is a broken shape. The pooled white of a cloak. I push myself out onto the platform and feel it give as I crawl towards the shape on my knees. I see the back of his head. There is blood in the pale curled hair. I feel something building in my throat so huge and hard that I don't want to open my mouth and let it out because it will rip me apart.

I can't reach him. There is nothing else that matters except the distance between us. Everything goes dark, and I inch forward. Though the chamber is open to the air, it is black all around me and the plaster dust comes down. I use my back to prop a huge piece of tiling and push it. Then I can reach him. I reach out to his head, his hair. I touch his hand. It is warm.

I can't bear to turn his head to me. I stay like that for a while, just cupping his head in my hands. Then I lean over so that I can move his body clear of the rubble.

Lucien's face but not his face.

The high forehead, the hair rippled back off it. I stare at it and my head does not hear what my eyes are telling me. Or is it the other way around?

It is not Lucien. It is Sonja.

Birdsong

I do not know how I get down but that I get down. Edging backwards; slipping; falling. I escape from the broken innards of the instrument.

I leave Sonja there in its heart. Held in its clasp and in her mastery and sacrifice.

Out of the hall and onto the lawn, and on my knees I spit out dust.

After a while I sit up and I see the whiterobed figures rushing around me. Magisters pull off their robes as they run. They form strange patterns. They turn to each other like strangers, and their mouths move in silence as if they've never had to learn to converse. I watch them move toward each other and then back away, unable to seek consolation. And all of the different permutations of faces that are unaccustomed to the expressions of hopelessness and despair.

There is no joy in it. I look at the grass in front of me and after a while I understand that their mouths are not moving in silence after all. They are speaking. I simply cannot hear them. There is a slow rushing sound in my ears. I reach up to touch them and the fingers of my hand come away wet with blood.

How the hell did she do it? Lucien flanked by the tall figures of the poliss, followed by the young magister who would soon be dead. Sonja stumbling out of the hall, pushed by her father. Her path twists in my head like a well-executed run in the under, a melody always two steps ahead. I sit on the grass and I puzzle it and still I do not understand. When did she decide? Her feet, in their dance ahead of me, treading their skilful bluff. Clear and measured and irreproachable. Memorise the music. Steal the knife. Read in your brother's face the understanding of his betrayal. Listen to his death sentence. Call out once in protest.

I see her running through the corridors of the hall, corridors filled with the last of that golden light. In her hand she holds my knife. Quick in her memory, the key tune that will open the chamber door. Beneath that, the whole wild close-beating company of her ambition and her loss – the music that she played and learned although it was not for her.

By the time she reaches the instrument, the poliss have already left. They have deposited the young traitor in the dominant chamber with the magister, hands firmly tied. They have done their duty and are ready for their breakfast. Nobody could expect a young girl to pose a threat. A young girl not even noted for any particular musical gift.

My thought turns to Magister Joachim, as I found him in the heart of the collapsed chamber. I think of his calm expression and I hope like hell that he was killed in the Carillon's collapse, as I had thought, and not before. When I remember Sonja's face as she turned from the sight of Martha's body I am not fully sure of this.

I sit on the grass and I know that I have to leave. I must search the rubble again, then the emptied rooms of the Orkestrum, then the tunnels, the corridors. I need to move now and keep moving lest the tense hope that's subito sprung up in me collapses along with everything else. But I can't seem to move. My legs do not respond.

I look up and through the crowds one of the whiterobed figures is walking toward me, steady and tall. He crosses the grass. I watch as he gets closer and I wait for his path to change, for his face to contort. Then at last my body answers and I scramble to my feet and after a while he reaches me where I stand. His body is marvellously whole. Unbroken. He stretches his hand out to mine and then his arms are around me and we stand like that for who knows how long, in the shadow of the broken instrument.

After is a different place than I had thought, if had let myself think of it at all. It is making the dangerous trip back into the instrument to rescue Sonja's body, and it is Lucien cradling her in his arms. His face cracked open in grief and the whole desperate unknown expanse of it stretching out.

After is knowing there is time for grief, and that time will be filled with it. Their heads inclined like that so you can't tell the difference between their pale curled hair. His hand to the curve of her face as if asking forgiveness. No help for any of it. Just a long path that we must go ahead on. It is the flint from Sonja's own pocket that lights the bier.

Smoke from the burning instrument rises upward into the sky. It twists in the air. The sweet wood, fine-tuned and jointed, goes up lento. We stand and watch it burn and the smoke smells like incense.

Later, in that time called after, we walk unquestioned through the Citadel. We pass people on their hands and knees with their faces twisted, still howling out their despair in silence. The ringing in my ears lessens, but does not stop.

The gatehouse is unmanned. Through the para windows is the picture of an abrupt exit. A lute hanging from a chair, still swinging from its broidered strap. Scores scattered on the floor. On a bench a half-eaten sandwich sits on stickwrap.

Past the tower we walk and through the city. And it is coming alive lento in the early light. Children clutching their half and three-quarter viols and cellos. Instrument makers holding lathes, planes, polishing cloths. The stall holders in markets stare out over dropped fruit, the white blown leaves of sheet music, the unfurled bolts of cloth. Families in stunned lines, mothers grasping babies tight and holding them into their shoulders, shielded from the gauzy wings of the smoke that stretch now through the town and through the market.

People out and clustering everywhere on the streets. They have emerged from shops and houses, from crosshouses and concert halls and workshops. They stand blinking in the light, and on their faces is the echo of the story that has been sounded. And I wish that I could say it was a look of wonder, or relief, or enlightenment. That I could see understanding there; pain, but the pain that comes from understanding.

But instead it is like watching someone wake from a dream. The look on their faces is of something crumbling around them as they watch. The look of something taken away.

It is an awful knowledge. Even if what you are coming up out of is a nightmare, waking is hard. When you were deep inside the dream, all was decided for you. Out in the morning is something else altogether. Something you have to choose for yourself.

The sky is lightening as we walk. Lucien is tall beside me and I turn to look at him. He stops. We are standing on a hill just past the city.

I can see to the east where the sun is still rising, and the full expanse of the sky stretches out.

The sky is empty. I feel that I have never looked at it before, in the quiet like this. The trees around us move in the wind and the wind's breath comes into me as we stand there and look out toward where the sun is taking its journey upward.

I see clouds moving. White and blown. Their rhythms are all different and unspelled. They tangle and reshape and you could give whatever meaning you liked to them. Whatever story you liked. I stand there and watch and I wonder if there'll be a time hereafter when the birds will come back. Whether they will want to return into this new and unremembered silence.

Lucien is moving off already and I follow him. We walk over the green grass together. I do not have to ask where he is going, because I know already.

Down to the river.

Acknowledgements

Thanks and love to Sandeep Parmar and Imogen Prickett, who were there at the beginning and throughout. To my darling siblings Christopher and Esther, and to Natalie Graham, Jacob Edmond, and Nikāu, Kāhu and Huia. Thank you to my parents Bruce and Barbara, to whom the book is dedicated. Thanks to Dawn and Allan Shuker, and to all the wonderful Williamses and Walronds. To Ayelet Gottlieb, Rowena Tun, Katy Robinson, Sienna Latham and Elizabeth Knox, for belief and encouragement. Thank you to my agent Will Francis, for his clear-sighted vision and general brilliance. Heartfelt thanks to the whole team at Sceptre and in particular to my editor Drummond Moir, who unerringly helped me towards the right resonances and rhythms.

Thank you to my daughter Lotte, who makes all the words new again. And to Carl, always, for your belief in me, and for your true, well-tempered love.